"Look. I thought of a way we could help each other out."

Melissa appeared mildly embarrassed. Seth never knew how to handle these awkward situations. Not that he'd been in that many of them, but in three years he'd had some offers, usually from nice women he didn't want to hurt. Like this one.

"I really don't think so," he said as firmly as he could, hoping to cut her off at the pass.

Her eyebrows rose. "You don't even know what I'm going to suggest."

Like hell. But he waited anyway. If she wanted to make this more difficult for both of them, he was too tired to stop her.

She licked her lips. That was a mouth made for kissing, Seth thought, surprised at himself for thinking it. What if she did ask him out?

What if he went? This was the first time he'd seriously thought he might. But then he remembered it wasn't his killer bod and winning personality she was after. It was her house she wanted.

D1132577

Dear Reader,

It's funny how themes play out in life as well as in books. This story is about picking yourself up after life knocks your feet out from under you. It's about people helping each other during hard times, with guts and humor. During the time I was writing this book, one friend lost her husband far too young, another faced cancer, another went through a divorce. During the same period, people fell in love, got married, ran marathons. Babies were born. Life's like that. Up and down. Sunshine and rain. In most lives, there's plenty of both. I wanted to chart one such journey, from darkness to light, as two struggling people and their families helped heal each other and became stronger in the process. I'd always wanted to write a Harlequin Superromance novel, having read and enjoyed them for years. I'm so happy I got the chance. I hope you enjoy *The Trouble with Twins*.

Come visit me anytime at www.nancywarren.net.

Happy reading!

Nancy Warren

NANCY WARREN
The Trouble with Twins

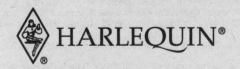

TORONTO • NEW YORK • LONDON
AMSTERDAM • PARIS • SYDNEY • HAMBURG
STOCKHOLM • ATHENS • TOKYO • MILAN • MADRID
PRAGUE • WARSAW • BUDAPEST • AUCKLAND

If you purchased this book without a cover you should be aware
that this book is stolen property. It was reported as "unsold and
destroyed" to the publisher, and neither the author nor the
publisher has received any payment for this "stripped book."

ISBN-13: 978-0-373-71390-5
ISBN-10:   0-373-71390-8

THE TROUBLE WITH TWINS

Copyright © 2006 by Nancy Warren.

All rights reserved. Except for use in any review, the reproduction or
utilization of this work in whole or in part in any form by any electronic,
mechanical or other means, now known or hereafter invented, including
xerography, photocopying and recording, or in any information storage
or retrieval system, is forbidden without the written permission of the
publisher, Harlequin Enterprises Limited, 225 Duncan Mill Road,
Don Mills, Ontario, Canada M3B 3K9.

All characters in this book have no existence outside the imagination of
the author and have no relation whatsoever to anyone bearing the same
name or names. They are not even distantly inspired by any individual
known or unknown to the author, and all incidents are pure invention.

This edition published by arrangement with Harlequin Books S.A.

® and TM are trademarks of the publisher. Trademarks indicated with
® are registered in the United States Patent and Trademark Office, the
Canadian Trade Marks Office and in other countries.

www.eHarlequin.com

Printed in U.S.A.

ABOUT THE AUTHOR

Nancy Warren is a *USA TODAY* bestselling author of thirty romantic novels and novellas. She has won numerous awards for her writing, and in 2004 was a double finalist for the prestigious RITA® Award. Nancy lives in the Pacific Northwest, where her hobbies include losing umbrellas, hiking, cooking, walking her border collie bareheaded in the rain, and classic movies. You can find her on the Web at www.nancywarren.net.

Books by Nancy Warren

HARLEQUIN BLAZE
19—LIVE A LITTLE!
47—WHISPER
57—BREATHLESS
85—BY THE BOOK
114—STROKE OF MIDNIGHT
     "Tantalizing"
209—PRIVATE RELATIONS
275—INDULGE

HARLEQUIN TEMPTATION
838—FLASHBACK
915—HOT OFF THE PRESS
943—FRINGE BENEFITS
987—UNDERNEATH IT ALL

Don't miss any of our special offers. Write to us at the following address for information on our newest releases.

Harlequin Reader Service
U.S.: 3010 Walden Ave., P.O. Box 1325, Buffalo, NY 14269
Canadian: P.O. Box 609, Fort Erie, Ont. L2A 5X3

To James and Emma for all the research help
and for your encouragement and support.
You are the best.

CHAPTER ONE

IT'S ALWAYS DARKEST BEFORE the dawn had to be one of the stupidest expressions Melissa Theisen knew. She'd worried and raged her way through plenty of middle-of-the-night blackness lately, and when the birds started chirping to announce dawn, she never felt brighter or better. She merely felt one day closer to the edge.

She watched as early morning light crept through the drapes of her Lakeview, Washington, home until she could make out the shapes of furniture in her bedroom. Her mahogany dressing table, and the matching chest of drawers empty of Stephen's things. The smooth expanse of quilt on his unslept-in side of the king-size bed. The crack in the ceiling above her head. Was it her imagination or was that crack expanding?

Giving up on sleep, she rolled out of bed and padded downstairs to put coffee on, showered while it brewed, then sat at her kitchen table sipping the first steaming mug while she read over the letter once more.

Stephen was two months late on child support payments. Worse, he'd missed his weekend visits with the kids. But not until she'd received the letter from the bank yesterday had she suspected the depth of his betrayal. From the midst of the careful, corporate wording, the word *foreclosure* jumped out at her like a skeleton leaping out of a closet. Oh, they weren't foreclosing quite yet, but the threat was there. Not only had Stephen stopped paying her, he hadn't paid the bank mortgage, either.

Ominously, he seemed to have disappeared.

A year after her divorce, she accepted that he wasn't coming back. But he'd never abandon his own children.

Would he?

The naive part of her wanted to believe that something had happened to him. The cynical side wasn't buying that for a second.

Draining her coffee mug, she rose and assembled the ingredients for oatmeal raisin muffins. It was part of her morning routine now, along with baking homemade bread—without a machine, thank you very much. As though knocking herself out to be the perfect homemaker could balance Stephen's role as the home breaker. The counselor she'd seen briefly after the separation had told her she was overcompensating for the lack of a father in her children's lives.

So what?

She liked baking. The activity soothed her and gave her some measure of control over the mess of her life. Not that she was fooling herself that a few muffins and a loaf of butter-crust whole wheat could make up for a missing dad, but she had to work with what she had.

By the time she woke the kids, the smell of comfort food filled the kitchen and she was dressed for the day.

She had to shake eight-year-old Matthew twice to get him to wake up. "Morning, sleepyhead," she said, smiling down at his sleep-pinkened cheeks and the one skinny leg sticking out from under the duvet cover patterned with vivid insects.

He groaned and rolled over. "Hi, Mom."

Knowing he wasn't fully functional until he'd been up for a few minutes, she ruffled his hair and left him with a reminder to make his bed. "Fresh muffins," she said, glancing back. "Your favorite."

Then she stepped into her three-year-old daughter's room.

Alice, like her, was a morning person. Fully awake, she sat in bed and chattered to her stuffed dinosaur. With the mixed herd of stuffed animals and dolls in her bed, she could amuse herself for hours.

"Mama," she cried, holding out her arms.

After a big smacking kiss for her daughter, Melissa performed the morning ritual of greeting the animals and dolls before helping her baby to the bathroom and then getting dressed. Alice was in a pink-and-purple fashion stage. Even at her tender age she was fussy about what she wore. Dresses were preferred, in pink and purple, obviously, but they also had to be good spinning dresses. If a dress didn't bell out when she twirled, well, what was the point?

Already, Alice was enrolled in tiny-tot ballet and had decided she was going to be either a dancer or a princess when she grew up. Such tough decisions when you're three.

Hand in hand, the two women of the house walked down the stairs. Melissa taking a moment to feel the tiny warm hand tucked into hers and watch the soft bounce of blond curls. The kids were growing so fast, sometimes she had to stop and concentrate on a small detail so she could hold on to it and hopefully program it into her long-term memory.

Alice was halfway through her second muffin and her apple juice when Matthew stumbled into the room.

"Before you sit down, can you get me a knife from the drawer, honey?" Melissa asked him. She removed the gingham frill from the top of her strawberry jam, ready to pair it with peanut butter for his sandwich.

"Sure." He yawned and yanked at the drawer. Even as she exclaimed, "Careful," she knew it was too late. The drawer front came away with his hand.

"Uh-oh," Alice said.

Uh-oh was right. How many times had she told them that drawer was loose? She couldn't afford a handyman, and her carpentry skills were in the slim-to-none category, edging strongly toward the "none" end of the range.

She quelled the urge to snap at him. It wasn't Matthew's fault. "Sorry, Mom," he said, looking stricken.

"It's okay." She took the drawer front from him and put it on the counter.

His gaze followed her movement, his expression serious and worried. "Ryan Doran's mom said I come from a broken home," he said hesitantly, staring at the broken drawer.

Oh, God. What to say?

"Superglue," she said, "fixes everything. We'll have that drawer back together in no time." In fact, there were two items in her toolbox. A single screwdriver with multiple heads, most of which were a mystery, and a tube of carpenter's glue, which was really amazingly versatile.

Matt nodded thoughtfully. "I told him it's not our home that's broken, it's our family."

ONCE SHE'D GOT Matthew off to school and Alice dressed, Melissa drove to the appointment she'd made at the bank after she'd received yesterday's letter. In the bank parking lot, still in her car, she read that devastating single page one more time. Helpless rage spurted through her. "Stephen Theisen, how could you do this to me?" She didn't even realize she'd vented aloud until her daughter chirped, "Daddy?"

"No, honey." Melissa turned to the child in the backseat, and her heart twisted. So much love and innocent trust shone from the cherubic face framed by a cascade of blond curls. "He's not here."

Alice opened her mouth and Melissa waited for, "I want Daddy," but after quivering a moment, the pink lips closed again. Melissa pursed her own lips hard to keep them from quivering just as childishly and opened the door.

Damn it, she hadn't lost everything yet, and she wasn't going to. The children had been deprived of their father, but they still had a home and a mother. They had friends and a decent school. And she would do anything, anything at all, to make sure they kept the precious stability of remaining in the only home they'd ever known.

Ten minutes past her appointment time, Melissa played with Alice in the waiting area and bristled with righteous indignation. Her ex-husband was supposed to pay the mortgage. Why was the bank bothering *her?*

A short, unsatisfactory interview with Mr. Cheney, the lending officer who had written the letter, explained why they were bothering her. If the mortgage wasn't paid, the loan would be called. Then foreclosure would begin.

"But," she argued, "I've got all the paperwork showing that my ex-husband signed over the house to me."

He checked the computer records and said, "Since you were on the original mortgage documents, you can pick up the payments without any problem." He glanced at her and then at Alice. "But the house is the collateral for the mortgage, Mrs. Theisen. Is there someone who could lend you some money to get yourself back on track?"

She blinked. "What about you? You're a lending officer at my bank."

He shook his head. "Sorry. You wouldn't qualify for a loan with us. No income, house payments in default." He was sorry, but that was it. When she tried to explain her situation, he looked at her as though he'd heard a thousand stories like hers and was tapped of sympathy. "Maybe you should trade down," was his only suggestion.

Trade down? A shiver of pure fear crawled over her skin at the words. She'd spent her childhood being moved from place to place, always trading down, never up. She envisioned the last home she lived in with her parents—the awful trailer across the highway from Big Bull's wrecking yard on Federal Way.

Mr. Cheney fished around in a drawer and came up with a couple of pamphlets, which he handed her. She read the title of one, "Avoiding Foreclosure," and crumpled the wad of papers into her bag.

In shock, she lifted Alice into her arms and stumbled out of the cubicle, heading numbly toward the daylight streaming in from an outside door.

"You're squishing me," Alice complained and wiggled out of her arms, then took her hand.

Around them, people ebbed and flowed to banking machines, tellers and suited bank reps like Mr. Cheney in cubicles. A sea of people with money to deposit, withdraw, invest. And she, Melissa Theisen, former wife of successful entrepreneur Stephen Theisen, had just been informed she was responsible for more than six thousand dollars in back mortgage payments, plus extra interest and late fees. She had thirty days to pay it and resume regular mortgage payments, or the bank would start foreclosure proceedings on the house.

Stubbornly, her Gucci flats, which had seen better days, refused to carry her out of the building.

There had to be another way.

Melissa hadn't done anything wrong. She'd followed the examples of those wonderful TV families. She'd married the right man, had had the right children. She'd entertained clients graciously. Done everything she could to help Stephen prosper.

She was rewarded by getting dumped.

Well, she'd had enough of men like Stephen and Mr. Cheney taking things away from her.

A guy in a baseball cap jostled her as she stood trying to figure out what to do. An armed guard lounged in a corner of the marble lobby and looked at her with mild curiosity. Fury at the unfairness of it all began to bubble inside her. No, she wasn't leaving this bank until she had a better solution than trading down. She stalked to the bank directory and scanned straight to the top of the listed names.

Seth O'Reilly, President and CEO of the First Bank of Lakeview, Washington. He was her man. Before the anger could dissipate, she picked up Alice and marched to the elevator.

The executive offices on the third level were hushed and unhurried. Melissa's worn shoes sank into teal carpet as she made her way forward.

"Can I help you?" a cool female voice asked.

"Yes. I'm looking for Mr. O'Reilly," she told the perfectly groomed, gray-haired woman behind the expensive-looking reception desk.

"Do you have an appointment?"

"No, I—"

"I'm sorry. He's in a meeting. Perhaps someone else can—"

"No. It's very important that I see Mr. O'Reilly today."

"He's not available today." The woman typed something on her keyboard and scanned her computer screen. "The earliest appointment he has is two weeks Wednesday."

"I need to see him today."

"Well, you can't."

Later, Melissa would realize that that was the moment she snapped. But at the time it seemed as though the only possible course of action was to find the one man who might be able to help her, and to do it immediately. She walked past the reception desk into a hushed labyrinth of offices and meeting rooms.

"Wait! You can't go back there. Stop! I'll call Security."

Melissa hardly heard the words.

She felt exhilarated by breaking the rules for the first time in thirty-four years. If a little rule-breaking would keep a roof over Alice's and Matthew's heads, it was a small price to pay. She stalked forward, knowing instinctively that the farther she got from the reception desk—and the public who paid for it—the closer she'd get to the real power in the bank.

IT HAD BEEN ONE HELL of a morning, and the day wasn't getting any better. Seth O'Reilly's stomach felt as if it was being attacked from inside with burning knives.

Which left him in no mood for the weekly executive meeting.

He eyed the silver carafe in front of him with a combination of fear and longing. Coffee was the worst thing he could inflict upon his already suffering body.

He tried to think about something else, but cups rattled against saucers to tease him, while the aroma of fresh coffee tickled his senses.

His doctor had warned him to stay away from the stuff—but then his doctor had never sat through one of these meetings. He poured a long, fragrant, black stream into the empty cup in front of him and drank deeply.

"Well, Seth? What do you think?"

Glancing up at the eleven faces around at boardroom table, he replayed as much of the discussion as he could remember. Stalling for time, he took another hit of coffee, then focused on the ad campaign the marketing director had presented.

A series of full-page mock-ups of newspaper and magazine ads stared at him from easels.

One showed a smiling middle-American family—one dad, one mom, one boy, one girl—in front of a brand new house complete with two-car garage and green velvet lawn. A second ad pictured a young Asian woman proudly polishing her new red sports car, while the third displayed a Generation X couple hanging an Open sign in front of a trendy coffee shop. All the ads carried the same headline— The New Face of Banking. And the subhead read, We're Banking On You.

Irritation spurted along with the gastric juices that were torturing his gut. "I think they're tired, trite and unimaginative."

A grunt of exasperation escaped from Mitzi Youngall, the bank's marketing director. "Seth, these ads went over great with the focus groups."

"You asked for my opinion. I'm giving it." He felt churlish, miserable and sick. He poured more coffee.

Mitzi tossed her newly platinum ringlets as she swung to gesture at the ads. "They're realistic."

"You want realism?" He poked his index finger toward the first ad layout. "There's a fifty-percent chance that family's going to break up, and the biggest argument will be over who pays for the kids' braces."

He pointed at the second ad. "That woman won't be smiling when she finds out she's sick of her car in a year and she's stuck paying for it for five. And as for those kids—" he jabbed his finger toward the spiky-haired, black-clad twentysomethings in front of the café "—in real life they're opening a goddamn hemp shop, not a coffee shop."

"With a smoking room in the back," Carl Fletcher, VP of customer services, added. "And I don't mean cigars."

A couple of wary chuckles erupted.

"Well, we can hardly show illegal activities in our ads," Mitzi snapped.

"Do you have anything else we—" Before he could finish his question, the door to the boardroom flew open, hitting the mahogany-paneled wall with a resounding thump. In charged a startlingly beautiful woman clutching a chubby toddler in her arms.

Everyone turned to stare at the woman, whose eyes snapped fire. Eyes so dark blue they looked purple, above lips so luscious they could advertise…anything at all, and he'd buy it. He blinked, wondering if he'd conjured this woman out of his boredom. But a second glance told him she was no fantasy; she was a flesh and blood woman—and she was rigid with anger. The dark blond hair pulled back off her face exposed the taut jawline. Her breathing was short and shallow, her creamy cheeks flushed, and she faced the room square on. He didn't need to be an expert on body language to see this woman was humming with fury.

Seth's masculine eye noted the tall, slender length of her body; his banker's eye noted that she wore an expensive coat and accessories that had seen better days. She also wore that attitude—and it crackled. Almost before he realized what he was doing, Seth found himself rising from his seat.

Her gaze snapped to his face. "Mr. O'Reilly?"

Yep, the voice was exactly what he would have expected. Crisp and ladylike. She was clearly furious, but she didn't raise her voice. He admired that kind of control.

He tried for a neutral expression as he answered calmly. "Yes, I'm Seth O'Reilly." Fifteen years in banking had taught him that irate customers were always easier to deal with if he could defuse their anger first.

Stella, the executive receptionist, and a uniformed security guard piled in behind the woman. "Sorry," she gasped, glaring at the woman. "I told her she couldn't come in here, but she barged past me."

"I'm a customer of this bank, and I'd like a moment of your time, please. Now." The words were delivered in the same softly determined voice, but Seth heard the quaver underneath and recognized the naked desperation in her eyes. Every chivalrous instinct surged within him. Maybe he couldn't cure cancer, but he could certainly help a mother who was having a problem with his bank.

He'd opened his mouth to speak when Carl Fletcher beat him to it. "As you can see, Mr. O'Reilly is busy now. I'm in charge of customer services. If you'd like to make an appointment, I'll try to see you next week."

"That's not good enough."

"Ow, Mama, you're squeezing me."

"It's all right, darling." That voice was definitely shaking now.

Seth surveyed the faces around the table. The expressions ranged from embarrassment to boredom. No wonder those customer ads were all crap.

Bert, the security guard, looked as though he wished the woman carried an Uzi instead of a child. He'd have a better idea of what to do with a gun-toting intruder.

"Ladies and gentlemen," Seth began. When he had the attention of his executives, he gestured to the woman inside the doorway. "*This* is the new face of banking. Stella, please seat this customer in my office." Then to the woman he said, "I'll be with you in a moment."

She was still steaming. He could see it in the line of her body, the way she held her chin up. For a second, he thought she might refuse to budge, but then, after glaring at him for another moment, she nodded stiffly and stalked out behind Stella.

The security guard wiped his forehead as he closed the door.

"Really, Seth, I would have thought this meeting was more imp—"

"That's where you're wrong, Carl. That woman is the reason we're in business. Never forget it."

He glanced coldly at each person in turn. "Excuse me, I have to see a customer."

Then he smiled for the first time that day.

CHAPTER TWO

MELISSA HAD EXPECTED THE bank manager to be old. Fatherly. Someone who might be won over by the thought of homeless children. She didn't want Seth O'Reilly to be close to her own age and good looking.

After Stephen, she no longer trusted handsome men.

With shaking hands, she settled Alice on the floor near a rack of glossy brochures advertising the bank's services, and perched at the edge of a gray upholstered visitor's chair.

After icily showing them into the office, Stella had marched off, leaving Melissa and Alice alone, and Melissa realized she needed a minute or two to calm herself. She'd never felt such anger—and never in her memory had she acted so brazenly.

Now that she had the attention of the man at the top, all she had to figure out was how to make the most of it. She took deep calming breaths while she tried to collect her thoughts. How would she convince the bank president that he had to let her keep her house?

A quick glance around the office revealed little in the way of inspiration. It was an executive office like a million others. Neat, professional, impersonal—except for the bag of crisply laundered shirts hanging from the door handle with the dry cleaner's tag still attached.

The dozen or so shirts themselves had about as much personality as the bag, spanning an entire spectrum from white to pale blue. Dull, corporate and respectable. She bet all his suits were navy or charcoal and all his ties had burgundy in them. He was probably a guy who always followed the rules; somehow, she would have to make him bend them in her case.

Apart from his dry cleaning, the only signs of the man's personal life were a squash racquet propped against one wall and a single picture on the rosewood desk in front of her. Leaning forward she turned the frame around and peered at two identical faces grinning back at her. The twin girls looked about ten years old. And, if a picture could tell a thousand words, this one told of pranks and mischief.

It wasn't the Raggedy Ann hair and freckles; it was the eyes—they were too round and innocent to be believed. And Melissa didn't fall for the "oh, what a sweet pair of angels" expression for a moment.

In her earlier career as a pediatric nurse—before being Mrs. Stephen Theisen had taken up all of her time—she'd treated all kinds of children. A lot of her patients had orchestrated their own hospital visits, falling out of trees or lighting themselves on fire—any number of disasters that poorly supervised brats could fall into.

The twins looked like high-spirited mischief makers through and through. And vaguely familiar.

"Their names are Laura and Jessica."

With a start, Melissa replaced the photo and stood to face Seth O'Reilly. "Thanks for seeing me. I thought I was going to be handcuffed and arrested like a bank robber."

He winced like a man in pain. He must take his job at the bank pretty seriously. "I'm sorry about that." It seemed as if he wanted to say more, but thought better of it. He squatted down to Alice's level and asked, "Would you like some juice?"

Alice was absorbed in assessing the various merits of a glossy new mortgage, a financial plan that made sense in today's volatile economy and a retirement package that promised she'd spend her golden years golfing and fishing. She glanced up from the fan of colorful brochures on the floor and, after sizing up the man for several unsmiling seconds, handed him a brochure with a crumpled corner.

He glanced at it. "You'd rather have an on-demand line of credit? Very sensible, especially if you're taking your mom toy shopping." He smiled at the little girl and, obviously deciding she'd found a friend, she smiled back.

Melissa hoped he'd be as nice to her.

Straightening, he turned and extended his hand. "Seth O'Reilly."

"Melissa Theisen." She shook his hand, glad he didn't seem worried about Alice mauling bank property. He had a nice, warm handshake, no he-man wrestler's grip, just a pleasant squeeze. He looked to be a pleasant, no-nonsense man as well, although the nurse in Melissa detected that his skin was unnaturally pale and his eyes had a dull glow she'd long ago learned to associate with pain. She hoped whatever he had wasn't contagious. The last thing she had time for now was a flu epidemic on top of eviction from their home.

"Would you like some coffee, Ms. Theisen?"

She'd like a reprieve from her mortgage and worries. She'd like to sleep at night. She wanted her old life back.

But a cup of coffee would be a start. "Thanks, cream and sugar. And Alice would love some juice."

The banker didn't push a button to summon an underling. He said, "I'll be right back," and turned toward the doorway only to pause when he spotted the dry cleaning.

"Sorry about this stuff," he said as he picked up the hanging bag and moved to open a closet door. Inside hung three jackets—one navy, one navy pinstripe and one charcoal. Half a dozen burgundy ties hung on a tie rack.

Melissa didn't realize she was smirking until he caught her at it.

"I don't really live here. I keep some things at the office because I don't have a lot of time in the mornings."

"I'm sorry. I wasn't thinking you live here, only...um...all your clothes look alike." *Oh, great. How to win friends and influence people—start by insulting the bank manager.*

The corners of his eyes crinkled when he smiled. For a second Melissa forgot why she was there and basked in the warmth of that smile. "It's the conservative look. They teach it in banking school."

A chuckle was surprised out of her. His sense of humor definitely didn't go with his boring wardrobe.

"Mornings are hectic enough. I don't have time to worry about putting the right shirt with the right tie. Everything I own matches everything else. Simple."

Now she understood. She'd felt the same way when, as a new mother, she'd cut her waist-length hair and tossed out her hot rollers.

"I'll get that coffee."

By the time he returned with a plastic tray containing two mugs and a glass of orange juice, Melissa had worked herself back to nervous. She took refuge in fussing around arranging Alice in a position where she'd be least likely to knock over her drink. Then she sat down and took a sip of coffee.

Glancing up, she saw Seth O'Reilly, now seated at his desk, do the same, and couldn't miss the grimace that crossed his face after he swallowed. Gastric trouble, she diagnosed mentally.

"You should try to avoid coffee," she said without thinking. Then gasped at her tactlessness. First she'd critiqued his wardrobe, now his health habits. Must be nerves.

"Great, now my doctor's sending out spies." He rolled his eyes in an expression of comical horror.

Melissa couldn't help but smile. "I used to be a pediatric nurse. Sorry."

"I didn't know caffeine addiction was rampant among children." He was teasing her, and the half smile on his face creased his cheeks into deeply attractive lines.

"You can get gastric troubles at any age," she said in her best nurse voice.

"Hmm. I'd drink Maalox instead, but I hate that thick milk mustache it gives me."

A typical stubborn man. She was glad he wasn't her patient. "Ulcer?"

He shook his head. "Acid reflux."

"Try herbal tea."

His disgusted expression told her what he thought of that idea. "If Dr. Ling didn't send you to check up on me, what can I do for you?"

Licking her lips, she glanced up into gray blue eyes fringed with black lashes. If he still felt discomfort, he wasn't showing it. He had a nice face. Not magnetically handsome like Stephen's, but nice. A face that grew more appealing each time she looked at it.

"You can let me keep my house," she blurted.

A crease formed between his eyebrows, and the look of

pain flashed again in his eyes. He reached for the computer keyboard on his desk, then, without so much as touching a key, paused and dropped his hands. His gaze shifted back to Melissa. "Why don't you tell me about it?"

"My husband—ex-husband—is supposed to pay the mortgage. It was part of our divorce agreement. But he seems to have disappeared." She stopped to swallow hard. She'd cried enough tears over Stephen; she wouldn't embarrass herself in front of a stranger.

"What do you mean he's disappeared?" He passed a box of tissues as casually as if most of his meetings were conducted in tears.

"He's g-gone. He's missed two of his weekends with the children." She yanked out a tissue and blew her nose. "I had no idea he'd stopped paying the mortgage…until I got this letter." She pulled the now wrinkled document out of her purse and waved it.

"You have a copy of the divorce agreement?"

She nodded.

"Where does he work?"

"He's self-employed. I tried calling yesterday, when I got the letter, but his office phone's been disconnected."

His focus on her sharpened and the crease between his eyes deepened.

"His home phone? Cell?"

She shook her head and sniffed. "Disconnected."

"Does he own his home or rent?"

"He rented an apartment downtown. I drove over there yesterday, after I got this letter." She swallowed. "He's gone."

Now he did drag the keyboard closer and started typing.

"Would you spell your last name for me, please?"

She'd already been through all this with Mr. Cheney, but

she didn't bother telling him that. Maybe his computer would give better news. Hah. And maybe this was all a bad dream.

Mr. O'Reilly took a longer time to scan the screen in front of him than Mr. Cheney had. He also pushed a few more buttons, clearly taking more of an interest in her case. Melissa began to feel hopeful.

Then she saw him glance at Alice, who was happily playing on the floor. There was pity in his eyes. "The mortgage hasn't been paid in more than sixty days. We've sent several letters to Mr. Theisen's current address and received no response. The last one went to the mortgaged property."

She nodded. "I got the letter yesterday. I didn't know anything about it." She felt her anger returning.

"I'm sorry, it's bank policy to call in a loan after ninety days of nonpayment, Ms. Theisen." He looked truly sad. *They must teach that in banking school, too—the Stanislavsky method of customer relations. Act like you care.*

"But I've got young children. I'm sure I can catch up with the payments now that I know about the problem. I need time. You can't throw us out on the street."

A glimmer of humor crossed his features. "In spite of the way you've been treated today, we do try to look after our customers. Under the circumstances, I can give you an extra thirty days to put a plan in place."

"Thirty days. I was supposed to get the house." She was speechless with shock and anger but at least the urge to cry had dried up. "This is *not* my problem."

"I'm afraid it is. The house is in your name all right, so whatever equity you've built up is yours, but the bank holds the property as collateral against the outstanding mortgage balance."

"You mean my house belongs to you?"

"We don't want it. The last thing a bank wants is a fore-closure. We'll help you any way we can."

"For thirty days." She pictured the trailer where her father still lived and shuddered.

Still watching her, O'Reilly heaved a sigh. "Do you have any idea where your husband is?"

"Ex-husband." Melissa glanced down at Alice, glad to see she was busy finger painting orange juice on one of the brochures, seemingly too caught up in her activity to listen to the grown-ups. "He hasn't been in touch with the kids in almost a month. And he hasn't paid child support in several months." She paused, knowing she'd been played for a sucker. "He said he was going through a cash crunch and promised to pay me everything he owed as soon as things got better."

"I take it things didn't get better."

"He's an entrepreneur. All our married life he had ups and downs financially. He used to be in car parts, then he moved to airplane parts." She shrugged. "And the airline business hasn't been so great in the last few years, but we always ended up fine. I trusted him to take care of his children. I assumed he was a better man than he's turned out to be."

"Have you contacted your lawyer?"

Melissa felt a flush heating her face. "We used the same lawyer. Stephen said it would be cheaper, and the agreement they worked out seemed fair."

Mr. O'Reilly scanned the computer screen. "You received your fair share of his pension and investments?"

She shook her head. "There's no pension or invest-ments. It was all tied up in the company. All I wanted was the house and the children." Her voice trembled again. "I can't believe he cheated us."

"You mean—"

"I know it was stupid of me. Believe me, I'm not as naive as I was. I called the lawyer, but he said there's nothing he can do. Stephen owes him money, too. Now I'm too broke to get another lawyer. To sue him, I have to find him."

"The police might be able to help. Do you think he's still in Washington State?"

"I doubt he's still in the country. Stephen used to talk about the opportunities in Eastern Europe." She glanced at Alice and lowered her voice. "There's a woman in the Czech Republic." She looked at the banker. "I only know her first name, Vladka. Oh, and that she's twenty-two and models."

When the kids had come home with expensive presents from their dad the last time they'd seen him, she'd been annoyed that he was buying their affection with gifts while holding back the support payments that kept them in food and clothes. It hadn't occurred to her until recently that he was giving them goodbye presents.

"I've called everyone I could think of. Our mutual friends, former clients of his. His parents went back to Germany after they retired. His mother's still alive, but she says she hasn't heard from him, either." She stared at the bank manager with the pain-dulled eyes. "How could anyone leave the family they were supposed to love?"

There was a strange moment when something flashed between the two of them, some pull of understanding or sympathy so powerful she felt her breath catch.

"Do you have other sources of income?" he asked brusquely, dropping his gaze to his keyboard.

"I do some landscape design, but the business is so young. It's not enough to support the kids and me. It covers groceries."

He nodded. "Have you thought about going back to nursing?"

"Of course I've thought about it. By the time I retrain and then pay for child care for two children, we'll hardly get ahead." She rubbed her forehead where a dull headache thrummed. "I've scaled back our expenses to the bone. My car's ten years old and I rarely drive it. We don't buy anything we don't absolutely need."

"You've built up some equity. The way house prices are rising in your area you could sell and move to a less expensive home."

"No!" He glanced at her, obviously startled at her loud cry. She forced herself to calm down. "I have watched my children suffer enough. Do you have any idea what it's like to see their confusion and hurt when they lose a parent?"

She saw his jaw clench once, hard, and then he nodded.

"At least they've got their home and their mother," she continued. "They can go to the same school and play with the same friends. I'll do anything to keep that much for them. Anything."

"It's not—"

"I've always paid my bills. Always. I don't have so much as an unpaid library fine in my past. I am going to make a good life for my children. I promise you."

Her passion must have reached him, and her determination.

"Here is the best I can offer. We can extend your mortgage to thirty years and renew you early at a lower rate than you're at now. It's going to cut your payments almost in half, but of course you won't be getting very far ahead."

"And the six thousand in back payments and fees?"

He stared at her for another moment, obviously

debating. She held her breath and tried to look like exactly what she was. A woman who stood by her commitments. Who paid her dues.

At last he said, "I'll add the fees to the mortgage principal. You'll pay it, but over time."

Relief made her feel dizzy. "That's okay. That's wonderful. When do I have to make the first payment?"

He sighed. Seemed to wrestle with himself. "Let's say sixty days from today."

"Thank you. I won't let you down."

"Mrs. Theisen, I suggest—" The phone on his desk rang and he frowned at it. "Excuse me," he mumbled and lifted the receiver. "Stella, I asked you to hold all my calls. What? Oh, put her through."

There was a pause, during which he glanced at his watch and the frown intensified and then, "Hi, honey, is there a problem at school?"

The look of concern changed to horror. She heard hysterical babbling sounds coming from the receiver.

"What? Where are you? How much blood?"

CHAPTER THREE

SETH O'REILLY jerked to his feet, glancing at Melissa with blatant fear in his eyes. "You're a nurse— My daughter's throwing up blood. I can be home in ten minutes. Should they call 9-1-1?"

"How much blood?" She repeated his question.

He looked completely baffled. "Hard to say."

She thought quickly, then shook her head. "The children are already panicked. I think it's better if you take her to the hospital."

He nodded once, then spoke into the receiver with a calmness at odds with the worry on his face. "Hang on, honey, I'll be right there." He hung up and turned to Melissa. "Would you come, too?" He didn't bother to disguise his fear.

"It could be flu." She stood watching him grab his coat, root for keys.

"Please?"

He'd helped her out of a tough spot, and even though it had been more than eight years since she'd nursed, her first-aid training was current.

"All right."

She glanced down at Alice, who'd picked up the atmosphere in the room and was staring anxiously at her mother. "We're going to help a little girl who isn't feeling too well."

Hauling Alice up in her arms and ignoring the crumpled mess of brochures littering the rug, Melissa scurried to keep up as Seth O'Reilly's long legs strode at top speed ahead of her. He yelled something to the astonished Stella on his way past. He didn't pause at the elevator but charged straight for the stairs. Melissa followed, her shoes clattering on the gray cement steps, one arm firmly around Alice, the other clinging to the handrail.

By the time she emerged from the street exit, he was a dark shape sprinting toward the parked cars. Even as she started forward, he leaped into a maroon Volvo. In seconds he was pealing out of the parking space and heading toward her. His impatience was palpable as she carefully buckled her daughter in the pull-down child's seat in the back.

Thank God they were in the safest car known to man, she thought, as they roared out of the parking lot. She buckled her own seat belt and turned a watchful eye on Seth O'Reilly. His face was set in a grim mask, all the emotions locked down, hands steady on the wheel. Only the speed at which they were traveling gave away his distress. She had a strong feeling he wasn't a habitual speeder.

"You won't help your daughters if you get in an accident," she warned him.

He didn't answer. Nor did he ease off on the accelerator. He removed one hand from the wheel, dug out a cell phone and pushed a button. The phone was shoved her way. "It's Jessica and Laura."

"Where are the girls?"

"My house."

"It's ringing.... Alone?" She couldn't help it if she sounded critical. They were too young to be alone.

"They're supposed to be at school."

"Where's their mother?" She couldn't imagine her kids approaching Stephen with a problem; it was always to her that they'd come.

"Their mother's dead."

"Oh. I'm sorry." A click sounded in her ear and then a recorded message. "There's no answer," she informed the man next to her.

She clamped her teeth together to keep from screaming as they careened round a corner, narrowly missing a milk delivery truck. O'Reilly ignored the shouted obscenities and accompanying hand gestures from the outraged driver.

They shot into a tree-lined boulevard not far from her own neighborhood. The homes that flashed by were a blur of well-kept Colonials and Tudors.

She was thrown against the passenger door by the g-force as he swung from one crescent onto another.

"Whee!" squealed Alice.

Moments later they jerked to a halt. He was out of the car and running up the path that bisected the only ragged lawn on the crescent. Quickly, Melissa helped Alice out of the backseat.

"Where we going?"

"We're going to visit a little girl who's sick. Can you be very good while Mommy's busy?"

Alice nodded solemnly, and Melissa couldn't help hugging her as she hauled her up into her arms once again and hurried up the walk mentally reviewing what she knew of internal bleeding.

The front door was wide open, and as she approached it she could hear the crying—in stereo.

Melissa sucked in a deep breath and crossed the threshold. After locking the front door behind her, she secured

Alice in the cluttered living room to the right of the front door. A quick survey told her there wasn't any clear danger to Alice, so she sat her on the floor near a pile of Barbie paraphernalia, with instructions to stay put.

Melissa followed the sounds of crying up the stairs and along a hall, where her nose was able to help pinpoint the twins' location. The air was toxic with the scent of vomit.

"Daddy, I can't stop throwing—" The tearful voice was cut off by a bout of retching.

Melissa poked her head around the open door to find one curly redhead bending over the toilet, heaving. An identical head was bent over the sink, similarly occupied.

Relief struck her immediately. If they were both vomiting then it was either flu or something they'd eaten. She could put away the sketchy knowledge of ruptured blood vessels and cancer.

"Do everything together, do they?" she said, stepping into the crowded bathroom.

Seth O'Reilly stood poised in the middle of the floor in his business suit—arms stretched to their limit so he could rub both heaving backs simultaneously.

He shot her a helpless-parent look that took her back to her days on the emergency ward. "Do something. They're bleeding their guts out."

"If they're both sick, it's a good sign," she said soothingly, keeping her voice calm but positive. How easily she slipped back into the nurse role.

Stepping behind him, she managed a good survey of the sink. "Which one started vomiting first?"

The one at the sink pointed to the one bent over the toilet.

"Still think it's flu?" Seth O'Reilly asked her.

"Could be." She did a rapid check for fever by putting

her forearm on the back of each bent neck. "They're a little warm, but that could be from exertion."

She gently lifted the wrist of the girl closest to her and found the pulse rapid, but nice and strong. "What did you girls eat last?"

The one over the sink groaned and started heaving. The one at the toilet stopped crying long enough to gasp, "Brownies. We made them ourselves."

Melissa glanced at their father, who appeared horrified at the news. "Hang on, I'll check the kitchen," she said.

She ran down to the kitchen and sure enough there was a large cake pan, empty but for a couple of remaining lumps of tar-like substance.

Pigging out on a whole pan of brownies was enough to make anyone sick, in Melissa's opinion, but not so violently. Puzzled, she studied the perfectly ordinary brownie recipe staring at her from an open book on the counter.

Everything the girls had used seemed to be on display, from baking chocolate to an oozing jar of corn syrup, to sugar and vanilla. There was nothing unusual, except that the flour canister in the far corner looked undisturbed.

In the interests of medical research, Melissa pinched off a lump of the brown stuff in the pan. It smelled like chocolate. She bit off a tiny piece and chewed. Careful not to swallow, she rinsed her mouth with water. Along with the strong chocolate taste, she noted a peculiar flavor.

She sorted more carefully through the ingredients strewn all over the counter. The only thing she didn't instantly recognize was an unmarked white plastic container with white powder inside. Beside it, a Pyrex measuring cup had powder residue almost up to the two-cup mark.

Using the tip of her tongue, Melissa tasted the powder

and wrinkled her nose: baking soda. The girls had obviously mistaken it for flour. No wonder the little stinkers were heaving their guts out.

And in the midst of the kitchen counter was a pitcher of bright-red cranberry cocktail and two nearly empty glasses of the red stuff. So much for the "blood."

With a muttered prayer of gratitude that they'd ingested nothing worse than bicarb of soda, she went back upstairs, sticking her head in the living room on the way by to see Alice happily trying to wrestle Ken into one of Barbie's evening gowns.

Back in the bathroom, the crying had started up again. "My stomach hurts," wailed one little girl, doubled over. The other one was now sitting on the toilet seat as though she knew she'd never get far.

Seth O'Reilly had his arms wrapped round the girl with the cramps. "I'm taking them straight to the hospital."

"Seems they made a pan of brownies using bicarb of soda in place of flour, and drank it down with cranberry juice."

"And you think that's funny?"

"That's what was turning their vomit red. Not blood."

As her words sank in, he slumped against the vanity, panic ebbing out of his face. But the concern was still there. "Thank God. But they're really sick. What should I do?"

"It won't do them any permanent damage. If they were my kids I'd put them to bed." She shrugged. "But the hospital can give them a shot to stop the vomiting. It's up to you."

He pulled the second girl into his embrace and hugged both children to him fiercely. "Right, come on girls. We'll have you feeling better in no time."

"Who's she?" asked one.

"This is Mrs. Theisen. She's a nurse and she's here to

help you." O'Reilly glanced over at Melissa as if wondering how to proceed next.

"Why don't I get the girls' coats and maybe a couple of buckets."

"Coats are on the hooks by the back door. There should be some buckets in the garage."

She found the jackets on the floor in the living room. There might have been buckets in the garage, but Melissa figured she'd end up in the hospital herself if she tried to wade through all the junk in there. Back in the house, she emptied a couple of overflowing waste-paper bins to serve the purpose.

"Alice and I live near here. Maybe you could drop us off?" she asked once everybody was buckled into the car.

"Aren't you coming with us?"

"I can't. I have to be home when my son gets out of school at three o'clock. It's after two now."

He glanced at her and she could almost read his mind. He was going to suggest she call a taxi, but knew she couldn't afford one.

"Please, it's on your way," she said, and quickly gave him directions.

When they reached her house, he barely waited till she had Alice out of the car before speeding away, leaving Melissa saying "I hope you feel better," to the empty road.

"HI, MOM, I'M HOME." Matthew's voice bounced high with excitement. At eight, he still thought she was the greatest being in the universe, and he held a special place in her heart as the only male who'd ever really loved her.

"Hi, darling, how was your day?" Melissa gasped as he squeezed her in a bear hug.

"Hi, Maffew." Alice ran up to get her turn at a bear hug, then laughed as her big brother lifted her feet clear off the floor.

"Guess what?" With all the importance due the only member of the family whose daily activities took him outside the home, Matthew plunked down at the kitchen table for his regular recitation of the day's events.

"What?"

"We're going on a field trip to see a play about space. It's gonna be so cool. I'm thinking about being an astronaut when I grow up, so it'll be real good to go."

At the words *field trip,* Melissa's heart sank. Field trips cost money. "I thought you were going to be a doctor?"

"Nah. Myron Oberfeller's dad's a doctor and all he does is look up people's noses. I tried it a few times at school. It was awesome when Ryan Doran had a bad cold, but mostly it's pretty boring."

Stifling a smile, she said, "I think Dr. Oberfeller is an ear, nose and throat specialist. Other doctors do more interesting things."

"That's okay. I've pretty much decided on being an astronaut." Now that he had his career settled, Matthew glanced around the kitchen hopefully.

Melissa prided herself on the wholesome home baking she served her family, but today she hadn't had a lot of time for baking. She sliced carrot sticks and dug out a dozen chocolate chip cookies from her emergency stash in the freezer. She had a packet of brownies in there, too. She shuddered and pulled out the cookies, which for some odd reason her kids preferred frozen, then poured the milk.

There was a knock at the kitchen door, and Matthew bolted out of his chair.

"Wait till I see who it is," Melissa reminded him.

"It's Josh," he said with the intense frustration of an eight-year-old who wants to play with his buddy *now*. Melissa was fairly certain he was right, but she still checked the window above her son's head to be sure. And broke into a smile.

Josh wasn't alone. His mother and little brother, who was only a few months younger than Alice, were also there.

"Hi," she said to them all. "Come in." As the boys ran by her, Melissa greeted Pam Bryant, her neighbor and friend. "Coffee?"

Pam grinned. "I brought my own Sweet'n Low."

The kids made short work of the cookies and carrots and then asked to go downstairs to the basement playroom. The moms helped the three-year-olds with the stairs after the older boys bounded down. Once they were ensconced down there, the two women could relax knowing everybody was safe.

Melissa brewed coffee and offered to warm up more cookies.

"No," Pam groaned. "Don't tempt me. I need to lose ten pounds before we go to the Caribbean."

"You're going to the Caribbean?" Melissa turned around to stare. "Oh, how wonderful. White sand beaches, turquoise water—"

"Two-piece bathing suit."

She laughed. "What's the occasion?"

Pam paused for a tiny second. "Our tenth anniversary."

Melissa would never see her tenth wedding anniversary, but she didn't let that stop her from being happy for her friend. "Hey, that's great. You know, Greg almost deserves you."

"He thinks I'm crazy to diet, too."

"I'm so glad I know you two. Greg reminds me that there really are good men out there. And you remind me that some women do have good judgment."

"Stephen was a charmer, Melissa. He fooled everyone."

She nodded, poured the coffee and sat down across from her neighbor. "He certainly fooled me." She proceeded to tell Pam about the bank's letter. For a long while during her marriage and even for the early part of the separation and divorce, when she'd been so shocked and had tried to convince herself that this was some crazy phase Stephen was going through and that it would pass, through all that she'd kept her troubles to herself. But one day Pam had come across her crying and she'd sobbed it all out. From that day, she'd realized the value of a friend who stood by her, let her say really awful things about Stephen that she needed to get off her chest, let her rant and rail and whimper.

In the year since the divorce, they'd become closer than sisters.

"Oh, my God," Pam said when she finished her story. "That bastard. We knew he was a bad man, but even I didn't think he'd turn out to be a deadbeat dad."

Melissa blinked. Her friend was right. *Deadbeat dad.* It was a phrase you read in tabloids. Not something that applied to a man you'd loved and had children with. Except in her case, it did.

"What are you going to do?"

"I'm not letting go of this house," she said fiercely. "The bank president turned out to be a pretty good guy. He's working out something so I pay a lower monthly mortgage payment. Of course, I'll pay it forever, but if I can just hang on until the kids are out of school…"

"If you need a loan, to get you through the next few months…"

Her eyes filled with tears. "I'm fine. But thank you from the bottom of my heart for offering."

"Hey," Pam said, her own eyes filling. "It's what friends do. The offer stays open. I still have a nest egg from when I worked. Greg doesn't have to know anything about it."

"I thought I had time, you know? With Stephen paying the mortgage and child support, we were okay. I had time to build my landscape design business." She shook her head. "Now I've got sixty days to figure out how to do it all myself. I'll have to find a job."

There was half a cookie left on the plate, and Pam popped it into her mouth almost as though she didn't realize she was doing it. She stopped midchew and moaned. "Oh, honey. You are the only woman I know who bakes better than my mom. Hell, who even bakes anymore? You cook healthy food, you raise gorgeous kids." She swallowed and said, "I know what you should do, you should run a school for moms."

Melissa laughed. "Better still, I should be a stand-in mom for kids who don't have one." And she told her neighbor about the banker's unsupervised daughters and their little baking experiment.

"Oh, my God. They could have killed themselves. Why weren't they at school?"

"I get the feeling that their dad is having a rough time controlling two high-spirited, motherless girls."

"Of course," Pam said, slapping her forehead. "That's what you should do."

"What?"

"Run a private day-care center from your home." She

leaned forward, her eyes widening as she got excited by her idea. "You're a trained pediatric nurse, you bake everything from scratch and your house is so child-friendly it's ridiculous. A friend of mine has been complaining about trying to find decent child care. You'd be perfect."

Melissa stared at her friend for a long moment and then nodded slowly. "You're right. That's the perfect solution. And I know a couple of kids who could sure use my help." She bit her lip. "Will you watch my kids for an hour or two after dinner?"

"Sure."

"I've got to pick up my car and then I've got some marketing and promotions to take care of."

"I'll drive you to your car," Pam offered.

"I owe you."

"Hah. Don't worry. I plan to use your day-care services."

"Anytime. But for you there will be no charge. We're friends."

CHAPTER FOUR

SETH GLANCED IN THE rearview mirror at the two children's bodies sprawled in sleep, red curls mingling. They were going to be fine. His heart squeezed with a painful feeling of relief. And guilt.

He wasn't good enough.

If only Claire were still here, none of this would have happened. She'd have made them a pan of goddamn brownies if they wanted them. And she'd for damned sure have made certain that his kids weren't sneaking home at lunch hour to an empty house.

Claire.

He tried not to think of her. It hurt too much. Going to the hospital had brought it all back. St. Vincent's was where she'd given birth to the twins.

And where she'd died.

And where, that last day, he'd promised to be mother and father to the girls.

He was failing miserably, and the torture chamber that used to be his stomach punished him for his failings on a regular basis.

This time he'd been lucky. The doctor hadn't even pumped their stomachs, merely put them both on IV drips for a few hours with some antinausea meds and something to rehydrate them. His daughters were going to be fine. But he felt his reprieve like a warning; his current child care arrangement wasn't only unsatisfactory, it was downright dangerous.

The car headlights guided him into the driveway. When he cut the engine everything went black, and Seth cursed himself for not flipping on some lights earlier.

The house appeared dark, cold and uninviting. He wished with all his heart and soul that Claire were here waiting for him. Claire with her good-natured laugh and generous loving. "Aw, baby, I miss you," he whispered under his breath as he dragged his exhausted body from the car.

And froze.

His heart jerked painfully against his ribs when a female figure rose gracefully from the front steps and glided toward him.

The hair stood up on the back of his neck and he felt his flesh break out in goose bumps as the apparition moved closer. "Claire?" his voice croaked.

Even as he whispered the name, he knew it wasn't his wife. The woman coming toward him was too tall and too slim.

"It's Melissa Theisen," she answered softly, her voice floating smoothly through the night air.

Disappointment crushed him. He wanted his wife, even if just for a brief ghostly visitation. He was tired, lonely and worried about his children. The last thing he needed was this woman with her mountain of problems.

He could hardly shoulder his own burdens, never mind hers.

She hadn't been so all-fired-up wonderful as a nurse, either, now he thought about it. He sighed. That wasn't fair. She'd been perfectly professional, but the twins needed their mother, not a nurse. He hadn't thought the evening could possibly get worse. Looked like he was wrong.

"This is a surprise," he managed to get out.

"How are the girls?" He could just make out the pale blur of her face as she stopped in front of him.

"You were right. They spent a few hours on an IV drip and they've been sent home to sleep it off." He opened the back car door and unbelted Laura.

"If you hand me your house keys I'll open the door for you," that calm voice suggested. He hesitated, then handed her the keys. By the time he had Laura hoisted in his arms, the outside lights were on and the front door wide open.

Trudging into the house and up the stairs with his sleeping burden, he felt suddenly grateful for the woman snapping lights on upstairs and pulling the bedsheets down so he could slip Laura into bed. She'd guessed wrong, but he didn't think the girls were in any shape to notice until morning they were in the opposite beds.

"Would you like me to put her nightclothes on while you get her sister?"

"Thanks. Her pajamas are...ah..." He glanced around the cluttered piles of clothing all over the floor until he recognized a cotton nightshirt with a picture of one of those nauseating boy singers on it. "Here."

He bolted back downstairs and by the time he returned with Jessie, Laura was tucked in and sleeping peacefully.

Within a couple of minutes, Melissa Theisen had Jessie settled in efficiently, and she'd done something to the beds so they appeared smooth and freshly made.

She nodded and quietly left the room.

He kissed them each on the forehead, promising silently

to do better for them in the future. He crept out of the room—or tried to. A stray fashion doll, naked as the day she was molded, tripped him up and sent him crashing against the door jamb.

One of the girls muttered in her sleep, then sighed.

He cursed softly. The entire house was a pigsty. He'd let it go because the current housekeeper was a trained teacher who couldn't find a job. She'd seemed like a responsible young woman, and knowing that she wanted to be a teacher, Seth figured she'd be fantastic with kids.

Now that he saw just how irresponsible she was, he hoped she never got a teaching job. In his opinion, the education system was in enough trouble.

When he returned downstairs, Mrs. Theisen stood at the bottom with a brown paper bag from which wafted a mouth-watering aroma. "I brought you some vegetable soup," she said. "If the girls wake up hungry, this would be good for them. Easily digestible and very nutritious. I brought enough for you, too."

"You didn't have to do that," he said, feeling awkward and embarrassed.

"Well, I wasn't merely being neighborly. I do have an ulterior motive."

He tried to keep his face neutral even though he wanted to kick something. This was not the first "casserole" he'd received that had come with thick strings attached. "I see." He knew her financial situation, possibly a little better than she did herself. If she asked him out, on this very day when she'd discovered she was in a financial jam, he wouldn't know how to turn her down without embarrassing the pair of them.

God, why had he put himself in this situation? If he

hadn't panicked when he'd got that call and thought he might need her training…

He took the bag she offered and, since he couldn't put it on the floor, he walked through to the kitchen, suggesting she follow.

"What a mess," he said when he saw the baking disaster in the kitchen. He'd forgotten all about it.

"Would you like me to help you clean it up?" she asked.

"No," he said, more forcefully than he meant to. He blew out a breath. "Sorry. I'm pretty beat. Why don't you tell me what's on your mind." He motioned to the kitchen chairs. She pulled one out and sat.

He put the bag on the counter. "Thanks for your help today." Pushing a stack of newspapers to the floor, he sank into a matching chair and leaned back, exhausted. He was almost relieved that Mrs. Theisen was here. She'd shared part of the crisis with him, and even if she did have a not very well-hidden agenda, he was touched that she cared enough to check on the children and bring them soup.

He felt like he'd aged ten years in one day, rushing the twins to the hospital then soothing them through the examinations, rubbing their backs each time a new spasm of retching shook their slight bodies and, finally, watching them sleep as the drugs took effect.

The only time he'd left them was when he'd phoned that useless housekeeper and fired her.

"You're welcome." She smiled at him faintly and he thought again what an attractive woman she was. Gorgeous, he imagined, when her eyes weren't etched with worry and she put some effort into hair and makeup.

There was silence for a moment. He couldn't summon

up small talk so he left it to her. Finally she asked, "Who's Claire?"

"What?"

"You called me Claire."

"Claire was my wife." He let his tone resonate with finality.

"What happened to her?" She asked the question as normally as if she were asking what he liked for breakfast. He felt as though something was smothering him. His chest labored to draw breath.

"Cancer. She got breast cancer and they did the old poison, slash and burn treatment. But it spread, first to her spine, until she couldn't walk." He let all the anger and viciousness he harbored spill out as though it were this woman's fault Claire had died. He knew it wasn't, but she should at least have the decency to leave the woman dead and buried, not question him for all the gory details. Well, if she wanted details he could give her enough to make her sick to her stomach. "Then it spread to her brain and some days she didn't know who she was, didn't recognize her own children. Didn't understand why she was in so much pain." He gasped at the anguish he was feeling.

"You must have loved her very much," she said softly, and he realized it was hopeless to try to intimidate a former nurse with illness horror stories. She'd probably seen it all.

"Yeah."

"She was lucky."

Something exploded in his brain. "Lucky? What's so lucky about having your flesh and bones, even your brain, eaten away by disease? What's so lucky about dying at thirty-five?" His voice was raw and hoarse.

"I meant she was lucky to be able to leave this world

knowing she was loved, and that there was someone to care for her children when she was gone."

"Huh. And a piss-poor job I'm doing at that. The twins are only ten years old. They could have set the house on fire while they were making brownies, or cooked up something even more poisonous."

"You said you had a child-care provider?"

"She was supposed to be here all day. Instead, she snuck off—to her boyfriend's, probably."

"From the state of the house, I'd say she was doing a piss-poor job, too."

Even though she was repeating his own words, the sound of a vulgarity coming from Mrs. Theisen's mouth shocked the hell out of him.

"Yeah. I fired her."

She nodded. "Good." She glanced at him, then at the brown paper bag on the counter. "Would you like me to warm that soup for you?"

"I'll shower and change before I eat." He was pretty sure he smelled like vomit.

"Look. I thought of a way we could help each other out."

She appeared mildly embarrassed. He never knew how to handle these awkward situations. Not that he'd been in many of them, but in the past three years he'd had some offers, usually from nice women he didn't want to hurt. Like this one.

"I really don't think so," he said as firmly as he could, hoping to cut her off at the pass.

Her eyebrows rose. "You don't even know what I'm going to suggest."

Like hell. But he waited anyway. If she wanted to make this more difficult for both of them, he was too tired to stop her.

She licked her lips. That was a mouth made for kissing, he thought, surprised at himself for thinking it.

What if she did ask him out?

What if he went?

This was the first time he'd seriously thought he might, but then he remembered it wasn't as if she was after his killer bod and winning personality. It was her house she wanted.

So he squelched the tiny spurt of male interest and waited.

"You remember when we were talking in your office today, about my situation?"

"Of course."

"Well, obviously I'm going to have to do something to earn enough money to pay for the mortgage and bills."

"Right. We already talked about this."

"I think I've found a way to do that."

"Already?"

"I'm going to start a day care in my home. I'm an excellent cook, a trained pediatric nurse, as you know, and I renew my first-aid certification every year. My home is clean and child-proofed, I have a fenced-in yard and I live within walking distance of the school."

"That's a good plan," he said, stifling a yawn. "Do you have any kids lined up?"

"That's why I'm here, Mr. O'Reilly. I'm going to suggest you and your daughters might benefit from the arrangement."

He stared at her blankly for a second, then almost laughed. On the good side, she hadn't asked him out, although his ego was oddly stung.

"I'm not sure that's a good idea, Mrs. Theisen."

She looked as taken aback as he must have when he found out it was his girls she wanted instead of him. "Oh."

There was an implied question mark at the end of her,

"Oh," so he went on. "I think it might be unethical for me to use one of my bank customers as a day-care provider."

She stared at him with her eyebrows slightly raised, and he could see she didn't believe him for a second. Well, why would she? His doctor and dentist both banked with him, as did his grocer and any number of other people whose services he used. He couldn't explain why he felt uncomfortable about her proposition. He simply did.

"Well," she said, rising, "I'll let you get on with your evening then. I'm sorry to have disturbed you."

He got to his feet, too. "You didn't disturb me. You were a big help today. I appreciate it." He held out his hand and she shook it. Odd to be so formal with a woman standing in his kitchen at seven-thirty at night.

She walked toward the front door and he followed her. In her jeans and sweater she was sexy as hell, which wasn't something he wanted to notice right now.

At the door, when she turned again to say goodbye, he blurted something he'd been thinking about while he sat beside his sleeping girls in the hospital. "Why did you let your ex-husband go so long without paying anything?" If she'd called the guy on it earlier, she might have at least been able to keep his payments current before he vanished to the other side of the world.

As he contemplated her in exasperated silence, her head dropped and color flooded her pale cheeks. How did she do this? One minute she was the cool, capable nurse, the next she was this vulnerable helpless woman.

In the long silence he heard a dog barking somewhere outside, but, even though he strained his ears, no sound at all came from the girls' room upstairs.

"I thought he'd come back," she whispered at last.

His spine prickled. Any fool could see it was hopeless. Mr. Theisen was a deadbeat dad, a subspecies of men who would leave the country rather than support the family they'd helped bring into the world. The woman standing staring at her shoes was crazy and pathetic to think he'd come back.

As crazy and pathetic as Seth himself, who no more than half an hour ago had whispered his dead wife's name out in front of the house.

"If I hear of anyone looking for a decent day care, I'll tell them to call you," he said.

"I'd appreciate that," she said. "Good night." And she was gone.

CHAPTER FIVE

UP IN HIS BEDROOM HE shrugged out of the scratchy, puke-smelling suit and dashed into the bathroom for a quick shower before dressing in jeans and a navy polo shirt. He kept his eyes averted from the queen-size bed, still covered by the same yellow chintz comforter Claire had chosen the year before she'd died. *Yellow is the color of hope,* she'd said.

His eyes burned. He stabbed his feet viciously into sport socks and grabbed his sneakers.

Back in the kitchen he warmed the soup the Theisen woman had brought. God, she was amazing. Not only was there a Tupperware container of soup, but she'd included another square plastic container of corn bread.

Okay, he thought, as he settled down with the first home-cooked meal he'd eaten in a long time by someone who, unlike him, could actually cook, she'd gone the right way about advertising her services. Not only was the flavor fabulous, but the soup tasted wholesome. He somehow knew the herbs in there were from her garden and that no cans, packages or shortcuts of any kind had been used.

Wow.

Maybe if he'd tasted the soup first, he wouldn't have turned her down so hastily. He buttered a square of corn bread and discovered it tasted as good as he'd imagined it would. But no. That woman had a mountain of problems and if he ended up having to foreclose on her home, he didn't want to have his kids involved.

Turning her down had been the right thing to do.

But, as he rolled up his sleeves and washed up the brownie disaster, he kept seeing her, the way she'd efficiently figured out what was wrong with the twins, the natural way she'd tucked them in, as though she did it every night.

Well, maybe she wasn't for him, but he bet whoever ended up using Melissa Theisen's day care was going to be very happy.

Tomorrow, he'd take a day off, watch the kids, work from home and find some other arrangement. He wouldn't use the same agency who'd found him the useless unemployed teacher. He rubbed a tired hand over his face, so hard that his wedding ring scratched his cheek. Maybe his sister would have some ideas. Janice was a grade-school teacher and a resourceful woman.

Dishes done, he wandered into the den and accessed his office e-mail from his computer. With luck, everything was running smoothly, he could leave Stella a voice mail that he wasn't going to be in tomorrow and then head to bed.

"Damn it all to hell!" he raged aloud, when he saw the subject of several e-mails.

Couldn't one single thing go right? Amid the crisis with the girls he'd forgotten that tomorrow was the directors' meeting. If he missed that, he might as well kiss his job goodbye. He had to present the bank's strategic plan for the next twelve months at ten o'clock tomorrow morning. He'd intended to spend the bulk of today preparing his presentation. First Mrs. Theisen, then the twins' illness had knocked the whole thing out of his mind.

The plan was in place, including Mitzi's crap ad campaign, but he still had to write his speech notes and polish up his presentation.

He started typing, then stopped. What was he going to do with the girls tomorrow? He'd been told to keep them home from school for a few days. He certainly wasn't about to unfire the nanny for one day.

Frustration settled in his stomach and the gastric juices began churning his guts into the pit of hell.

He picked up the phone on his desk and called his big sister. "Hey, Janice," he said when she answered, feeling better just hearing her voice. As she'd grown older, she reminded him more and more of their mom. "What's up?"

"I'm considering petitioning Congress to outlaw cell phones to any child under twenty-one. I had a girl's cell phone go off in the middle of a math test. I confiscated it and later her father called. Not to apologize, you understand, but to warn me never to touch his daughter's personal property again." She blew out a breath. "How was your day?"

"I win in the crap day department. Mine was worse." He told her about the brownies and the hospital visit and Janice made all the right sounds of outrage and sympathy. Being able to tell her about it made him feel a little better. "So, now I'm stuck with no child care tomorrow and two sick kids."

"Oh, Seth. I'm so sorry. Look, I can call in a sub and take a day off tomorrow. Believe me, after the cell phone incident, I need a mental health day."

"I love you for offering, but no. I'll find another way." There was a short pause. "You know Mom would fly home and help out." Their parents had retired to Florida two years earlier. They'd owned the condo in St. Pete's for a few years before that and he knew that they'd held off moving to support him and the twins through Claire's illness and death and the first terrible year after she'd died.

"I know she would. But then Dad wouldn't want to be left alone, so they'd both come and it's not fair on them. They're enjoying their lives. Besides, it would only be another temporary fix. No. I've got to find a better solution." He scratched his head. "If only the twins weren't so…"

"Troublesome?" his sister suggested with a wry note.

He made a face he was glad she couldn't see. "I've spoiled them, haven't I?"

"Well, you let them get away with murder, but you've also got two great kids who are getting through a difficult time as best they can. Anyhow, they come by their pranks honestly. Remember what we were like?"

And just like that, he laughed. "Mostly, it was you who thought up the stunts and me who got caught."

"They're going to be fine, Seth," she said, answering the concern he hadn't voiced. "They'll grow up to be wonderful people. We did."

"I know you're right. Thanks. It's tough having nobody to share the worry and the responsibility."

"I know. I guess Claire's parents wouldn't—"

"No," he said with finality. He'd met his wife at college back east. She was from Chicago and her family still lived there. Claire's parents had never really got to know Laura and Jessie all that well, and after Claire died, the contact dwindled to gifts, and a phone call at birthdays and Christmas and a check each year toward their college fund. He couldn't understand how her parents could dismiss all that was left of Claire, but he suspected they found too many painful memories of their dead daughter in the twins, who looked so much like her, and he tried to understand.

Claire's brothers and sister all had their own families and seemed to take the lead from her parents.

"I do have one option," he said, and he told Janice about Melissa Theisen.

"She sounds perfect," his sister said after he'd described the way his bank client had helped him through the brownie fiasco and he'd outlined her qualifications. Seen through his sister's eyes, of course, Mrs. Theisen *was* perfect. "Why are you so hesitant?"

He didn't mention one of the reasons. That he was attracted to a woman who was as messed up emotionally as he was. "I don't know. Maybe because she was talking about being a landscape designer earlier today and now she suddenly opens a day care. And if we have to foreclose, well…"

"Oh, honey. I wish I had an easy answer for you. Look, the offer stays on the table. If you want me to take a day off tomorrow, you know I will."

"Thanks, Janice. You're the best." He rubbed a hand absently over his belly. "But I'll figure this out."

"SORRY, I'M LATER THAN I thought I'd be," Melissa said when Pam opened the door. "I had to wait for them to get back from the hospital."

Her neighbor glanced at her wrist. "Fifteen minutes late. I'll have to punish you by feeding you coffee. Come on in, I just made some decaf."

"You sure you don't want me to take the children straight home?"

"They're watching the new Disney video. Nothing could drag them away until it's over and the princess bags her prince. Besides, Greg's got a partners' dinner tonight. I can use the company."

Melissa snorted, following her neighbor into her warm, oak kitchen. "I'm thinking about launching a petition against all movies where princes and princesses end up happily ever after. Why poison their little minds with… what are you doing?" While she'd been speaking, Pam had dragged a chair across the floor. Now she climbed up on it to reach the cupboard above the fridge.

"I sense we need a little kick in our coffee," Pam said, dragging out a bottle of Irish cream liqueur, which she handed to Melissa. With a grunt, Pam clambered down and bustled around collecting mugs and the coffeepot.

Melissa watched, amused, as her friend poured rich, dark streams of coffee into two mugs and then sloshed a healthy dose of liqueur into each mug. "Hell, we might as well go all out," she announced and opened the fridge and pulled out a slim carton. "Real, one-thousand-calories-a-teaspoon whipping cream."

Soon they were sitting at the kitchen table, frothy coffees in front of them. Melissa sipped, enjoying the tickle of cream against her upper lip, and the kick as the drink hit her stomach. For a moment life felt like it used to.

"Well?" Pam asked, reminding her abruptly that life was actually completely different than it used to be.

She shook her head. "He said no."

"How could anyone say no to you? What's the matter with the guy? Is he too cheap to pay for decent child care?"

"We never even discussed money. It wasn't that." Her eyebrows drew together in a frown. "I don't have a clue why he turned me down. He said something about ethics, but I don't think it was that."

"Maybe he really wants the kids looked after in their own home," Pam suggested. "And getting the child-care provider's exclusive attention."

"Maybe. And they could certainly use a housekeeper. That place is a mess."

"Don't be disappointed. We'll put the word out. We'll have you turning away customers in no time. I guarantee it."

Impulsively, Melissa reached across and touched the other woman's hand. It was freckled and warm. "You've already helped, taking the kids tonight. And coming up with such a great idea in the first place."

"I'm pretty proud of myself for thinking of it. You'll be terrific."

"Do I need some kind of a license or something?"

Her friend shrugged expansively. "I don't know. You can check it out tomorrow."

Excited chatter erupted from the basement. The movie must be over, thought Melissa. Feet pounded up the stairs, and four bright faces burst through the doorway into the kitchen.

"Hi, Mom," Matthew shouted, running forward and then sliding to a halt in his stocking feet when he realized his friend Josh was watching.

Alice had no inhibitions about hugging in public. She threw herself into her mother's arms. "Mama."

WHEN SHE'D FINISHED TUCKING the kids into bed, Melissa ran a bath—one of the few indulgences she still allowed herself.

She was a little punchy from lack of sleep and a day that had been pretty much all dramatic peaks with not enough valleys in it to catch her breath and regroup.

The knowledge that Stephen had abandoned them still stung cruelly, but there was a sneaking sense of determination that Melissa hadn't been sure she possessed. She knew, as well as she knew anything, that she was going to be okay. With a lower mortgage payment, some day care clients and her landscaping business, she was going to survive. All on her own, thank you very much.

Her first attempt at recruiting day-care clients hadn't gone so well, she reminded herself as she stepped out of her robe and sank into the warm, bubbly water.

Those girls were obviously a handful, but the mother in her responded to their plight. Sure, it was bad to have your father abandon you, but to have your mother die of cancer was so much worse. Although Seth O'Reilly was no doubt a top-rate bank manager, she got the strong feeling he was out of his depth in his domestic life.

Oh, well, if he didn't want her, he didn't want her. Bubbles tickled her neck and her breasts peeked through the white foam, pink and wet. And it hit her. He did want her. That poor, broken man, calling to his wife's ghost on the front lawn, had wanted her in that elemental way a man sees a woman and responds. There'd been a time when that had happened so often she barely noticed, but in the last couple of years, she'd caught that look, that certain current of energy, so rarely she'd almost forgotten what it was like.

Was that why Seth O'Reilly had turned down her offer? Because he was attracted to her? She tipped her head back and inhaled the gardenia fragrance. Probably it was just as well. She didn't have the time or the energy to let a man down lightly. Better they remain strangers.

He'd awakened feelings, though, feelings she'd almost forgotten she owned.

She'd noticed him eyeing her curiously. She so rarely bothered to dress up these days, or waste the time and energy on makeup that she hadn't immediately interpreted his admiring gaze. She thought about him. Realized she'd found him appealing, too.

If anything, his painful love for his dead wife increased his attraction. Fidelity was an attribute she no longer took for granted.

While she was in the tub anyway, she decided to shave her legs. And she really needed to do something about her nails. Just because she was alone was no reason to let herself go.

In the middle of the second leg, the phone rang. It was a habit to bring the portable into the bathroom with her, so she was able to reach one bubble-dripping hand out of the tub to the small wicker table that held candles, some fancy soaps and a basket of polished rocks with inspirational words on them. She picked up the phone. "Hello?"

"Mrs. Theisen? It's Seth O'Reilly."

Now, there was a voice she hadn't expected to hear. "Um, yes?"

"I hope I'm not calling at a bad time."

"No. It's fine." What on earth did he want? She flashed back to the way he'd looked at her earlier. *Oh, no,* she almost moaned. Please don't let him ask her out. She didn't feel up to rejecting the man who'd so kindly helped her sort out her finances today.

Regardless of the fact that he didn't want her looking after his children, she didn't want to hurt him.

"I have a problem," he said, sounding tired and serious.

"Join the club."

He chuckled, but his exhaustion was clear. "I was

planning to stay home tomorrow with the girls, but I've got a critical meeting in the morning."

Okay, it seemed like he wasn't asking her out. She let out her breath, relaxing so the water sloshed up over her shoulders. "Uh-huh."

"Frankly, I'm reconsidering your child-care offer. Pardon me for asking, but are you reliable? I can't keep changing sitters—it's bad for the girls."

"Pardon me, Mr. O'Reilly, but I am completely reliable, my home is spotless and my brownies haven't killed anyone yet."

"Okay. Can you start tomorrow?"

"Well, since it's an emergency, I suppose so."

"What's your address?" he demanded. "I was in such a hurry earlier, I didn't pay much attention."

She gave it to him. "I live even closer to the school than you do." She'd figured out that the twins had seemed vaguely familiar because she'd seen them at the school. Being twins, they stuck out in a crowd. She'd never seen Seth O'Reilly at the school as far as she knew. With a little shiver, she wondered if she'd ever seen his wife.

"I'll be right over."

"What?" she squeaked, sitting up so fast bubbles and water streaked over her torso. The half-shaved leg splashed as she dropped it back into the tub. "It's ten o'clock at night."

"I need somebody to look after the girls tomorrow. If you want my business, I'll have to check out your home."

"But—" She was about to tell him she was naked and wet, then thought better of that idea.

What on earth had she done? "I'll be charging higher rates than most child-care providers because of my medical training," she said, in a last ditch effort to head him off.

"I'll be right over."

She hung up and scrambled out of the tub, threw on some clothes, ran a brush through her damp hair and dabbed on lip gloss.

She ran downstairs to make sure everything was tidy, and realized the stupid broken drawer front still sat on her kitchen counter. She ran down to the basement, found her glue and ran back up.

Following the directions, she squeezed glue onto both the drawer front and the parts left behind and stood with her hip against the loose piece.

Was she a handy woman or what?

AFTER BEGGING HIS good-natured sister to watch the kids, Seth was at the Theisen house in less than five minutes. An elegant Tudor, it rose a foot or so higher than its neighbors as though even the houses in this neighborhood were playing Keep Up With The Joneses.

The outside lights illuminated a lush garden straight out of an upscale magazine. Annoyance sparked through him. The first thing that woman needed to do was get rid of her fancy gardener. She had to save her money to pay the mortgage and feed her family. He trod up a whimsical, winding flagstone pathway with dark leafy shapes shadowing either side, leading to two steps. Ignoring the doorbell, so as not to wake her kids, he banged the lion's head door knocker. In the dim light, its brass glowed as though it was polished regularly. He couldn't help but compare the outside of her house with his; she must employ an entire staff to keep the place up.

She must have been waiting for him, for the door opened almost immediately. His eyes widened when he saw her. This woman holding the door looked like she'd just stepped out of the shower, smelled like it, too, he noted as he entered the house. Her blond hair curled around her flushed face in steamy tendrils. She was pretty even without makeup, he decided, and she smelled like flowers.

He'd never seen such a kissable mouth. Full and bow-shaped, the lips parted under his stare. He felt a shaft of heat rush through him, as unfamiliar as it was exciting. It had been a very long time since he'd thought about kissing a woman.

And he wasn't thinking about it now. He forced his gaze away from her lips and shut the front door behind him. *Check out the house*—that's why he was here. Glancing around the front hall, he noticed how neat it was. Blue-and-white striped paper on the walls, unmarked by fingerprints, gray blue carpeting that still bore the ridges of a recent vacuum job.

"Would you care to come into the kitchen?" she asked in her soft hostess voice.

Nodding, he followed her lead. Peeking into the unlit living room, he got the impression that it was rarely used. It seemed lifeless somehow, and the formal dining room across the hall looked like it hadn't seen a dinner party in a while.

He followed Mrs. Theisen's back. She wore pale yellow jeans and a flowered T-shirt, and he approved of the way they looked from behind. He ran his eyes up and down the slim form, noting the elegant set of her shoulders, the straight spine and the bewitching sway of rounded hips. He definitely approved.

The kitchen was obviously the heart of the house. It was done in blues and yellows that looked vaguely French. They sat at a wrought iron table with a spotless glass top and regarded each other. Seth wasn't sure how to begin, what he wanted to ask her. She seemed suddenly shy.

"Would you like something to drink, Mr. O'Reilly?" she asked. "Herbal tea?"

"I'm fine, thanks." He smiled, trying to ease the atmosphere between them. "After the day we've spent together, I wish you'd call me Seth."

She appeared to consider his words for a moment, as though looking for a trick but finding none. The corners of her mouth tilted upward. "And I'm Melissa."

Her house was obviously clean and well organized. A quick inspection showed all the outlets had childproof covers. His own pair were more devious than any toddler. He wondered how she was planning to keep them out of trouble.

"Well, Melissa..." He tried to lounge back in his chair, but the wrought iron curlicues gouged into the muscles under his shoulder blades, jerking him upright in a hurry. "What do I get for my money?"

If she was taken aback by his bluntness, she didn't show it. "Apart from emergency medical response on demand, I'll also provide wholesome home-baked snacks after school, I'll supervise the girls' homework, encourage them to play outside in nice weather. You can drop them off in the morning on your way to work. I'll walk them to school with my eight-year-old son."

"What if I'm late picking them up at night? Do I get charged overtime?"

It was obvious she hadn't thought of this possibility. He watched her struggle with herself, clearly wondering how far she could push him. "Of course," she finally answered.

"I tell you what, let's try it for a month and see if it

works out. You'll have to keep them home from school tomorrow." He paused, then voiced his biggest concern, "The girls are a little...lively sometimes. Do you think you can handle it?"

The slightest smile of superiority teased her lips. "In my experience, Seth, the best way to keep active children out of mischief is to keep them busy. I'll do my best." She rose. "Would you care to see the backyard?"

He nodded. Anything to get out of the torture device she called a chair and quickly hauled himself to his feet.

She crossed the kitchen to a pair of French doors and flipped on a light switch. As he came up behind her he could see an immaculate fenced yard with a swing set and child's playhouse. A round patio table and chairs were pushed to the side of the deck awaiting better weather.

The backyard looked fine. Too fine. "Who does your garden?" he asked. He'd try to slip in a subtle reminder that she needed to cut nonessentials like professional gardeners out of her budget.

"I did it myself," she said, not without pride. "Gardens are my passion."

What a fool he was. She'd told him this morning she designed gardens. "It's beautiful," he said. So was the line of Melissa Theisen's jaw since she'd relaxed and stopped clenching it. Her neck was slender and the skin appeared silky soft. If he moved forward an inch, his chest could touch her back. He breathed in the aroma of gardenia and woman, and was torn between an urge to pull Mrs. Theisen round and kiss her senseless, and an urge to run raging into the night. For, standing here, surrounded by the scent of her, he couldn't for the life of him remember what Claire had smelled like. He tried to recall the scent of her perfume or shampoo, but the flesh and blood woman in front of him overpowered his memory.

He caught the gleam of her eyes reflected in the glass door and realized she was staring at him, wide-eyed and frozen. Jerking backward, out of the spell of her woman's magic, he drew in a ragged breath.

"I'll drop the girls off at eight tomorrow morning."

She turned slowly, and he noticed a flush on her cheeks. "That's fine Mr....I mean Seth." The use of first names seemed a strange intimacy suddenly. He wished he'd kept his big mouth shut. Nobody thought about kissing a woman they called Mrs.

He unhooked his jacket from the chair and shrugged into it. The sound of something falling and hitting the ground with a smack had him turning.

"Oh, I thought I fixed that," his hostess said with an irritated tone. On the floor was a wooden drawer front. Everything in her kitchen was so pristine that the broken drawer made him feel more at home somehow.

He walked forward and picked up the wooden slab. It was solid maple he noted. No particleboard for the Theisen home. "How did you fix it?"

"A tube of glue. It's about the only handyman thing I know how to do."

He nodded, oddly pleased that he could do something better than she could. "It needs a vise. To hold the pieces together until they're dry."

"A vise. Oh."

He stifled a grin. "Want me to take it home? I can bring the drawer back in the morning."

Her eyes closed for a moment. Then she opened them and he saw she wasn't annoyed, as he'd feared, but grateful.

"That would be so wonderful. You know, I try to watch home fix-it shows, and I have a couple of books, but I don't think I'm the handyman type."

"Well, I can't cook worth a damn."

A silent laugh shook her. "Between the two of us, we make a great single parent."

He was too busy pulling the drawer all the way out and placing the plastic thing holding the cutlery onto the counter to answer her.

"I'll bring this back tomorrow with the girls."

She followed him slowly to the door. "Do I need to worry about the twins sneaking home for any more illicit cooking sessions?"

"Not anymore. I confiscated their house key."

"Good."

"See you tomorrow." He opened the front door and plunged into the darkness before she had even reached the door. He felt a sudden urge to run.

CHAPTER SIX

MELISSA HADN'T FELT sexually stirred in a very long time. Even before her marriage was over, she'd lost respect for Stephen, and with that loss went her pleasure in physical intimacy. When she found out he was cheating, they'd stopped having sex altogether. To have this angry, grieving man be the one to reawaken her desires was just perfect.

When had it even happened? One minute she'd been showing him the backyard, and the next minute she'd felt his warmth at her back, felt longing coming off him in waves, and to her complete surprise, had experienced an insane urge to respond.

"Melissa, you sure can pick 'em," she said aloud.

Flipping off lights as she went, she made her way up to bed, then lay awake for a long while wondering.

First, she wondered where Stephen was. Did he ever think about them? Was he sorry? She'd read about deadbeat dads in the newspaper and never understood how a man could run away rather than support his own children.

She was going to have to track him down somehow and make him resume his responsibilities.

From Stephen, her mind drifted to another tall, handsome man who'd come into her life and pretty much shunted it onto a whole new course, all in one day.

Seth O'Reilly would have been faithful to his wife forever—she could tell from his obvious pain that his love had been the forever kind. It seemed an unfair irony that the man who'd loved his wife so faithfully should lose her in such a cruel way, while the man who'd had it all, healthy wife and children, should abandon them like flotsam on the shores of his life.

Seth had been furious when she'd said his wife was lucky. He couldn't understand the stab of envy that had shot through her for the woman who'd been loved so deeply that her husband was still calling out her name long after she was dead.

What would it be like to be loved by a man like that, Melissa wondered as she rolled over and tried to find a more comfortable spot. What would it be like to love a man like that, a man you could trust? To know that when he had to work late, he kept his pants on. To know that when he was out of town on business, he slept alone.

That love extended to his children. She smiled in the dark, recalling the panicky affection in his eyes as he tried to comfort both vomiting girls at once. She shuddered to think where her own children would have ended up if she'd been the one to die young and Stephen had been left with two children.

She was completely unprepared to entertain a couple of convalescing ten-year-olds tomorrow. Darn, she'd meant to ask Seth to send along some of their toys and games. They certainly wouldn't want to play with a three-year-old's toys, and she couldn't imagine any of Matthew's would hold much appeal, either, except maybe that game cube thing that had been his father's parting gift.

Don't even go there, she warned herself, feeling the

familiar bitterness begin to rise. If she started herself on the "How could Stephen have…" path, she'd never get any sleep, and she had an inkling she'd need to be on her toes tomorrow.

FEELING LIKE SHE'D tossed and turned all night, Melissa finally got out of bed at six-thirty, flipping off the alarm that was set for seven.

Tired and dispirited, she put on coffee then jumped into the shower while it brewed.

Toweling off, she glimpsed her naked body in the mirror and sighed. Nothing was quite as perky as it used to be, although she was slim enough—too thin, really. Since she'd given up her fitness club membership, her body had lost its tone.

At least her breasts were still round and firm, that was something. As if it mattered. She'd been discarded. Stephen had taken everything she had to give, from her virginity to her trust, and treated them like worthless junk-store gifts to be used, broken and discarded.

She was thirty-four years old, she reminded herself. Not old enough for the scrap heap. Still, she dressed quickly. An image of the taut young nymphet Stephen had finally left her for flooded her mind while she automatically dried her hair, wondering how soon it would turn gray.

By eight o'clock, her own children were breakfasted and dressed, and she'd sent them up to tidy their rooms and make their beds before school. Alice imitated her older brother in everything, and Melissa knew she longed to follow him to school almost as much as her mother dreaded the day she'd send her baby out into the world.

By eight-fifteen, Melissa was beginning to wonder

whether the bank manager had had a change of heart, or a better offer for child care. But, as she was getting ready to walk Matthew to school at eight-thirty, the Volvo pulled into the driveway and one very harassed-looking father emerged, followed more slowly by two little girls with sullen faces that told their own tale.

Even though she knew she was the probable source of the long faces, Melissa had to bite back a smile. Seth O'Reilly was a poster boy for the hopelessly manipulated single dad. His face was red, as though he were bottling up a mighty temper, when he stomped up the path with two identical red knapsacks that looked high tech enough for a Mount Everest climb. He dumped the bags unceremoniously in the front hall. His gray-blue eyes looked like a stormy winter ocean, and there was a large nick on his chin where he'd cut himself shaving.

"The girls aren't too happy about this arrangement," he grumbled. As if that was news, when she could see them crawling up her driveway with mutiny written all over them. The tune to Aretha Franklin's Respect started playing in Melissa's head, only she substituted the letters *T-R-O-U-B-L-E*.

A double portion.

Instinct warned her not to leave those two unattended in her house even for the fifteen minutes it would take her to deliver Matthew to school.

Earlier, while her children had made short work of a cheap but nutritious hot oatmeal breakfast, she'd told them she'd be looking after the girls.

Matthew had looked disgusted that more girls would be invading his home—until he found out they were twins. That put them firmly in the cool category. He eyed them now with open curiosity, his eyes huge blue pools as he discovered they really were identical.

Seth said, "Sorry, I gotta go, I'm late." His face was drawn and tired, his eyes underlined by dark half circles. He was backing away even as she opened her mouth to ask him questions.

"But, what about—"

"I'll call from the office," he muttered, then turned and strode back to the car. As he passed the twins, still only halfway to the front door, he grabbed each in turn for a quick hug, only to be treated to two icy rebuttals. The girls' actions did nothing to improve her appraisal of them.

"Oh, here," he said from the car and reached into the backseat, emerging with her kitchen drawer.

She walked down and took it from him, noting how solid it felt, as if it might actually stay fixed this time. "Thank you."

He nodded, got into the driver's seat and pulled away before she'd recovered from the fact that he was dumping two very grumpy-looking girls on her for the day.

"Matthew, honey, go knock on Josh's door. You can walk to school with him today."

"But…" His eyes were still glued to the twins.

"Don't worry, the girls will still be here when you get home from school. You'll get to know them then." If you still want to, she thought, noting the glances of open disdain the twins were throwing his way.

"Hi!" he chirped, with his eager, friendly smile.

"Hey," they both muttered, sounding as though they were speaking around wads of bubble gum.

"I see Josh on his front step, go on Matthew," she urged, giving him a quick hug and a pat on the backside. With a cheery wave, he took off down the sidewalk, and she watched him all the way to his buddy's house.

Pam was now out front with her coat on. Matthew jogged up to join her and her son, and Melissa watched him chatter excitedly to the pair. Pam's head popped up from where she'd been bent over listening, and she peered over to where Melissa stood giving a thumbs-up sign. Her friend threw her fist in the air and mouthed "Yes!" before heading off toward the school with the two little boys in tow.

Now that she had Matthew on his way, Melissa turned her attention to her day care's first customers. They didn't look thrilled. Without a word to her, they trooped into the house, and with a child's uncanny instinct, headed straight for the kitchen.

"Girls." Melissa stopped them in their tracks with her nurse's voice, pleased to see it hadn't lost its ring of authority after eight years of disuse. "When you arrive in the morning, I'd like you to take off your shoes and put them in the front closet. You can hang your coats there, too."

They dragged themselves back up the hallway and one after the other kicked their shoes off into the closet that Melissa had opened for them. Biting her tongue against further rebuke, she handed each of them a hanger and watched them shove their red-and-navy jackets on the wire. She was impressed at the way they both managed to hang their jackets so that they sagged disreputably. Without a word she put the jackets away, knowing they would fall to the ground long before the day was over.

Leading them into the kitchen, Melissa asked, "How are you feeling today?"

"Gross," replied one.

A glance at their pale faces confirmed it. "Have you been able to eat anything since yesterday?"

A firm shake of the head from one and gagging motions from the other answered in the negative.

Knowing they should at least get some electrolytes in their bodies, she sent them into the TV room with a couple of blankets and pillows and glasses of watered-down apple juice. "This is an exception to my rule," she warned them. "I don't usually allow television until after school when all your homework is done. I'm letting you watch TV today because you're sick. Understood?"

She got a couple of lackluster grunts out of them.

One day at a time, she reminded herself. Today she was earning real money. Not enough to solve all her problems, but enough to solve a few.

When she heard music that didn't sound like it came from a children's show, she popped into the den, where the girls were curled up watching a music video channel. Alice sat on the couch beside them, enthralled by some spiky-haired women who looked like aliens belting out lyrics with only two decipherable words: *hot* and *deep*. Alice had a thumb in her mouth and her favorite stuffed dinosaur in her lap as she watched the screen with wide-eyed fascination.

Melissa stomped to the TV and grabbed the remote— "Let's find something more suitable—" and punched around until she found Bert and Ernie in an intense discussion about paper clips.

With identical snorts of disgust, the twins peeled themselves off the couch and trudged to the front entrance, where they'd left their knapsacks. Melissa watched them haul out handheld video games and drop where they stood. Soon the front hall sounded like a miniarcade, but she decided she'd let it go. So long as they didn't damage her home or hurt her children in any way, she'd let them be. For now.

Back at the kitchen table, Melissa found an old envelope and a pen and started a to-do list. She hated writing on the backs of envelopes, hated the way the ridges spoiled her handwriting, but nice fresh pads of paper were one more luxury she could no longer afford. She'd discovered it wasn't losing the big things that bothered her. It was the little ones. She could forgo new clothes, hair appointments and even, after a struggle, Swiss chocolate.

It was the dumb little things like foregoing boxed tissues and pads of writing paper that irked her the most.

With a shudder, she propped her head on her hand. And wrote:

1. Find Stephen.
2. Research lawyers.
3. Increase income.

They looked so neat, those prim little instructions to herself, telling her how to fix her life. She chewed her lip for a while, thinking. From the front hall, little pings and beeps sounded along with girlish shouts of triumph or groans of failure.

The most important item was to track down her ex-husband. He'd betrayed her so often she shouldn't be surprised. But she was. She couldn't believe he'd gone off and abandoned his children, gone back on his promise about the house.

Maybe something had happened to him?

What if he was dead? But a moment's reflection told her that was unlikely. If he'd had some kind of accident, he wouldn't have given notice at his apartment and closed up his office. No. He'd run away from his responsibilities. A bad habit of his. At least if he'd died, she'd have the life insurance money for her kids.

By lunchtime, she was feeling a little more hopeful. She'd discovered a legal aid clinic that specialized in helping women and that was open in the evenings. She'd made an appointment.

Her mind revolved around where Stephen might have gone and what had happened to his successful business while she warmed up soup, arranged rice crackers on a plate, sliced an apple and poured three glasses of watery juice.

Then she went in search of the girls.

They were no longer in the front hall, although everything they'd pulled out of their backpacks was scattered all over the floor. Her lips pursed when she heard the music coming from the TV room.

Sure enough, the three of them were sitting on the couch glued to the same music station she'd already switched off once. This time the group was a quartet of white-suited young men, so squeaky clean they looked like they'd been bleached. All blond, pale-skinned and in white suits and shoes they crooned some sappy love song.

"I thought I told you—"

"Shh—it's the Bravo Boys!"

"I don't care if it's the Three Tenors break-dancing, you aren't watching it," she said, aiming the remote toward the screen.

"No. Please just let us watch this. It's 'Born To Be Bravo,' my favorite." They sounded so desperately serious, Melissa paused with the remote in midair.

She had to admit there wasn't anything to pervert Alice's

innocent mind on the TV screen. If anything, the boys were so cute they were nauseating. Melissa had a flashback of a Duran Duran poster that used to hang in her room when she was a teenager and paused with her finger still on the off button. The twins were rapt—and so was Alice.

"Born To Be Bravo" would never win a Grammy—she hoped—but at least the lyrics were expletive-free and far from disgusting, although the level of schmaltz could well be toxic. It was certainly an upbeat melody, probably the kind that got stuck in your head on an endless loop—like the jingle on a toothpaste commercial.

When the song ended, she clicked off the TV and sent the girls to wash up for lunch. Sure enough, they clambered up the stairs banging their feet rhythmically, chanting, "Born to be bra-bra-braaavo!" Alice's tiny voice wavered along with them, a beat or two behind. Melissa couldn't help but grin.

CHAPTER SEVEN

"I HATE SOUP."

"You haven't even tried it yet," Melissa reminded the girl scowling at her. The four of them were sitting at her kitchen table for lunch, though it felt more like they were two battalions preparing for war.

"I hate all soup."

"Can I have milk instead of juice?" the other twin asked.

Spoiled brats. Melissa's fists clenched, and she counted silently to ten. "The soup and crackers—and the juice— are easy on your stomach."

"Dad never makes us eat stuff we hate."

"He doesn't let our babysitters make us, either."

Deciding nonconfrontation was her best course of action, Melissa put her spoon into her soup and started eating.

She refused to react when the twins walked away from the table, leaving their lunches barely touched. She needed to talk to their father about how she planned to handle the girls, and for this first day, she was curious to see how they behaved. Although *curious* was quickly turning to *appalled.*

After lunch, Alice went down reluctantly for her nap. "I want to play with the two twins," she argued.

"They'll still be here when you wake up. Besides, they'll be resting, too," Melissa promised her.

And rest and quiet was exactly what the twins needed. Knowing they would want to watch more TV, Melissa was determined, so long as they were under her care, they wouldn't spend all their time drooling over the Bravo Boys.

It was time she took charge. She went to her room and dug out *Anne of Green Gables* and *Little House on the Prairie* from among her favorite books from childhood.

As she returned downstairs she heard the hum of the TV, as she'd expected. Marching into the room she stopped dead. She'd anticipated the music videos. But she certainly hadn't expected to find the twins curled on the couch surrounded by potato chips and candy bars.

"What on earth?" she cried angrily.

"Dad said we could bring some snacks," replied the one she'd come to see as the bolder of the two, her chin jutting forward. The smell of grease and chocolate hung in the air, and Melissa stared at the bold twin—Laura, she thought—until the girl's defiant gaze faltered. She was beginning to see subtle differences between the twins, but it would be a while before she's be able to distinguish them unerringly.

Cellophane crackled beneath her fingers as she scooped up the load of junk food from the couch and ordered the girls to wash their hands once more.

"But I didn't finish my Doritos."

"In my house, you follow my rules. No snacks between meals if you don't eat your lunch."

They glared at her as if she were an ogre before stomping off, muttering to each other.

If they thought she was evil to take away their junk food, she must have dropped even lower in their estimation when she produced the books.

"We don't have to do homework, we're sick."

"This isn't homework. It's called reading for pleasure."

Glumly, Laura took the proffered book and then balked again when she read the cover. "Don't you have *A Series of Unfortunate Events?*"

She shook her head.

"*American Girls?*" Jessie cried, glancing at the cover of *Little House on the Prairie.* "*Redwall? Saddle Club?*"

"Sorry, I only have the books I used to read when I was a little girl."

The two identical looks of horror caused her lips to tremble with barely suppressed amusement. "That was just after the printing press was invented."

"You read this stuff?"

"Well, only because the Bravo Boys weren't born yet."

"My Dad—"

"Would you like to phone your Dad and check if it's okay to read a book at my house?"

The panicked glance the twins shared confirmed what Melissa had begun to suspect: they were on their worst behavior for her benefit. Without another word, they opened their books and at least made a pretense of reading.

"I'm going to start dinner now. If you have trouble understanding any words, you can bring the book into the kitchen."

"But we're too sick to read," Jessie whined.

"Then you can nap in Matthew's bed."

They had their heads down, eyes to the page in seconds. *Challenge is good. What doesn't kill you makes you stronger.* She continued her silent pep talk as she started preparing dinner. While she was peeling onions the phone rang.

"Hello?" she answered, sniffing.

"Melissa?"

She sniffed again, and wiped her streaming eyes with her sleeve. Oh, for a tissue. "Hello, Seth."

"What is it? Have the twins made you cry?" Seth's voice sounded full of dread.

She chuckled. "I'm peeling onions. The twins are fine."

She heard scuffling noises in the hall and suddenly the bold twin bounded in the room gesturing frantically. It took Melissa a minute to figure out that the flapping, pointing and silent begging were a plea for her not to tell Seth about the junk food stash in the backpacks. Interesting. Maybe he wasn't a complete pushover after all.

The sigh that rumbled out of the receiver said more than any words could. "Tough day?" she asked.

"Annual directors' meeting. It went all right, but I had trouble concentrating." He paused. "I was worried about the twins."

Was he worried she was being mean to his sweet darlings? His sympathy would have been better placed with their caregiver. She kept these feelings to herself, however, and asked what time he'd be picking them up.

A groan of frustration was her answer. "There are a couple of urgent items I've got to clean up. I was hoping you could keep them till seven tonight…at your overtime rate, of course."

She hesitated. Frankly, she had been counting the minutes till she could get rid of the twins, but she heard real anxiety in Seth's voice. And he *was* paying her overtime. "All right," she finally agreed.

"I'll tell you what." She heard the relief in his tone and was glad she was able to help. "Put the onions away, I'll have pizza delivered to your place for dinner."

"We'll take a rain check on pizza. The last thing those girls need is more junk in their stomachs. I'll make them something wholesome."

He chuckled, and the sound did something to her stomach that she didn't even want to consider. "If it's wholesome, they probably won't eat it, but you're the boss."

She was thinking that if he used that laughing, sexy voice all the time, the bank would be swamped with female customers. And even though he and his daughters seemed to have taken over her life in a matter of twenty-four hours, she felt her lips turning up in response. "See you later."

Surprisingly, he turned out to be wrong. Maybe it was because they hadn't eaten anything but a few filched potato chips and a lunch they'd only picked at, but the twins wolfed down the chicken and vegetable stew she'd made and got through most of a loaf of whole wheat bread. They looked suspiciously at the rice pudding, but once they'd tasted it, they made short work of that, too.

And they surprised Melissa by displaying excellent table manners.

Matthew was so much in awe of them that he spent the entire mealtime staring at first one, then the other twin. Maybe they were used to that kind of attention; they didn't even seem to notice. Alice didn't stare. She merely copied everything they did.

"How did you get on with *Anne of Green Gables,* Laura?" Melissa asked. They hadn't come to her all afternoon for help, so she was suspicious about how much reading they'd done. She'd peeked in on them once and found Laura reading and Jessie sound asleep on the couch.

"It was okay." The girl shrugged and fell silent.

"Did you have any trouble with big words?" Melissa persisted.

"Not really."

Had the girl read any of it? Or had she heard Melissa's approach and stuck the book in front of her face before she got caught doing something else? "What did you like about the book?"

Laura stared hard into her rice pudding. Beneath the rioting auburn curls, Melissa made out a different shade of red staining her cheeks.

Nobody said anything for several seconds.

Just as Melissa was about to ask her what she'd really been doing all afternoon she burst out with, "That Anne was an orphan. If our dad dies we'll be orphans, too, and nobody will want us." She raised a face wet with tears, her eyes huge.

"Laura, that's not true." Melissa's heart turned over at the real fear she saw in those big, wet eyes before the child turned and dashed out of the room. "Laura, come back," but the running footsteps kept pounding down the hall and up the stairs.

Before Melissa could stand, Jessie let out a sob, and knocking her chair over in her haste, jogged after her sister, beginning her own noisy brand of wailing.

Melissa stood up. "Excuse me, children," she mumbled. What had she done?

She started to follow the twins, but, glancing at Alice, saw her daughter's face start to pucker. She wouldn't understand what the crying was about, but she'd responded to the emotion she'd witnessed.

Matthew looked anxious. He was pulling on the cowlick in the centre of his hairline, a habit he had when he was upset. "We don't have a dad. Are we orphans?"

Sudden tears pricked Melissa's own eyes. "Of course you have a dad. And he loves you. And you have me." She felt as though a vise was squeezing her ribs. "I won't let anything happen to you...I promise." By this time, tears were streaming helplessly down her own cheeks and Matthew's eyes had flooded.

Alice howled, "I want my daddeee!"

At that moment Seth O'Reilly walked into the kitchen. "Nobody answered the door. I...what the—?"

SETH BLINKED HIS EYES AS though he could reopen them and find the world was back to the familiar place he knew.

It wasn't.

Melissa was melting into a puddle right in front of him, and strangely, he felt a strong urge to take her in his arms and comfort her. Except that she was already moving to offer comfort to her sobbing children.

He glanced around for his own children. What had they done now? Fear clenched his gut. "The twins?"

Melissa pointed upward, her body shaking badly. "I'm so s-sorry." She could barely speak. "The b-book. It's all my fault."

He bounded out of the kitchen and up the stairs without bothering to ask permission. "Girls?" he shouted as he ran, terrified of what he might find. He'd never thought of a book as being a deadly weapon, but with the twins you never knew. His terror eased a little when he heard distinct, noisy sobs coming from down the hall.

They were lying curled up together on a single bed in a room so dominated by pink and purple it must have been Alice's. A quick survey showed him they weren't obviously hurt. There was no visible bleeding or broken body parts. Some of his panic dissipated and he crossed quietly to perch on the bed beside them.

"Hey Red, what's up?" he said softly, using the nickname he'd had for them since they were toddlers.

"Dad-ee!" they cried in unison and somehow both ended up on his lap, clutching at him. "Don't d-die," Laura begged him, turning a tear-swollen face up to him.

Even as he opened his mouth to utter an automatic soothing promise, a pain sharp and cruel pierced his chest. How could he promise something he had no control over? Who'd have thought Claire would die? Claire, who'd embraced life and who would have done anything to spare her children pain. "I'm right here," he said with a catch in his own voice. It was the best he could offer.

"I don't want to be an orphan," Laura sobbed. "They make you work like a c-cleaning lady and send you on trains to people who don't even w-want you."

"Who does?" Seth was floundering way out of his depth. Cleaning ladies? Trains? Death? What kind of a babysitter *was* Melissa Theisen? "Nobody's going to make you a cleaning lady," he soothed.

"That's what happened to Anne. And she finally finds a place she likes but they d-didn't like her because she was a girl. Why couldn't we be b-boys?"

"Well, I'm glad you're girls." Seth latched on to the one part of her complaint he understood. "Your mom and I always wanted a girl, and we were so lucky when we got two of you." He squeezed their slim shoulders to him in a hug.

Jessie's body shuddered on a hiccup.

"Who's Anne?" He never remembered hearing about anyone at school called Anne. He thought he knew most of their friends outside of school. No Annes there, either.

"Anne Shirley."

"Anne Shirley?" Now where had he heard that name before? Then he remembered, Melissa had mentioned a book. "*Anne of Green Gables?* That Anne Shirley?"

Laura nodded and sniffed.

"Anne Shirley is a fictional character. And that book was written a long time ago. That's never going to happen to you."

"Then who's going to look after us when you die?" Laura demanded.

"First of all, I'm not planning to die for a long time. And if something did happen, your Auntie Janice would look after you. You know that."

"But she has her own kids," Jessie objected.

"She'd let us live with her to be cleaning ladies and do all the cooking and the wash," Laura warned.

"Well, she wouldn't be getting much of a bargain," Seth said drily. "You two would soon have her whole house looking like your bedroom." He squeezed his arms around them in another big hug. "And after yesterday, I don't think she'll be asking you to do any cooking."

A reluctant chuckle answered him.

"How was the rest of your day?"

He caught the guilty glance they exchanged. "Fine."

Dropping kisses on their fiery curls, he said, "Wash your faces and come back downstairs."

Considerably calmer now, he made the return journey to the kitchen. Melissa had settled her kids as well as dried her own tears. She glanced up guiltily when he entered. "How are they?"

"Drying off."

"Matthew, take your sister into the den for a few minutes

while I talk to Mr. O'Reilly. You can watch TV." She gave them each a loving pat as they trotted out of the kitchen. The Theisen tear storm had apparently passed.

She waited until they were out of the room before speaking again, her face creased with worry. "I'm so sorry, Seth. I—"

"*Anne of Green Gables.* I heard."

"I loved that book so much as a child. And since it's about a spirited girl with red hair, I thought Laura might enjoy it. I didn't think about how it begins, with Anne as a rejected orphan. I'll put it away and find Laura something else to read."

"No, wait. I know I read the book in school, but I'm a little fuzzy. Doesn't she run around after some boy named Gilbert?"

Melissa said, "No. She doesn't. Gilbert runs around after her, and she won't have anything to do with him. He has to win her slowly, with a lot of hard work." She sighed blissfully. "I loved that book."

Sounded like a bunch of BS to him. "Why do you women always love to make men suffer?"

She rolled her eyes. "We're entering dangerous territory. The point is, Anne overcomes all the obstacles in her life and finds love and happiness."

Seth was nodding his head as though she'd helped him win an argument. "Then let's let her finish reading the book. Life is tough. Laura's already learned that." He sighed and shifted his hips back against the kitchen counter. "She's the older twin, you know, definitely the dominant personality."

Melissa nodded vigorously, and he smiled a little. She'd figured them out pretty fast.

"She's having more trouble than Jessie getting over her mother's death. I've been trying to smooth her path, prevent her from being upset. And she pulls pranks like the brownie disaster." He shrugged. "Maybe reading a book about somebody else who gets over a similar situation will help her."

His stomach churned, recalling her plea to him not to die. "At least it brought out a fear she hasn't talked about before."

"That she'll be orphaned?"

"Yeah." He swallowed a sudden lump in his throat. "I told them my sister Janice would look after them." He shrugged his helplessness. "It's the best I can promise."

She nodded, a crease between her eyebrows. "She made me suddenly realize that if anything happens to me, my children will have nobody." Her voice trailed away, and she turned quickly, moving with jerky steps toward the kitchen sink.

She paused there, leaning against the edge of the countertop. She appeared to be staring out the window, but Seth didn't think she saw anything. Even though her shoulders didn't move, he knew she was crying.

Before he knew what he was doing, he was gripping her shoulders and turning her to face him. He wanted to offer comfort, but what could he say? She was right. He'd seen this situation before. Unless she was very lucky, or her ex suffered a sudden attack of conscience, Stephen Theisen was as good as dead to Melissa and the children.

"Don't you have any family?" he asked.

She shook her head. "I'm an only child. My mother's dead and my father…" She gulped. "No. There's no one."

The raw pain and fear he saw connected with his own pain and fear. He couldn't offer her any real consolation, but he could hold her while she cried, give her the temporary comfort of a shoulder to cry on. Gently but firmly he pulled her into the circle of his arms.

She tried to pull away, making little sounds of distress, but suddenly she gave in and clung to him.

Melissa fit into his arms perfectly, the top of her head nudging his chin. The bones of her back were slender and prominent beneath his hands. Her frame seemed too delicate for the strength of the sobs that shook her. Her hands gripped his shoulders and her tears soaked through his shirt.

But even through her terrible grief, he was aware of the woman's body shuddering against him. His response to the feel of her shocked him. He felt every curve of her. Warmth radiated from her body where it pressed against his.

And the way she smelled. He'd forgotten how exciting all those fragrances were. The hair products that were scented like flowers. The powders and lotions so numerous that Claire's side of the medicine cabinet overflowed into his half. Razor, shaving cream, toothbrush, toothpaste, deodorant. That's all he needed. He used to tease Claire about renting a storage locker to keep all her junk in. Now he had lots of empty shelves. And he missed the little spills of makeup goo on the counter. But most of all, he missed the delicate, flowery scents.

He missed the taste of lipstick during a wet, hungry kiss. He missed the taste and touch and smell of a woman. And not just Claire. He was appalled to discover he was eager to sample the woman in his arms. At least his body was.

He'd meant to offer comfort. It was an effort of will to prevent his body from letting her know in no uncertain terms what her movements were doing to him. Grief was making her body rub against him in a way that was giving him all sorts of ideas he didn't want to have.

Shifting his hips back slightly didn't help. She clung

closer, so far gone in her indulgence of tears she didn't know what she was doing.

"Shh. It's going to be okay," he murmured over and over, stroking her hair as well as her back. Touching those silken curls was another big mistake.

A mental cold shower was in order. And fast. *Down, Boy.* Profit and loss figures from the yearly income statements. He tried to recall all the numbers from this morning's meeting. The bank's profits were up. The board of directors was pleased. Everyone was pleased.

He wouldn't have even got to the meeting if it hadn't been for Melissa.

Not only had she been there all day with the twins and fed them healthy food, but she'd convinced Laura to read a work of literature instead of watching TV. No other baby-sitter had ever bothered.

A wet sniffle coming from the direction of his right shoulder called his attention back to the matter at hand. The sobs seemed to have ended as quickly as they had begun. She didn't raise her head, though. Instead, her hand reached out behind her, fingers splayed, bouncing along the countertop, searching.

Puzzled, he let his gaze scan the counter, but he didn't think it was the pot scrubber or the dish detergent she was after.

The hand suddenly clenched and pulled back. "I'm out of tissues," she mumbled into his chest.

Seth smiled into her hair, dug into his pocket and pulled out a handkerchief, which he placed into her hand.

With a muffled "thanks" she kept her head lowered while she wiped her eyes and nose. Only then did she raise her head and look at him. "I'm sorry. I shouldn't have done that," she whispered.

"Feel better?"

Her face flushed. "A little. Mostly, I feel stupid."

Stepping back, he shot her a smile he hoped was brotherly. "Crying is supposed to be therapeutic."

"I've never found it good for much except sore eyes. I try to be a doer, not a crier," she said on a hiccup.

"And how are you doing?"

A frown appeared. "I found out I'm not the only person whose spouse ever went AWOL. I have an appointment with a legal aid clinic for women. If I could find Stephen…" She glanced up quickly. "I made an evening appointment so I'll be here for the girls, of course."

Seth tried to look positive, but it was tough. He'd seen a few of these cases at the bank. Everybody hated them. He didn't think Stephen Theisen planned to keep paying child support for children he no longer saw and mortgage payments on a home he no longer inhabited.

If Melissa's hunch was correct and he was in Eastern Europe, things didn't look good.

The sooner Melissa realized she was on her own, the better. But he was too tired and too smart to tell her that. She'd find out soon enough.

She blew her nose once more, then started to hand the soggy handkerchief back, only to stop with an embarrassed, "Oh! Why don't I wash this and return it."

He would have taken it, but he could see she was uncomfortable and with a shrug said, "Sure, thanks. No starch."

She grinned at his lame humor and tucked the hanky in her own pocket. "Would you like some chicken stew?"

Homemade stew. He'd been smelling it in the air since he walked in. It reminded him of his own mother's kitchen. Melissa's food smelled like a warm hug at the end of a tough day. If it was anything like the soup she'd brought over last night… But he paid Melissa to look after his kids, not him. "No thanks, I had a big lunch," he lied.

"Same time tomorrow?" she asked while they both tried to pretend they hadn't heard his stomach growl in hunger.

"Yes, I'll get the girls. Oh, and here." He dug into his pocket and pulled out the check he'd written. "A week's pay, plus time and a half for the overtime tonight. I don't think I'll be late again this week, but if I am I'll add that to next week's check. Is that acceptable?"

She flushed slightly as she took the folded paper in her hand. She didn't open it but stared at it with her head bowed. "You know, I used to babysit for people all the time. Working moms, neighbors with dentist appointments. I've never taken money. If we'd met under different circumstances, I would have been happy to look after your girls. I wouldn't have charged you."

That urge to comfort was back again. He smiled down at the top of her blond head. "Working for money is nothing to be ashamed of, Melissa. Welcome back to the real world."

Her head jerked up. He was surprised it wasn't anger, but amazement in her face. "You're right. I've been living in a dream world. I was like one of those TV women from the sixties, Mrs. Cleaver, maybe. I just wanted to stay home with my kids, that's all."

"Mrs. Cleaver always scared the pants off me when I was a kid. That hair never moved. Did you ever notice that? And she had that smile that looked like it wouldn't budge even if she was force-feeding you the peas on your plate." A shudder of memory went through him.

Her expression lightened even more. Now, if he could get a smile on her face before he left.

"But Mrs. Partridge, there was a cool mom. Although I'm not sure I'd have wanted my mom in my rock 'n roll band. Still, she was pretty sexy."

"She was a single mother, too. And she sure made it look a lot easier than it is."

"Hah, she wasn't as bad as Mrs. Brady, tossing two single families together like it was as easy as baking a batch of chocolate chip cookies."

"No. I imagine that's a very difficult thing to do." Melissa was blushing slightly, and then it hit him what she was thinking. Good God, she couldn't be thinking…

Hard to tell. She'd dropped her head and started fiddling with the check again.

"Hey, Red!" he bellowed up the stairs, "Time to go."

The bustle of sticking the girls in their coats, collecting their belongings and saying their goodbyes got him out of the door without having any more intimate conversation involving the Brady Bunch. He hoped she didn't think he'd been hinting. He didn't want a desperate woman getting any ideas about him.

Any more than he wanted to have any ideas about her.

The Brady Bunch. Get real.

CHAPTER EIGHT

SETH BANGED THE PROUDLY shining lion's head, wondering how often Melissa polished him, and when she found the time. She was one remarkable woman. He couldn't believe his luck.

They were into their third month of the new babysitting arrangement, and so far, things were going so well that his stomach had almost stopped eating away at itself.

The twins were happier than they'd been since their mother had died. They were doing better at school, acting more like little girls than hellions—most of the time.

Even their room was marginally tidier. He'd caught them making their beds without being reminded on one memorable occasion.

Melissa was making her mortgage payments. Her daycare included another child around Alice's age, who was usually gone when he came to pick up the twins, and she seemed fairly busy with the landscaping. Thank God. He would not have wanted to foreclose on this woman's house. Of course, she was treading perilously close to the financial edge, but she knew it and she was doing everything she could to make things work. He admired her.

It wasn't Melissa who opened the door, as he'd

expected, but Jessie, looking both important and mysterious. Always a bad combination in his experience.

"Hi, Dad." She opened the door wider, and he stepped into the hall. It was the first time anyone but Melissa had opened the door to him. His stomach clenched.

"Hi, Red. Where's Mrs. Theisen?"

"She's on the phone. She's been on for ages."

His stomach sank. How long had the twins been unsupervised? "Oh. And what have you been doing?"

Jessie swept her gaze in all directions like a cartoon spy before whispering, "We're having a secret meeting."

"What about?" Secrets, in his experience, usually turned out to be unpleasant surprises for parents.

His daughter put her finger to her lips and motioned him upstairs.

He relaxed a bit, knowing she wouldn't invite him to join the secret unless it was something she thought he would approve of. Which narrowed the possibilities from life-threatening to merely dangerous. Until he remembered the time the girls had invited him to watch their play, *Mary Poppins,* with his golf umbrella as the featured prop. Laura was practically out of their bedroom window, preparing to jump, when he'd lunged across the room and grabbed her ankles. Melissa's second-floor windows were even higher than his. He increased his pace to a run, heading toward the sound of children's voices hissing in exaggerated whispers.

With a sigh of relief, he saw nobody was on the roof or doing anything more death defying than hanging their heads over the bed. They looked a little red in the face, the row of four all regarding him upside down.

"Hi," he said.

"Shh!" they all hissed fiercely.

"This is a secret meeting, Dad. You gotta promise not to tell Melissa," Laura ordered him.

"Why are you all upside-down?"

"It's our secret signal."

"Well, I'm happy to join the meeting, but I can't do it upside-down."

"Well, since you are kind of old...if you promise not to tell, I guess it would be okay," Laura decided.

"I can't promise not to tell unless you give me a hint what this is about."

"Dad, you're so lame," his oldest informed him. "It's Melissa's birthday on Friday, and we're planning her surprise party."

A wave of relief rolled over him, as well as pride that they were planning something nice for Melissa. "I guess I can keep that secret. What do you have planned so far?"

"Spray streamers that come in a can." Laura held up a hand and stuck one finger in the air. Without the extra hand to give her balance her head tilted alarmingly, but she didn't seem to notice any discomfort.

"They spray out like a bunch of different-colored worms all over the place," Matthew added.

Seth imagined how thrilled Melissa would be when she found her pristine house covered in canned confetti, and he shuddered.

"We're all pitching in some allowance and buying chips and pop and stuff," Laura stuck another finger in the air. "Can you drive us to the store on Thursday night?"

"Sure."

"And me and Jessie are going to bake a cake." When she jutted her upside-down chin at him in her usual defiant mode, she nearly toppled over and had to stick her other hand on the ground to rebalance.

Visions of bicarb brownies and a barfing birthday girl danced through Seth's head. The twins had come so far since the brownie disaster, but he sure as hell didn't trust their baking skills yet. "How 'bout I buy the cake?" he tried.

In unison Laura, Jessie, and Alice, who'd managed to get herself upside-down alongside the others, shook their heads. His stomach started to burn.

A cake.

They wanted to bake a cake, and they had no mother to help them. And yet he could read in their sparkling, upturned eyes how important this was. "Tell you what," he heard himself say. "We'll make it together."

Yips of joy greeted his announcement. "No mixes, Dad. She never uses them. It has to be from scratch."

Hell, how hard could baking a cake be, anyway? He had a shelf full of cookbooks. And he could always call Janice if things got too scary.

"And you have to get Melissa out of the house so we can decorate and stuff," Laura said.

If they really thought a three-year-old could keep a secret, he wasn't going to spoil the fun. "How am I going to get her out of the house with you guys all here?" he wanted to know. "And who's going to look after you?"

"Auntie Janice could watch us. And, um, you could tell Melissa you want her to go with you to the parent-teacher interview." Was it his imagination, or had his daughter's face just gone an even deeper red?

He rubbed his stomach. "What parent-teacher interview?"

"There's a note in my backpack," Laura mumbled.

"What have you been doing now?" He felt his good mood crash like the stock market on Black Monday.

"Nothing. That teacher's so mean. She picks on me all the time. It's because we don't have a mom," she said in a wheedling tone he didn't believe for a second. "Please take Melissa with you on the interview. She can tell Mrs. Picky that we're always good here."

"Your teacher's name is Mrs. Picard. Maybe she wouldn't be so mean if you showed her some respect."

"Well, anyhow, she wants to see you on Friday after school. If you take Melissa with you, we can decorate while you're gone."

"You'd better tell me about it, Laura, before I agree to any party. And you can do it right side up."

With an angry grunt, Laura hauled herself up on the bed and glared at him. "Tracy Moore said Benny lip-synchs. She called him a cheater."

Benny? She was championing a guy called Benny? "Benny who?"

Laura rolled her eyes around in her head. "Benny Samson. The Bravo Boy."

He raised his eyebrows and waited, forcing his expression to remain calm. Every time he thought about those mini men from Glad, he mentally ground his teeth together. His daughters were ten. Ten. At ten, he'd been playing marbles, not thinking about the opposite sex. This whole boy thing was starting way too young.

He glanced over at their identical Raggedy-Ann hair and faces. If his girls had to start having preteen crushes, he could maybe handle it if they gushed over the latest James Bond, or one of the young Russian hockey players. Any normal, redblooded man. Anyone but those nauseating Bravo Boys. "Maybe he does lip-synch."

"He does not! And that's what I told Tracy, but she just kept going, 'Benny is a cheater, Benny is a chea-eater.'"

"And for this, your teacher wants an interview?"

Silence.

"Laura?"

Silence.

"Jessie?"

More silence.

"Your teacher will only give me her version. You'd better tell me yourself what happened."

"I might have called her stupid." Laura's breath started getting uneven.

He kept his mouth shut and waited, knowing from the way her lips were working that there was more to come.

"Then she told me she's not allowed to play with us anymore 'cause her mom said that ever since our mom died we've turned into little m-monsters." She choked on the last word and her eyes filled with tears.

"Oh, Red—"

"So I told Tracy I'd rather have no mother than a stupid bitch like hers." With a sob she tore out of the room and a moment later he heard the bathroom door slam.

Jessie's head hung down, and he could see she was fighting tears.

"Jess?"

"Everybody has a mom but us," she mumbled to the floor. "Even the kids whose parents got divorced still get to see them both."

He knew he should be outraged that his daughter had called a classmate's mother names. But the thing was, he agreed with Laura's assessment of Tracy Whatever's mother. And he could think of a few other adjectives to add to *stupid*, like *heartless, sanctimonious* and *freakin' lucky to be alive.*

With a sigh, he got up and wandered to the closed door of the bathroom. "Laura?"

"Go away."

"Honey, I'm not mad at you. I'm glad your teacher wants to see me. I've got some things to say to her, as well."

He heard some shuffling and a loud sniff on the other side of the door. "You're not mad that I swore?"

Parenthood was a constant minefield, and he'd just stepped on a good one. "Of course, I'm mad that you swore. But I understand. Sometimes I swear, too, when I'm really mad."

"Yeah. You say sh—"

"Okay, okay," he interrupted. "I shouldn't do it, either. Can you come out now?"

He heard water running, then it stopped and a moment later the door opened. Laura stared up at him with a mixture of belligerence and pleading.

Maybe he should give her a lecture, a grounding, force her to apologize. *The hell with it.* He opened his arms and she tumbled into them, squeezing him so hard he thought both their hearts would break.

"Seth? Are you up there?" Melissa's voice floated from downstairs.

He whispered into the tangled red mass of Laura's hair, "We'll sort this out later, huh?"

She nodded and pulled away to scamper back to the others.

"Hi, Melissa." He stood upright and ran lightly down the

stairs to where she waited at the bottom, a look of suppressed excitement on her face.

He realized with a shock that she was beautiful with that hopeful glow highlighting her features. Every time he saw her, there seemed to be a line of worry marring her forehead. "I got here a few minutes ago, but you were on the phone."

"Oh, sorry. My head's in a whirl."

He smiled at her. She looked years younger. It was easy to see what a knockout she'd been before her life had turned sour.

"Looks like you got some good news."

She twirled like a princess at a ball. "I got the job of landscaping the display home in that new upscale subdivision down on Essex Street."

"That's great." In the three months that she'd been looking after the girls, he and Melissa had become friends. She'd sent the baking to Jessie and Laura's class for the Christmas party, and she and Seth had sat together at the annual winter concert, where all the kids but Alice had had a part.

He realized he'd come to look forward to picking up the girls, when he and Melissa would share a little of their day.

"Well, it is great. Because, if the people who buy into the subdivision like what I do, they'll hire me, too, right? This could lead to a lot of work for me. I've even been toying with the idea of expanding my services to include doing the actual landscaping." He followed her as she walked to the kitchen.

"That's a pretty big job."

"I know. And I'd need employees and things."

"Capital."

She grinned at him. "Good thing I am on such excellent terms with my local banker."

"Have you thought about—"

"Oh, don't worry. I won't do anything until Alice is in school full-time. Right now, the design work is keeping me busy. It's amazing how many people know people. Word gets around."

"It's not that I'm not supportive of the idea, because I am, but I don't want you getting any more strung out financially than you can help." He frowned, hating that he had to bring their business connection into her kitchen. "The thing is, you don't have much of a cushion if anything goes wrong."

She slumped into one of her torture chamber chairs, and he reluctantly sat opposite. Her fingers tapped the wavy glass of the table. "I know. Believe me, I know. It keeps me awake at night."

"This is a pretty big house for three people, Melissa," he said gently.

She rubbed at her forehead. He'd noticed she always did that when she was stressed. "Do you think I grew up with this? Scaling down is the story of my life." She glanced around the kitchen as though for the first time. "I grew up in a crummy old run-down house that seemed like a palace once we got thrown out. I was seven, and that was the first time we scaled down."

"Melissa, I…" What? What could he say to make any of this easier?

"It was always somebody else's fault when my dad lost a job. His drinking had nothing to do with it."

He suddenly pictured Melissa as a little girl, a little girl who looked a lot like Alice, living in squalor, and his belly squirmed.

"We played the same scene over and over. He'd get fired, then hang around home drinking. Mom worked as a cashier and waitress to keep food on the table. She always made excuses for him. It was because of his war injuries, she used to tell me."

"What war?" He calculated swiftly. "Vietnam?"

She shook her head and the overhead light reflected gold in her hair. "He did a short stint in the military, but got thrown out after a drunken brawl. His real war was against anyone who told him what to do."

"Like a boss, for instance?" Seth was getting a strong mental picture of Melissa's father, and he didn't like what he saw.

"Yep. After a while we didn't move for jobs anymore, we just moved to cheaper places. I don't think I ever did more than a single year at any one school."

Her index finger traced patterns idly on the glass. Seth fought the urge to take her restless hands in his.

"By the time I was a high-school sophomore, my mom came into a little money from an aunt who'd died, and she bought the trailer we were living in. My dad's still in it. It's an awful place, in a derelict trailer park across the highway from Big Bull Auto Wrecking. But, by some quirk of fate, the high school I got bussed to was pretty good. That's where I met Stephen."

He didn't want to talk about Stephen. He didn't really want to talk about her past, either. For some reason, it made him feel guilty. But it explained so much about this mania she had about keeping her house. "How did you get to be a nurse?"

"I won a scholarship. Lived in a dorm and swore I'd never go back to that trailer park. I married Stephen the year I graduated. Mom was so happy the day I got married, but when we moved into this place, I thought she'd burst with pride. I'm glad she passed away before Stephen left me."

Seth put a tentative hand out and touched her shoulder. Such slender shoulders for such a heavy burden. "I'm sorry, Melissa."

"Well, I inherited a lot of things from my mom. The work ethic, the love of cooking and bad taste in men. Stephen took out a million-dollar life insurance policy right after Matthew was born. He said if anything happened to him, he wanted to know his family was looked after. How could anyone change so much? How could he do this to us?"

There was no answer. How could any man desert a woman as special as Melissa? He sure as hell wouldn't.

"Not all men are bad, you know."

"I know." She sighed and leaned back. *How did she do that without armor?* "My friend Pam up the street? She's never lost the extra pounds from her last child. Her husband tells her not to diet. He likes her exactly the way she is. Imagine." She rose and went to the oven to check on something that smelled amazing. As he watched her in the kitchen, he noted one of the cupboard doors hanging askew. She liked things so neat and organized that he knew that must be driving her nuts.

He got up and followed her, moving the door back and forth. "Looks like you need a new hinge."

She sighed. "Among other things. I wish I was handy."

"What other things?"

She was bent over an oval baking dish, turning chicken pieces that were in some kind of Italian tomato sauce.

"I've got cracks in some of the walls from when the house settled. The upstairs bathroom faucet leaks. One of the boards on the back veranda seems soft." She shrugged. "Little things I need to figure out how to fix. Dumb things."

"Was Stephen handy?"

She gave a snort of laughter. "Not remotely. But when he was around, we could afford to hire people."

He took another look at the hinge. "I think I could fix that."

She glanced at him over her shoulder. "Thus proving that you are a better man than Stephen?"

"You already know I'm a better man than Stephen," he said evenly. He'd never been violent, but he was aware of a strong impulse to pound the long-gone and unlamented Stephen Theisen.

"Yes," she said, turning away quickly. "I do. You're one of the good guys, too."

He stared at her back, so straight and elegant. He was aware of an urge to kiss the junction of her shoulder and neck where the skin looked so soft he almost knew how it would feel under his lips—warm and silky.

"Have you even dated anyone since he left?"

Her hands stilled. "No." She bent to replace the casserole and when her head was practically inside the oven she asked, "You?"

"Two dates. One very bad blind date and one awkward dinner party where I was paired with a single woman I've known socially for a while."

"Oh." Did she sound relieved that he wasn't dating?

Was he relieved that she wasn't?

Something was definitely between them, some spark of attraction that they both pretty much ignored.

Maybe it was time to stop ignoring it.

CHAPTER NINE

"BE CAREFUL NOT TO scratch it," Melissa cried out as two hefty guys in blue overalls manhandled the gleaming burled walnut dining table out the front door.

Not that she should care. It didn't belong to her anymore. A beam of sunlight hit the surface and reflected the deep colors of the wood: brown and amber and a swirl of butterscotch. The rich patina was due not only to the quality of the walnut and the age of the piece—she had to take some credit for the hours she'd spent polishing that table in the years it had been hers.

"What are you doing?" Seth O'Reilly's unmistakable voice carried through the open door a moment before she glimpsed him hurrying up the front path.

"Redecorating," she called out breezily. Darn it, she'd especially booked the pickup for midday when everyone from curious neighbors, to questioning kids, to nosy bank managers should be otherwise occupied.

"Hold it right there," Seth ordered the guy closest to him, who paused and turned inquiring eyes on Melissa.

"Nonsense, keep going," she said, making forward motions with her hands, and glaring at Seth, who fumed on the other side of the walnut barrier.

"This is crazy. You can't sell your furniture." Seth stood in the middle of the steps directly in front of the table.

"Would you keep your voice down?" She checked up and down the street, but Seth's yelling hadn't brought curious heads poking out windows. She breathed again. "I've already sold it," she said. And given herself an emergency financial cushion that she'd appreciate a lot more than a dining table she rarely used.

Seth's face flushed, "You can't—"

"Look, pal, this thing weighs a ton. How 'bout you kiss and make up after we go, huh?"

After glowering at the man, then at Melissa for another moment, Seth stepped aside and watched in silence as the men eased the table the rest of the way out the door and headed for the truck waiting at the curb.

As soon as the table was clear of the door, he strode over the threshold. "What are you doing?"

"I needed a change. I'm tired of the traditional look—I decided on a more minimalist style."

Seth glanced into the dining room, where a lone table lamp sat on the floor. China was stacked neatly along one wall. He could see indentations in the blue carpet where the furniture had been. "Minimalist, huh?"

"I decided on a Bedouin dining room. My guests will eat cross-legged on the floor." She glared back at him, daring him to say one more word.

A reluctant grin tugged at the grim line of his lips. "Maybe you'll set a new trend."

"I got five thousand bucks for that dining suite, so if you're here to evict me, you've wasted the trip."

He smiled, one of those rare smiles of his that made her go weak at the knees. "I came to see if I could take you and whatever kids are in residence to lunch."

"Oh." She took a step backward. The hall seemed to

have shrunk since he'd started looking at her with that warm expression in his eyes. "Lunch."

"It's a common custom to eat something in the middle of the day." The expression turned teasing. "Even the Bedouins take lunch, I believe."

She stalled for time. "I've only got Alice home today, but she isn't very good in restaurants."

"That's why I had the deli pack us a picnic. It's such a nice day, I thought we'd eat by the river."

He'd arranged a picnic lunch. That was so thoughtful of him, but also ambiguous. What did it mean? Was this like a date? How did she feel about going on a date with Seth? While she stood there not knowing how to respond, he said, "I want to talk to you about the girls."

"Oh. Well, in that case." She stopped herself and then caught him grinning at her. "I'll get Alice."

MELISSA LICKED a dab of mayonnaise from her lip and sighed, lifting her face to the spring sunshine warming her skin. The river burbled its way past the park where they were sitting at a picnic table watching Alice tackle the jungle gym in the adjacent playground.

The weather was surprisingly warm for early March, and, after weeks of rain, it was beyond nice to feel the sun on her face.

Odd to feel so content when she'd parted with one of her prized possessions, but Melissa was a lot less bothered by the loss of her precious dining suite than she'd expected to be. She'd spent months searching for the right furniture, and that suite had fit perfectly into the dining room. It was old and grand, and if she tried hard enough, she could pretend it had been in her family for years.

Stephen had told their dinner guests that once. He always insinuated that Melissa came from a privileged background. She used to believe it was to save her embarrassment. Now she knew better. He'd wanted to impress on their friends and his business associates that he'd won a prize in Melissa. The real Melissa apparently wasn't enough of a prize.

There was a lightening somewhere in her chest. Maybe getting rid of that table with its twelve matching chairs, buffet and china cabinet was like setting a lie straight. Cleansing.

And she'd save hours in polishing time. She breathed deeply of the soft spring air. "Thanks for bringing us here."

"I'm enjoying it myself."

This impromptu picnic was like a miniholiday, as pleasant as it was unexpected. She glanced at her companion and provider of the feast. With his white shirt rolled up at the sleeves and his tie loosened, he looked exactly like what he was, a businessman father stealing away from the office for lunch in a park.

Only Alice wasn't his child, and she wasn't his wife.

She gazed at him, at his black hair lightly threaded with silver, the straight nose and firm jaw, the deep smile lines in his cheeks. A nice face, an attractive face. She wondered what it would be like if appearance was reality and he was hers.

He sat facing the playground, as she did, his back against the table top. He took a bite of his sandwich and she watched his square hands with their blunt-tipped fingers. Strong hands for a desk jockey. Her eyes traveled to his forearms, muscular with black hairs catching the sun. "How do you stay in shape?" she found herself asking.

He finished chewing and swallowed. "Squash. Four lunchtimes a week." He turned to her. "I cancelled today."

Feeling absurdly flattered that he'd cancelled another commitment to be with her, she took refuge in scolding. "I hope you still eat something in the middle of the day. With your stomach trouble, you should eat regularly."

"Yes, nurse," he replied with false meekness.

What was she doing? She had no right talking to Seth O'Reilly that way. He was her bank manager and employer, not her child or her lover.

"Alice, why don't you try the other slide?" she heard him say, and jerked her attention back to where Alice wobbled uncertainly on the bottom rung of the biggest slide in the playground. Melissa half rose and then sank again as her daughter moved to the small slide without complaint.

He's a good father, a mushy voice crooned within her chest.

With a start she pulled herself away from the direction her thoughts were headed.

"You wanted to talk about your daughters?" she asked tartly.

He turned his head to look down at her, a frown drawing his eyebrows together. "I'm sorry, I didn't mean to interfere with Alice."

"Oh, no. It's not that...I mean...Seth, why did you bring us here?"

Consternation turned to puzzlement. "I don't know," he said slowly. "I thought about our conversation yesterday. We're obviously both pretty gun-shy, but..." He gazed off at the river for a long moment. "I wanted to spend some time with you," he said at last, and she could tell from his tone that he was as surprised to say it as she was to hear it.

Something funny happened in her chest. Like her heart tried to cram about a year's worth of heartbeats into a nanosecond. "Oh," she said. Could he possibly be interested in her? Not as a loser bank customer, or as an efficient day-care provider, but as a woman? Even as the possibility fluttered across her imagination, he doused it.

"Oh, hell, forget I said that."

She was only too happy to forget it. More complications in her life, she really didn't need. "Consider it done. Um. What about the girls?"

Another age seemed to go by before he answered, and Melissa felt a struggle going on inside him. It must be as tough for him to face an attraction to another woman as it was for her to think that way about another man. She watched Alice taking turns on the slide with an adorable giggling blond boy and listened to their shrieks of laughter. A smile tugged at her lips as the kids shared the instant intimacy of children.

She and Seth were at the opposite end of the intimacy spectrum, forced into closeness by circumstances and doing their best to remain strangers.

She felt rather than saw the movement beside her as he wiped his hands on a napkin and then picked up his soft drink. "Laura's in trouble at school."

"What?" Melissa was genuinely surprised. She'd seen enormous progress in the child's school work and attitude in the months she'd known her. In fact, once she'd realized she wasn't going to get away with her old lazy habits at Melissa's house, she'd exhibited a natural curiosity and intelligence that made Melissa as proud as if Laura were her own child. Jessie, who followed her sister in everything, had improved enormously, too.

"She got into a fight at school and the teacher overheard her call some girl's mother names."

He recited the facts tersely, and by the end Melissa was furious. "How could any mother be so cruel? Laura's been doing so well. I hope this won't set her back."

"Her teacher's asked to see me Friday after school. I think it would help if she saw there was an important woman in Laura and Jessie's life. I want her to meet you."

An important woman? He thought she was important to the twins? Well, he was right. But she was surprised he'd noticed. And she'd love to tell that teacher a thing or two. Even more, she'd like to have a few words with one very insensitive mother. "I'd love to come."

"I was hoping you'd say that."

"But what about the kids? Who'll look after them while we're gone?"

"If it's all right with you, I've asked my sister Janice to watch them at my house until we get back."

"Oh. Janice… Your house?"

"Janice would be more comfortable there. She's great with kids. Her own are teenagers, so they can fend for themselves."

"Well, I guess that would be all right, then. If you're sure your sister won't mind."

"She'll love it."

Friday was her birthday. Oh, well. It's not like she had anything better to do than attend a parent-teacher interview.

Seth stretched his arms over his head and Melissa's mouth went dry as she watched the pull of muscles beneath the white shirt. Catching her gaze he held it a moment then said, "How would you like to take a walk along the river?"

"I'd love to." She raised her voice. "Alice, let's go for a walk."

"I'll get her," Seth said. As he walked to take Alice's hand, the three-year-old cried, "Daddy."

For a stricken moment, Seth and Melissa stared at each other. "She copies the twins in everything," she said, trying to make light of the comment.

They avoided looking at each other by packing up the picnic remainders. They went for their walk, but the brightness of the day had dimmed.

SETH WEDGED HIMSELF into the child's chair, feeling like Gulliver in Lilliput. It didn't help that Mrs. Picard had chosen to sit facing him and Melissa in her adult-sized teacher's chair.

He didn't like her. Not only did her ridiculous chair power game annoy him, but her face looked like some giant hand had accidentally squeezed it too hard. All her features were shoved together in the middle of her face in a prissy frown.

There were lots of fabulous teachers, men and women who took pride in their work and inspired kids. He knew that. Well, he couldn't imagine a better or more dedicated teacher than his sister. So far, the girls had been lucky enough to experience some first-rate educators. But unfortunately, not this year.

It was like going back in time. The room smelled like chalk, old apple cores and the bodies of ten-year-olds. He glanced over at Melissa squeezed into the desk next to him and had to squelch an urge to reach over and pull her hair. Or slip her a note.

As though aware of his gaze, she looked his way and he knew, from the twinkle of mischief in her eyes, that she'd read his thoughts.

Suppressing a grin, he turned to the unsmiling face above him. Mrs. Picard had a file folder open on her lap and was regarding it sternly. She made them wait for a minute while she completed reading.

"Have Laura and Jessica told you why I requested this meeting?" she asked at last, her eyes boring into both of them, as though daring them to come up with the wrong answer.

"Yes." He bit back the "ma'am."

She nodded. "Good. I've called you in today because this is by no means the first such incident. Laura used foul language about another student's mother. I feel it is only fair to inform you that the mother in question has also been to see me. She is naturally extremely upset."

"But she—"

The teacher raised a finger. "Please, Mr. O'Reilly, allow me to finish. You will have your turn."

Damn, he'd forgotten to take an antacid pill before the meeting. He tried to ignore the pain as anger prodded his gut.

"I believe it would be appropriate for Laura to be taken to Mrs. Moore's house and forced to apologize for her behavior."

Seth tried to rise, but he was jammed tightly in the desk. He wanted to be standing above Mrs. Picard when he told her what he thought of that idea. But Melissa beat him to it.

"And will that woman apologize to Laura for *her* rude comments?" Her voice was strong and clear, and angry. "Laura's a ten-year-old, a child who's lost her mother. Mrs. Moore's comments were cruel and insensitive, and maybe her daughter would have done better not to repeat them to the twins."

There was utter silence for a moment. If possible, Mrs.

Picard's mouth pursed even more. "You, I believe, are the babysitter."

But Melissa wasn't intimidated so easily. Seth watched in admiration as she said, with her quiet dignity, "I'm also their friend."

Turning her attention to Seth, the teacher said, "I have here a written record of the times one or both of the twins have been reprimanded."

"You keep a rap sheet on ten-year-olds?" Seth spluttered.

She shot him an acidic glance as though to say, *Now I see where the girls get their rudeness from.* "Laura is the worst offender, but Jessica follows her lead. I believe the girls are a bad influence on each other. Now, the school cannot force you to make Laura apologize. That is up to you and your conscience. However, I intend to split them up into different classes."

"Split them up?"

"For their own good."

"But they've always been together. Since their mother died, at least they've had each other." The school bell rang. Idly, he wondered why when all the students had left for the day.

He hated the idea of splitting up the girls. And he was determined not to let it happen. He'd go to the principal, the school trustees, as high as he had to. Once again, he tried to wrestle himself out of the chair.

And once again, Melissa's voice stopped him. "Mrs. Picard, I've noticed a real improvement in the girls' behavior over the last weeks, would you agree?"

"I would have said that, before this last incident, yes."

"Perhaps you would consider giving the girls a trial period to see if the improvement continues?"

"Does Mr. O'Reilly plan to make Laura apologize to Mrs. Moore?"

"No," Seth said.

"Then—"

"Mrs. Theisen is a trained pediatric nurse. She's an expert on treating children who've dealt with trauma. Since she's been working with the girls, we've all seen an improvement. You've admitted it yourself. If she believes a trial period would be beneficial, I think it's worth a try."

He could see the old biddy's wheels turning. Did she dare defy an expert? He was still holding back his trump card, hoping he wouldn't have to use it.

"I'd be happy to work with you on this Mrs. Picard." Melissa smiled. "I believe at this stage in their recovery, separating them could have disastrous consequences."

The teacher's eyes narrowed even more. She was obviously out of her depth. "You have professional credentials and references I assume?"

Melissa's eyebrows rose. "Of course."

"They may stay together for the time being, but I'll be watching them carefully," she said to Melissa.

Seth finally ejected himself from the desk, and he and Melissa got out of the classroom as quickly as possible. Their steps echoed down the linoleum hallway, past the rows of pint-sized lockers. Once out of sight and hearing of Mrs. Picard, Seth grabbed Melissa's hand, and bringing it to his mouth, kissed her knuckles. "Thank you."

She squeezed his hand briefly, then pulled away, and he noticed the delicate color creep up her cheeks. "And thank you for making me into some bogus expert."

"Not bogus." He pushed the metal bar on the outside door and held it open for Melissa. As they passed out into late afternoon sunshine, he said, "Even Mrs. Picky had to give you credit for what you've done for the girls, especially Laura. Maybe I haven't said anything, but I've noticed it, too."

She blushed even deeper, and he knew his words had pleased her.

"And thanks to you, I didn't have to play my trump card on the wicked witch of the west."

"Trump card?"

"The school principal is one of my squash buddies."

She laughed, a sweet, sexy laugh. "I'm beginning to see where Laura gets her craftiness."

"Let's go get the kids," he said as they made their way to his car. He'd been careful not to do anything stupid like wish her a happy birthday, but now that it was time for her birthday surprise, he felt as jumpy and excited as the kids had been for the last couple of days. Melissa didn't say anything, but he had to wonder if she suspected.

"Don't forget to drop me at my place so I can pick up my car," she reminded him.

He wanted to drive her to his house. Wanted to prolong their conversation and their time alone together, but he'd make her suspicious if he didn't drop her off, so he said goodbye in her driveway and roared off to warn the birthday party surprise crew.

CHAPTER TEN

MELISSA SLUMPED FOR A moment behind the wheel, giving her cheerful act a break. Thirty-five years old today, and what had she achieved in her life? She'd become a cliché—the divorced single mom, dumped for a younger woman. And on top of that, she was fighting to hang on to her home.

She was as much a loser as her mother.

No, worse. Even her mother had managed to hang on to her husband.

Melissa gave herself a mental shake. She had two beautiful children, and more work than she needed between the garden designing and the day care. She didn't relish living on the financial edge, but she felt herself moving slowly toward safer ground.

As a birthday present to herself, she decided to take a night off from worrying. Putting the car in gear, she headed for Seth's place. After she picked them up, she'd take the kids out for pizza. When was the last time they'd had a treat like that? And after they were in bed, instead of spending the lonely hours on work, she'd grab a good book and run herself a bubble bath.

Melissa pasted the smile back on her face as soon as she reached Seth's house. It took a while before anyone answered the door. As she was about to ring a second time, it opened and there was Seth grinning down at her. Her phony smile was suddenly twenty-four-carat genuine as she beamed back at him.

"Hi," he said. "Kids are waiting in the living room. Come on in."

The living room? A stifled giggle and furious whispering came from somewhere behind his left shoulder. Surely they hadn't remembered. Another quick glance at Seth's face and she could see they had remembered. He was as keyed up as a little kid.

"Oh, Seth."

"Don't spoil it," he whispered, and grabbing her arm, dragged her into the living room.

"Surprise!" Young bodies bounced out from behind the furniture, and they all threw themselves her way. Foggily she noted balloons, clumsily twisted crepe paper and long, looping strings of colored goop all over everything. Then she was being hugged and Happy Birthday'd by four kids at once. Blindly, she hugged them back.

Above their heads her eyes met Seth's, and she thanked him silently. Something crazy happened when he gazed right back at her, something soft and sweet and very, very new. Melissa experienced a sudden surge of elation; she felt her heart pick up the pace, her mouth dry and her breathing ragged.

He took a step toward her, his eyes dark and serious, and then, as though he'd just noticed they weren't alone, he stopped.

Everything that had receded in that moment came crashing back.

Especially the noise.

All four kids were talking at once, shouting, really, as

they tried to claim her attention. They were telling her how many times they'd almost blown the surprise, whose idea it was to get the potato chips, how many cans of spray streamer they'd emptied.

"How about we let the birthday girl take off her coat," Seth suggested. He stepped forward to help her out of it and managed to turn the simple courtesy into a caress that left a wake of gooseflesh down her arms.

A woman with a big smile who looked to be in her early forties emerged from the kitchen. "Hi," she said. "I'm Janice. Happy Birthday."

"Thank you. I think." She shook Seth's sister's hand and decided she could see a faint resemblance, though Janice seemed a lot more content, at peace.

"This is your chair, Mom." Matthew pointed to one of the Queen Anne chairs decorated with balloons, bows and ribbons.

"I feel like a queen," she assured him after he arranged a footstool under her feet and thrust a bowl of potato chips at her.

"Do you want some swamp water?" Jessie asked. "We bought four kinds of soda, then decided to mix them all together."

Melissa swallowed and hoped her smile didn't waver. "Why thank you, Jessie."

"Tell you what, Jess, you get the kids' drinks. I have something special for the adults." He turned to Melissa. "I got champagne, but if you prefer something else, name it."

"I love champagne. I haven't had it in ages."

"Three glasses, coming right up."

"Not for me, bro," Janice said. She turned to Melissa. "Tyson, my oldest, is playing basketball tonight. I have to go watch." She glanced from Melissa to Seth and back again. "Have a great evening, you two," and then she was gone.

He looked as though he was going to say something, then changed his mind. He disappeared into the kitchen just as Alice walked in, proudly holding a lumpy red-wrapped package.

"It's a present," she confided in a whisper and placed it at Melissa's feet.

"Come here, you," Melissa exclaimed and hauled her giggling daughter onto her lap for a giant hug.

Soon she had a stack of presents at her feet and a full glass in her hand.

"Open mine first," Alice begged.

"I'll open them from the youngest to the oldest. Is that all right with everyone?"

After a chorus of "yes" she picked up the lumpy red parcel carefully and slowly unwrapped it. Inside was a terra-cotta plant pot painted with bright craft paints. "Oh, Alice, It's beautiful. Why, look at that big, happy yellow sun, and an apple tree, and so many different colored flowers, and there's even a rainbow."

"And that's you." Alice jumped up and ran over to point at the stick figure with a huge smile. "You're in your garden."

"This is the most wonderful present, Alice. Thank you."

"Jessie helped me," Alice told her, pointing at the blushing girl.

"I knew you liked plants and stuff," Jessie mumbled.

"Thanks. It's perfect."

With a big smacking kiss, she set Alice aside as Matthew stepped forward to present his gift, a grocery-sized box wrapped in newspaper. He opened it for Melissa and pulled out a mobile on a bent coat hanger.

"This is me in outer space. See, here are all the planets and that's my spaceship. Seth lent me a book about space so I could get the planets in the right order." Somehow, Mr. O'Reilly had become Seth to the kids, ignoring that one awful moment when Alice had called him Daddy. She wasn't sure when the Seth thing had happened or whether she approved.

But the twins called her by her first name, so what could she do about it? When she thanked him for helping her son, Seth looked as embarrassed as his daughter had.

"We can hang this in the kitchen so I can enjoy it every day."

"And when I go into space, you can look at it and remember where I am."

The laughter helped ease the lump in Melissa's throat.

"You next, kid sister. You're five minutes younger than me," Laura said.

After rolling her eyes, Jessie said, "Mine's the yellow one. I bought them with my allowance," she informed Melissa, who was exclaiming over the package of spring bulbs.

Laura presented her with a pastel drawing of a girl who strongly resembled Laura, holding a hank of her red hair and frowning. *Carrots* was scribbled underneath.

"Why that's *Anne of Green Gables*. Laura you are a very talented artist."

"I know you like that book."

"I love it. It's something we have in common. Thank you." She rose and crossed the room to hug first Jessie, then Laura.

When she returned to her seat, there were two neatly wrapped packages still at her feet. "But what are these?"

"The green one's from Auntie Janice," Laura piped up. "The huge one's from Dad."

"Janice? But—she shouldn't have bought me a present." She opened it. "What a pretty vase. I'll be able to put the flowers that grow from your bulbs in here, Jessie."

The last package was the biggest of all. When she tore off the paper she found a hardware store box. Inside was wall plaster and a metal applicator, tile grout, some assorted tools and a hinge exactly like the one on her kitchen cupboards.

She glanced up. "Thank you, I think."

"It comes with a handyman," he explained. "I'll come over and fix the cracks in the plaster and the other things you mentioned. I noticed your upstairs tub needs grouting. Make a list. You've got yourself a weekend handyman."

"A handyman," she breathed in rapture. Maybe it was sexist, but she didn't care. She'd tried to figure out the basics of home repair, but she couldn't even hammer in a nail straight.

"Everybody else got a hug, doesn't my dad?" Laura asked loudly.

Melissa laughed shakily. "Yes, I guess he does." She rose, and slowly crossed the room.

He stood to meet her, the expression in his eyes intense, hungry. He put out his arms and pulled her flush against his solid body, where she clung for a moment, letting her head rest against his shoulder. She heard the beat of his heart— a little fast perhaps for a man who played squash four times a week, but still slower than her own frenetic pulse.

"I can't thank you—"

He interrupted her words with a quick, hard kiss on the lips. "Happy birthday, Melissa."

CHAPTER ELEVEN

IT WAS JUST A little birthday kiss. A peck, really, yet she felt she would have fallen on the floor if she hadn't been clinging to Seth. Her lips still tingled with the remnants of heat from his mouth. She wanted—

"I'm starving. Can we have pizza now Seth?"

"Ma-atthew! Come in the kitchen," Laura ordered, then she gestured frantically at the other kids who scrambled to obey.

"Oh, dear. Is she upset?" Melissa pulled away and straightened her perfectly straight blouse.

"No-o. I'm not the child expert you are, but I think she likes to see us kissing." Seth picked up his glass and drained it.

In the awkward silence that ensued, Melissa busied herself picking up wrapping paper and folding it neatly.

Seth fiddled a CD into the player, and soon Diana Krall drowned out the rustling of the gift paper.

"Shall we see if dinner's ready?"

She nodded her agreement, and they headed into the kitchen, where pizza steamed on a round oak table laid with what was obviously the best china.

It seemed so right, sitting there with Seth and his children. Although, she knew it was corny, she was beginning to believe in the Brady Brunch as she looked around the table. Jessie was helping Alice to a slice of pizza. Laura scolded Matthew in a low voice about the way he picked every vegetable off his pizza.

And there was Seth, caressing her with his gaze every time their eyes met. She almost choked when she caught him staring at her mouth. She licked her lips, wondering if she had a blob of pizza sauce on them. Seth seemed transfixed by the movement of her tongue.

She felt hot and excited and nervous. Like a woman being pursued by a man. And she realized that's exactly what she was. Her pleasure was totally out of proportion with the casualness of the interest she was certain he felt, but it was still nice to feel desired. It had been such a long time.

After they'd all stuffed themselves with pizza, Melissa made a move to start clearing the table.

"Sit." Seth ordered. He and the girls cleared the table and then everyone but Melissa disappeared. Within minutes, she heard the ragtag sounds of the happy birthday song, and around the corner came the cake.

"We made it ourselves," Laura proudly exclaimed.

Melissa shot an alarmed glance at Seth, remembering the disastrous brownies the girls had once baked, but it was Jessie who calmed her fears. "Dad and Aunt Janice and me and Laura all made it together."

"And me and Alice helped decorate it."

"Oh, it's beautiful." And it was. From the candy heart decorations to the crooked lettering. "Come on, everybody help me blow out the candles." She pulled the kids around her.

"Wait."

She paused on a big indrawn breath and glanced up at Seth's command. A camera flashed.

As soon as the chocolate cake and ice cream was consumed, the kids begged to watch a video.

"I don't know. It's getting kind of late." Melissa checked her watch.

"You should probably have some coffee before you drive home. We have lots of room if the kids want to doze off here."

"Can we have a sleepover?" Matthew begged.

"Sleepover, sleepover." Alice jumped up and down.

"I don't know. I hate to impose."

"There's plenty of room, you're all welcome to stay," Seth said in a too-casual voice that sent shivers of excitement up her spine. He was inviting her for a sleepover, as well.

"Please, Mom. Please."

"I'd like you to stay awhile," chimed in a much deeper male voice.

"Well, maybe for a little while."

"Come on." Matthew wasn't waiting for her to change her mind. And with the maximum possible amount of noise, the four kids bounded off.

In the relative quiet after the stair-pounding died down, Melissa fussed about clearing the dessert things, keeping her hands busy while her brain reeled. Seth wanted her. Unless the champagne was making her delusional.

Bent over the table, picking up scattered birthday candles, she peeked up at him through her lashes. He seemed engrossed in measuring coffee into a filter, but she sensed he was as keenly aware of her as she was of him. It was as if an invisible current hummed between them. She tried to imagine what it would be like to make love with Seth.

"How do you like it?" he interrupted her thoughts.

Her eyes widened and her jaw dropped. She liked it pitch-black and under the covers, where sagging boobs and stretched abdomens didn't show. And she did not like discussing sexual preferences in a well-lit kitchen with a man she hadn't yet decided she would sleep with. She closed her mouth and glared at his back.

"Black? Cream and sugar?"

Coffee. Oh, God, he was asking her how she liked her coffee.

"Melissa?"

"Uh, cream and sugar please."

She cursed herself for a fool. But as she eased behind Seth to load the plates in the dishwasher she felt it again. No way all that heat was being generated by her. Working together in the U-shaped kitchen brought them into close contact.

Even as she ran water over the dishes and stacked each one carefully into the dishwasher, she sensed his movements where he worked scant feet away. The aroma of coffee filled the air. Idly, she hoped it was decaf. Any more stimulant and she might go spinning off into space.

"Here," he said, handing her a cup.

"Thanks." She followed him into the living room. So formal. For a few minutes, conversation was stilted. He told her a dull story about the bank. She told him a cute story about Alice and Jessie, then had an awful feeling she'd told him the same story the day before.

Suddenly, he laughed. "This feels weird, doesn't it?"

"Yes," she agreed. "It does."

"We're friends—at least I think we are?" He glanced at her, and she nodded confirmation. "But this feels like a date."

"I know." She didn't mention the strange undercurrent between them that was making her so jittery.

"What do you think would have happened if we'd met socially? Instead of the way we did?"

"What do you mean?"

"If I'd met you somewhere, a party through mutual friends, say, would you have said yes if I'd asked you out?"

"I don't know." She put her empty coffee cup down. "Would you have asked me?"

"I think so. I hope so."

She tilted her head to one side and studied him, trying to imagine meeting him for the first time without the fear of losing her house topmost on her mind. "I probably would have said yes."

"Okay." He crinkled up his eyes in a sexy smile. "So I'm asking."

"You're asking me out? On a date?"

"Yes."

"When? Where?"

"I don't know. Dinner. Next week sometime."

"Who'd look after the kids?" she asked, stalling.

"A sitter, I guess."

She blew out a breath. "I feel so old going out on a date. I'm thirty-five today."

"I'm thirty-eight. And we'll still be thirty-five and thirty-eight whatever we do."

He was suggesting they take this unspoken attraction out into the open. Was she willing to? She looked at him. "Okay."

"Excellent. How about next Friday?"

"Sure, so long as we can find sitters." She rose and carried their cups to the kitchen.

"More coffee?" he asked.

"I'd better not. I should get the kids home."

She put their cups in the dishwasher and noted the machine was full.

"Where do you keep dishwasher detergent?"

"Under the sink. Here let me." He moved forward but she was already there. As she'd bent and placed her hand on the cabinet handle, she felt the soft, warm impact behind her as he toppled over her. His hands grabbed the counter on either side of the sink and his hips plowed into her backside. If she'd needed hard evidence that he was as keyed up as she, it was pressed up against her.

Very evident.

And very hard.

For a stunned second, neither of them moved, then she heard her name in a strangled whisper. A whisper that spoke to her own secret torment.

She made some kind of a noise in her throat, not a moan or a sigh but a combination of both with a hint of nervous giggle thrown in.

His hands came down off the counter and wrapped around her, straightening them both in the process. He held her like that, his front warm and solid against her back, his arms wrapped around her torso, below her breasts. She let herself lean into him and absorb his warmth, his scent. In a slow caress he brought his hands to her shoulders and slowly turned her to face him.

She gazed into the blazing hunger of his eyes, and then his face blurred as he claimed her mouth in a kiss. It was as though she had walked across the Sahara and stumbled onto an oasis of sweet, pure water, so greedily did she drink in his affection. Circling her arms around his neck, she opened her lips and welcomed the hot wetness as his tongue slipped into her mouth.

She splayed her hands in the springy hair at the back of his neck, letting her fingers learn the shape of his head. She wanted to learn all of him. The curves and ridges of his entire body. And she wanted it now.

Her own lust embarrassed her.

Pulling away she dragged in a lungful of air. "This is crazy," she gasped. "I'm not sure it's a good idea." She'd gone as far as agreeing to a date. That was a big step for her.

"Don't analyze it, Melissa, please. Let it happen." The urgency and dark promise of his words sent passion skittering along her nerve ends.

He was right. If she stopped to think about it long enough, she'd call a halt. And she couldn't bear to stop, not now.

She ran her tongue over her swollen lips. "Let me check on the kids."

"Okay. But hurry."

She crept downstairs and smiled. They'd pulled out the Hide-A-Bed, and all four of them were sprawled on it, sleeping deeply. A woolen throw had fallen to the floor, so she picked it up and laid it over the kids. The TV blared. She flicked it off and left a lamp burning, then tiptoed back upstairs.

Seth was waiting for her. The dishwasher hummed, so obviously he'd turned it on. She knew how the thing felt.

"Everything all right?"

"They're sound asleep."

"Good." He reached out and dragged Melissa toward him. He kissed her gently, then ran his fingers down her cheek. "I feel like a teenager, sneaking around while his parents are asleep. You never imagine you'll have to sneak around behind your children's backs."

She laughed softly. And then he kissed her again, long and slow. His hands traveled over her back, cupped her butt and then moved up the front of her blouse. When he reached her breasts, she moaned. His lips moved steadily downward, stopping to kiss whatever they passed. Her cheeks, jaw, chin, neck. When his lips reached the vee of her blouse, he started undoing her buttons.

Nerves fluttered in her stomach. There was far too much light in the kitchen. "We should go upstairs," she whispered, "In case the kids wake up."

He hesitated, then with a quick kiss, grabbed her hand and led her down the hall and up the stairs.

She was so taut with a combination of desire and nerves—she was, after all, a woman who'd only ever been with one man—that when they reached the top of the stairs, she didn't notice the tension radiating from his body until they paused before a closed door. Turning her toward him he kissed her again, hard and hungry but with an edge of desperation. Then, taking her hand again, he brought her farther down the hall.

They entered a bedroom, and to her profound relief he didn't turn on a light, merely kept kissing her, all the while backing her toward the bed. The curtains weren't drawn, so moonlight gave the room a dim glow. It was a tidy room, almost sterile. Lamps on the bedside tables and nothing else. A wooden bureau with an empty vase.

A vague uneasiness settled in her chest, then he was laying her on the bed and, as his bulk blocked her vision, she gave in to the sensations invading her body. The knowledge that he truly desired her was as intoxicating as the feel of his mouth on hers. Warmth unfolded within her, traveling stealthily along her limbs until her whole body was pulsing with heat. His hands trailed over her, slowly, molding her shape through her clothes, stoking the fire. He kneaded her breasts, pinching the pebbled nipples lightly so she gasped, wanting more. His hands moved lower, over her abdomen, her hips and down to her knees, then they tracked up her pantyhose and under her skirt, moving slowly and relentlessly up her thighs. He trailed his fingers over the centre of her sensible cotton panties and she bit back a gasp of pleasure.

She'd never felt like this, never. She was close to exploding right there and then, from nothing more than a little fully-clothed foreplay. But she felt, with Seth, something she'd long ago lost. Trust. He would never deliberately hurt her. She knew it as surely as she knew his eye color. Secure in that trust, she felt herself blossoming, her sexual urges flowing like sap after the spring thaw. Beneath those demure cotton panties, she was wet and throbbing with the need to be filled. Even as she thrust her hips up toward him suggestively, her hands reached for his belt buckle.

With equal urgency, he grabbed at the waistband of her pantyhose and started to pull, peeling the fabric from her skin with hands that were not quite steady.

Perhaps a breeze picked up outside, blowing clouds away from the moon, but just then a shaft of moonlight illuminated the bed, and her, as bright as day.

She shivered theatrically, pretending cold although her body burned with lust. "Let's get under the covers. I'm freezing."

He lunged up and dragged down the bedspread. Melissa moved to help him, but her questing fingers found only a blanket, and the dimpled surface of a mattress, no sheets. Where were the sheets? A slight musty smell rose from the disturbed bedding. The pieces began to fall into place. The impersonal feel, the lack of any signs that Seth inhabited the space. "This isn't your room, is it?"

A glance at his face showed him looking both guilty and confused. "It's the guest room," he admitted. "I thought... ah...it was safer, in case the kids came looking for us."

"Don't you have a lock on your bedroom door?" she asked softly, dread building in her stomach.

"Well, yes. But—"

"Then I want to go there." Had she been wrong about him after all? Maybe she couldn't trust him.

"Look, can't we—"

"I want to make love with you in your bed, where you sleep, like I'm part of your life, not some temporary guest." Didn't she deserve at least that? Or was this some casual thing, a one-nighter with a sex-starved divorcée. A pity— No. Even as the thought entered her mind, she knew Seth wouldn't treat her so shabbily. Anguish was coming off him in waves.

"All right," he said almost angrily. "Come on."

They padded back down the hall, not holding hands this time, to the doorway where he'd paused earlier. He had intended to take her to his bed then changed his mind. She was getting a really bad feeling about this. Coward that she was, she wished she'd shut up and let nature take its course in the guest room. But it was too late to turn back now. With a deep breath, Melissa entered his bedroom. It was dark, but she had to see the room, she knew that. So she snapped on the overhead light.

"Oh, Seth," she said with all the pity in her heart.

CHAPTER TWELVE

THE ROOM WAS A SHRINE TO a dead woman. He was living in his own personal Taj Mahal. Pictures of a young woman with mischievous eyes, and a short, sassy crop of curly red hair smiled at Melissa from half a dozen picture frames.

She moved silently to a wedding photo. A much younger Seth, with a smile that held no shadows, hugged his bride. Beside that photo was Claire with the newborn twins, and pictures of family vacations, Christmas, happy family mementoes.

It wasn't only the pictures, it was the bright yellow, flower-printed chintz draperies and bedspread that spoke of a woman's touch. The lacy pillows monogrammed with *C* and *S*. The brushes and perfume bottles on a spindle-legged dressing table. Melissa could have sworn there was even the faint scent of another woman in the air.

Her mind was obviously playing tricks on her. And yet… She glanced at Seth, standing in the doorway, looking so lost and confused she wanted to take him back to the guest room and simply offer him what comfort she could. But she'd learned a lot about grieving in her nursing career.

That light floral scent hovered in the air like a ghostly presence. Which was ridiculous. Unless…

Melissa grasped a drawer handle on the dresser and pulled.

"No! Don't—"

But it was too late. She'd already spotted the neatly folded nighties and lingerie, and she knew without looking that the rest of Claire's clothes would be neatly stacked in the drawers and probably still hanging in one of the double closets.

"Oh, Seth," she whispered again, her heart breaking for him. The scent was stronger with the drawer open, and in a rush of embarrassment that she had barged into his private shrine, she swiftly closed the drawer. When she straightened and turned around, Melissa was alone in the room.

She heard Seth's tread thumping down the stairs and decided to give him a few minutes to recover. She needed some time herself.

The lump in her throat threatened to choke her. She picked up the nearest photo. Claire in a flowered summer dress laughing at the camera as though she'd been caught unawares. "You were one lucky woman," Melissa whispered. "Please understand, I don't want to take your place, I want to help him. How do I do that?"

But the pretty young woman kept smiling. If she was sending any message, it was that Melissa was on her own.

Carefully, she replaced the picture exactly where it had been and quietly left the room.

She found him sitting in the darkened living room sipping coffee. He didn't offer her a cup, didn't even acknowledge her presence, but Melissa knew he needed her as strongly as if he'd sobbed on her shoulder.

She went to the kitchen and poured herself a coffee, adding cream and sugar from the set Seth had prepared earlier, then returned to sit across from him.

They sipped silently for a while.

"The girls look a lot like their mother," she said at last.

"I'm sorry." His voice was gruff and full of pain.

"I'm sorry, too."

He was staring at the floor, his elbows resting on his spread knees, the cup held in his hands. "I thought I could handle it. You're the first woman I've wanted...since...I mean... Oh hell, you know what I mean."

"Yes. I misunderstood. When you took me to the guest room, I thought it was an insult."

His eyes burned when he glanced up. "I wasn't only trying to get laid. I wanted you."

"I'm glad."

He'd wanted her, but not enough to brave his own demons. Melissa sighed. She had to put away her own feelings. Later she could think about how she'd been rejected in favor of a dead woman. But now, Seth needed help and she had training in grief counseling. As much as the woman in her was tempted to run, the professional in her had to stay and help him.

"Do you know about the stages of grief, Seth?"

"Yes. Anger, denial, bargaining, depression and something."

"Acceptance." She let a hint of humor creep into her voice. "You've obviously mastered the first four stages. It seems to be the final one that's giving you trouble."

"I have accepted it. She's been gone for three years for God's sake."

"Three years and how many weeks, days, minutes, seconds?"

He let out a startled exclamation.

"Leaving everything exactly as Claire left it is denying that she's not coming back."

"I'm not a freaking psycho. I know she's not coming back. I never got around to getting rid of all that stuff."

"I know of an excellent women's shelter that would put her things to good use. Don't you think she'd want that?"

"Damn it, I know she would. She'd want us to be up there humping our brains out on her old bed, too."

"I'm not trying—"

"No. She would. She made me promise I'd get on with my life and find someone else, for me and the girls."

Melissa swallowed. "She was a good woman."

"Yeah, she was. The last couple of weeks, the way I've been feeling every time I'm around you…I thought I was ready."

"But you're not." She sighed, knowing there was something she could do to help him.

He shoved a hand through his hair. "I made a nice mess of your birthday. I'm sorry."

"Don't be. I understand." What she planned to do would hurt him, and make him angry with her. She knew that. Sometimes healing really hurt. "Seth, I want you to do something for me."

He glanced up warily, his face gray. "What?"

"Tomorrow, I want you to take the girls out for the day. And I want you to give me the key to your house."

He closed his eyes briefly as he understood the unspoken message. That she would be cleaning out his wife's things while he was gone. "I don't think—"

"It's time, Seth."

"I thought maybe the girls would want—"

He wasn't going to make this easy. "I'll tell you what. I'll label everything and put it away in storage boxes. Nothing will be gone, but Claire's things won't be in your room anymore." She felt the way his body jerked physically when she said Claire's name. She bet everyone else he knew never mentioned his wife. They'd think they were saving him from bad memories, and he wasn't the kind of man who'd bring up a subject that he thought would be uncomfortable for other people. So he'd bottled all that stuff inside.

She didn't need to ask him if he'd ever had counseling. "Claire will always be a part of your life and the twins'. She's a wonderful part of your past, and a piece of her lives on in those girls." She put her coffee cup down and moved toward him, kneeling so she could look up at him. "But it's time for you to get back to living."

He dropped his head and nodded once. Then he raised his hips and dug in his pocket, pulling out a bunch of keys. They clattered jarringly in the quiet room as he separated one. Leaning forward he snapped the lone silver house key onto the coffee table in the middle of the room, still without looking at her. "Call Janice. She'll help."

He needed to be alone for a while. She was forcing him to take the last step in accepting that his wife was gone forever. For now, she was the enemy, and she understood that. She only hoped he would recognize how difficult it was for her to play that role, when she so wanted to be close to him.

But there was no future for them together so long as his wife's clothes lay neatly folded in drawers and her scent permeated his bedroom. Of course, the step she was about to take might kill any hope they'd have had, anyway. But at least she might help him find peace and eventually he'd be ready to start again with another woman. It was a depressing thought, she discovered, imagining him with somebody else. It seemed like a lose/lose situation for Melissa.

She picked up the key, still warm from being so close

to his body, and rose. "I'm going to wake up my kids now. It's time we were heading home."

He made an effort to rouse himself, forcing a sorry attempt at a smile as he stood. "Yeah. I'll get you Janice's number, and then I'll help you get them in the car."

Matthew muttered in his sleep as Seth hoisted him in his arms. Alice didn't stir as Melissa untangled her from where she'd snuggled in Laura's arms. The two adults carried their sleeping burdens to the car, but the biggest burden was the unspoken one that weighed on them. The memory of what had happened upstairs, and the knowledge of what Melissa was going to do tomorrow.

Once the kids were buckled in the car, the engine purring softly as the inside began to heat up, Melissa tipped up her face to say good night. Her trite *"thank you for a lovely birthday"* never made it out of her mouth. One quick glance at Seth's painfully bleak expression, and she was out of the car and reaching for him, her heart yearning to give him comfort.

Wordlessly, he held her, so tightly she feared for her ribs. She closed her eyes and leaned in, offering him all the strength and understanding she had. Her head nestled against his neck. "I won't do it if you don't want me to," she whispered, not sure if either of them could bear the pain.

"You have to," he muttered.

"Yes, I think I do." Despite knowing what the cost could be to their budding romance. Would he be able to accept that she must hurt him in order to help him? Or would he forever hold it against her that she caused him this suffering?

At last she pulled away and slid back into the driver's seat. "Good night."

"We'll go out early tomorrow," he said in a voice that

pleaded with her to get it over with as quickly as possible. She nodded and then put the car in gear and backed away.

The last image she had was of him standing outside in his shirtsleeves, oblivious to the cold, staring straight ahead.

WHEN SETH WALKED up the stairs, he felt like an old man. The girls were sound asleep on the pullout downstairs, and he decided to leave them there for the night. He'd contemplated opening a bottle of Scotch and spending the rest of the night slumped in his favorite chair in the den, but he knew that desire for what it was—cowardice. Getting good and drunk wouldn't help anything.

His day-care provider and almost-lover was a master of the gotta-be-cruel-to-be-kind school of do-gooders. But he knew she was right. He'd made an ass of himself and denied both Melissa and himself some self-indulgent pleasure they could both use. She'd been so tentative at first, but once she got warmed up, she'd been all passion and fire. He ached all over again thinking of what they'd missed.

But Melissa had understood what he hadn't. There was a woman standing between the two of them.

Claire.

He touched the wedding ring on his finger. He and Claire hadn't had a perfect marriage—who did? They used to have the odd fight, and during the first year after the twins were born, they'd both been frazzled, but Claire had been exhausted, what with breast-feeding both kids, which she'd insisted on doing. If one wasn't crying in the night, or teething, or getting a cold or colicky, then the other was. It seemed that they'd barely ever had a full night's sleep. But they'd managed.

And she'd loved those tiny redheaded babies with her

whole heart. He found he was smiling as he went into their bedroom, his and Claire's, as he remembered a night when he'd walked in to find his three favorite redheads all sound asleep, one baby still attached to each breast, sucking reflexively.

The old anger rolled through him. It wasn't fair that someone like Claire should be taken so young. And so cruelly. Her daughters needed her. Who would teach them to be women? Who would help them through all that incomprehensible teen girl stuff that was right around the corner? He, being a banker, and a sensible man, had planned for the girls' education the minute they were born, just as he had begun saving for his and Claire's retirement from the day they were married.

She used to tease him about living for tomorrow instead of for today, but he liked to plan ahead.

Nowhere in the plan or in his worst nightmares had he imagined losing a woman so full of life. He picked up one of the photos on his dresser. It was the only one he had of her after her diagnosis. She was still smiling, and she'd promised him she'd fight that cancer with everything she had.

She had, too. A tear rolled down his cheek. She'd lost that brave battle, but Melissa was right. Claire had left a part of herself in the twins. The fact that Claire had lived and that he and she had loved each other was evident everyday in those two girls, who looked so much like their mother.

He wasn't keeping his end of the bargain. He'd promised Claire that he would make a good life for the girls. She'd told him, near the end, on one of her good days, that he would find someone else. She gave him her blessing. They'd both cried. And at the time, he'd believed it would never happen. He would never find someone to replace Claire.

And, he realized, looking at that bright, laughing face, he hadn't. He'd found Melissa. She wasn't Claire. She wasn't much like her at all. She was quiet where Claire had been outgoing, meticulous where Claire had been happy-go-lucky. They didn't look a bit alike or have any similarities but one. They were both terrific mothers.

Was that what he was doing? Falling for a woman because she was a good mother and his girls were in desperate need of one?

Even as the notion crossed his mind, he dismissed it. He placed the photograph back on his dresser. No. What he felt for Melissa was what a man feels for a woman. He wasn't certain how strong it was, or where it would lead—probably nowhere, now that he'd made a total fool of himself—but it wasn't because she was a good mother that he ached for Melissa.

He'd never fallen out of love with Claire, and he never would. He thought that Melissa, of all people, had understood that. He opened the closet and fingered a random dress that was no doubt totally out of style and would have long since been donated to charity if Claire were still alive.

In that moment he realized that packing away her things, like burying her body, didn't mean she was gone forever. Her memory would live as long as he and the girls did.

He stood there with his head bowed, knowing this was the last night he'd spend in this room that was still Claire's. He was still alive. Maybe it was time he started acting like it.

THE NEXT DAY, Seth put off returning home as long as he could. After breakfast in a pancake house, a shopping trip where the girls picked out new clothes that were totally overpriced and so flimsy they looked like they'd last about a week, lunch in another restaurant, a stop at the music shop in the mall to buy the new Bravo Boys CD, and two hours watching a teen romance movie where he munched antacids at the same speed the girls downed popcorn, they headed home.

He'd told Jessie and Laura over breakfast what Melissa and Janice were going to do today. They'd gone quiet for a second, shared a look, then Laura had said, "Okay."

And they hadn't mentioned it again. Somehow, he knew it was okay. Maybe because they were younger and more resilient, maybe because he'd sent them to the grief counseling he couldn't face himself, maybe because they were optimistic, like their mother. "You know, your mom would be so proud of you two if she could see you now."

"She does see us, Dad," Laura said, looking at him in surprise. "She watches us from heaven. She told us she would, don't you remember?"

He couldn't speak. He could only nod.

When he couldn't think of anything else to do, they headed home.

He drove so slowly seniors were overtaking him. But, as slowly as the car crawled along with the girls chattering in the back, it arrived in his driveway too soon for him.

"Hurry up, Dad, these bags are heavy," Laura complained as he stood outside his own front door, terrified to put the key in the lock.

He pushed the door open. Somebody had left some lights on, for which he was grateful. The main floor of the house looked exactly as he'd last seen it that morning. He swallowed while the girls clattered past him. "Let's try on our stuff," Jessie said as they hauled their loot up the stairs.

When the hall was quiet again, Seth took a deep breath and started up the stairs himself. *Just get it over with.* He refused to pause outside the closed bedroom door but pushed the door open and hit the light switch.

He'd half known what to expect. Even so, he felt the air grunt out of his body as though a medicine ball had slammed into his belly.

Nothing was the same.

Oh, they'd been busy, all right. He stepped forward and eyed the green plaid quilt on the bed—which was on the other side of the room from where it used to be. He gulped as he realized they hadn't taken only Claire's clothing away, they'd removed the dresser she'd kept her stuff in. God, Janice's husband or the boys must have helped, too. Humiliation burned within him along with rising fury. The whole room was different.

He stalked to the double closet and yanked it open, shocked to find her side stripped bare, even though he'd known it would be. A fireball of rage clogged his throat. Even the yellow curtains were gone. They'd even taken her goddamn curtains.

They'd left him nothing, those interfering do-gooders. Nothing but the pictures. Claire still gazed at him from half a dozen frames, but she seemed more distant. They weren't her anymore. They were only pictures.

He collapsed onto the edge of the bed. It didn't even smell the same. Those thieving women had taken everything. If they could have, they'd have sucked his very memories up in a vacuum cleaner.

CHAPTER THIRTEEN

AN HOUR AND TWO Scotches later, the doorbell rang. The girls were downstairs in their brand new clothes dancing to the Bravo Boys, having declared themselves too full of popcorn for dinner. That was fine with Seth. His stomach rejected the idea of food. The Scotch tasted like drain cleaner, but he figured he needed it.

As the persistent bell interrupted his reverie, he felt his eyes narrow in fury. He marched to the door ready to tell that damn Melissa she'd done enough for one day.

It wasn't Melissa standing on his doorstep, tears of sympathy in her eyes, a steaming lasagna in her hands. It was Janice.

He wasn't too pleased to see her, either, but for some reason, he wasn't as angry with his sister as he was with the babysitter cum psychiatrist who'd suddenly taken over his life.

"Can I come in?" Janice asked.

"I guess." He knew he sounded as sulky as a schoolboy.

"I thought you might be hungry." She hurried past him into the kitchen where he heard the oven door creak open and bang shut. He didn't move from the front door, hoping that was a strong enough hint that he wasn't interested in a social visit.

Her heavy tread came down the hallway toward him. He refused to turn around.

"I'm sorry, Seth. It wasn't easy for me, either." Her voice was raspy with tears. "I kept remembering..." She sniffed and he heard the stifled sob.

Turning, he grabbed her to him. Her hefty body shook with grief. "It's okay, Janice. It's okay."

"I knew it had to be done. In three years, I haven't had the courage even to bring up the subject. Melissa did most of it. I stood around crying all day." She sniffed louder. "Melissa warned me you might be angry, but I can't stand it if you are. Please don't be mad at us. Please."

"Melissa warned you?" His voice was sharp. How could she have known? Of course. She had training. He was probably as predictable as a textbook. "Why did she do it if she knew I'd get mad?"

"She cares about you, little brother. She warned me that you wouldn't like either of us for a while. She said I should let you alone, give you time. But I couldn't." She trembled again in his arms, and the lump in his throat eased.

"I'm glad you came, Jan." He squeezed and let her go.

She dried her eyes and gave him a big smile. "I'm glad, too." She touched his shoulder lightly. "This is probably the worst time for me to tell you this, but you know me, I've never been the tactful type."

"Tell me what?"

She sent him a sweet, sassy grin. "I like this one. You can't spend an entire day crying in front of someone and not get pretty close to them, you know?"

He nodded. He'd been so obsessed with his own pain he hadn't thought about Janice's. "That must have been hard on you."

"Well, it was. But I love you. I don't want to see you hurting."

"I know."

"Melissa's a very determined woman, so organized she scares me, and pretty damned bossy, but I like her a lot." She glanced up at him. "It wasn't that easy for her, either." His sister took a shaky breath. "Don't scare her away."

"Did she tell you about last night?" He didn't think he could feel more humiliated about last night, but the thought of Melissa and Janice chatting about him choking made him squirm.

They walked into the kitchen together. "She didn't have to tell me anything. I've got eyes. I haven't seen you look at a woman that way since..."

"Claire. I know. Janice, I screwed up royally last night."

"What are you talking about?"

"I—well, things got pretty hot—" God, this was hard to talk about with his sister.

"Yeah, okay, I get it."

"And I took her into the guest room. I couldn't take her into my bedroom."

His sister was staring at him, obviously torn between pity and horror. "You mean you couldn't take her into Claire's room."

He nodded. "She figured out pretty fast that we weren't in my bedroom and then she made me take her there."

"Oh, hon."

"And when we got to my room, and all Claire's things still around... I couldn't. We didn't..." He swallowed. "Do you think she'll ever give me another chance?"

"I don't know. She seemed fairly professional about

what she had to do today." She looked doubtful as she opened drawers and started setting the table.

"Listen, can you stick around for a while? Feed the girls? I'd...uh...well, I need to see her."

"Are you sure that's a good idea?"

"I'm not sure of any damn thing anymore."

Janice sent him one of the wide smiles she'd inherited from their mother. "Stay as long as you like."

Rejecting the car in favor of a brisk walk, Seth let the rhythm of his footsteps soothe him. But it was tough. All the awkwardness and humiliation of the night before rose in his mind. He'd made a fool of himself. And Melissa had acted like a dentist's drill, breaking through his protective barrier to get at the soft, hurting part. He didn't like being without his protection. He felt exposed and, if he was honest with himself, frightened.

She'd uncovered his secret pain. Gone through his wife's things. How could he make love to her when she knew him for the coward he was? How could he still want her?

The lights of her home welcomed him, even though he dreaded seeing her. He picked up the pace a little and was breathless by the time he banged the lion's head.

"Seth." Her surprise was evident in the lilting way she said his name. "Are you all right? I-I didn't expect to see you." She looked so concerned and so vulnerable standing there with eyes wide and uncertain, that the last of his anger died.

"No. I'm not all right. Not really." He shoved his hands in his pockets as though searching for a tip. "I guess it's going to take a while. But that was a brave thing you did. I wanted to thank you."

A smile both sad and sweet crossed her face. "Would you like to come in?"

"Yes. I would."

She pushed her hair behind her ears in a nervous gesture. "I was putting the kids to bed."

"Can I help?"

"Well, you could read Matthew a story." She sounded kind of doubtful.

"Yeah. That'd be great. I need something to do, something away from my own house." So, he was running from his ghosts. He knew they'd find him again, but a temporary reprieve would be good. Maybe by the time he'd read Matthew a story, he'd have a clue why he was here. Oh, hell. He knew why he was here. But what was he going to do about it?

Matthew was both shy and eager when Melissa explained Seth would be reading him his story. His hair was damp from a bath and he sported flannel pajamas with baseball players all over them. Seth experienced a flash of yearning. He loved his girls, but, before Claire had found out she was sick, they'd planned to have another child. Secretly, he'd hoped for a son.

"Which story do you want?" Seth asked.

"Dunno. You pick."

Seth scanned the shelves in Matthew's bedroom. Science, nature, space, everything educational. He felt a little intimidated. A *Hardy Boys* would have been nice.

He eyed the slugger jammies. "Don't you have any books about baseball?"

"No. I don't know how to play baseball."

"You don't know how to play baseball?" Knowing how to play baseball ranked right up there with knowing how to fly a kite or soap windows on Halloween—quintessential boy stuff. The poor kid might as well have not had a father.

Wide, assessing blue eyes, so much like his mother's, gazed longingly at him. Too scared to ask, but so hopeful Seth didn't have the heart to refuse the unspoken request. "Tell ya what. If it's nice out tomorrow, how about we play some baseball? Just us guys."

Matthew nodded, pure bliss evident on his face.

"We have to check first with your mom."

"Check what with me?" The way her voice sounded was as sexy as a caress. It did things to Seth he didn't want to think about.

Seth opened his mouth, but Matthew beat him to it. "Seth said he'd teach me how to play baseball tomorrow. Please, can I?"

"Baseball? I thought you didn't like team sports. You never let me sign you up for the teams at school." She sounded puzzled, troubled even. It couldn't be any easier for her being a single mom of a boy than it was for him to understand the whole girl thing.

Matthew was getting an anxious expression, which the little boy Seth remembered being could totally relate to. He didn't want to make a fool of himself trying to play a game he didn't understand. Quickly, before his well-meaning mom could ruin everything, Seth spoke up. "We're only going to horse around for fun."

Matthew's stress visibly drained from him as he nodded, the damp cowlick bobbing.

Besides, teaching a kid to play baseball might take his mind off his own troubles for a few hours.

Maybe she read his mind. Melissa glanced from one to the other and nodded. "That'd be great. Why don't you drop the twins here, and we girls will have our own fun."

He rolled his eyes in Matthew's direction, got a

goggle-eyed gagging look in return, and the male bonding had begun.

"Boys," Melissa muttered as she headed back down the hallway, her hips swaying in a way that made Seth very glad there were differences between the sexes.

He dragged a book about telescopes from the bookshelf, but they ended up talking about baseball anyway. "We'll have to catch a Mariners' game one day," he said, thinking how much fun it would be to take this boy to Seattle and watch him enjoy his first pro baseball game. Then a pang of guilt struck him. What was he doing? His actions encouraged Brady Bunch thinking. The last thing the eager little boy beside him needed was another adult male letting him down.

He sat there, his legs looking ridiculously long atop the bug quilt, reading doggedly on about telescopes until the boy dropped to sleep. Then he sat there some more, the soft, regular breathing soothing him as he stared at the open book. What was he doing here tonight? He had no business leading them on, Melissa and her kids.

He was a broken man, as he'd so spectacularly proved last night. He wanted Melissa in the way a man who hasn't had sex in over three years might be expected to want a woman. But how far beyond that he wanted to go, he had no idea.

The lights were dim all through the orderly, polished house as he searched out Melissa. He found her sitting at the kitchen table, drawing, a heap of what looked like textbooks surrounding her, some stacked in wobbling piles, some open; it was the most disorderly thing he'd ever seen her do.

He approached softly, admiring the line of her jaw, the way it elongated into her neck and disappeared behind her open shirt collar. Her expression was rapt as she stared at the page in front of her, frowned, erased something and reached for one of the books.

"Working on one of your garden designs?" he asked.

She glanced up with a quick smile. "I'm supposed to call it landscape design. Sounds more important, I guess." She found the book she was looking for and scribbled something on her page before addressing him again.

"This one's for my neighbor, Pam."

"That's great."

"If you like what I do, I'll do your garden next. It's good practice for me. Besides, I owe you for all you've done for us."

"You've done a lot for me, too."

He slumped against the door frame and addressed the huge thing that was sharing airspace with him and Melissa. "I knew it had to be done. I couldn't bring myself to get rid of her things. I knew she was gone, of course, and that she was never coming back. But—" he blew out an awkward breath "—I didn't want anyone else touching her things, either. Janice offered a couple of times, then gave up. It was tough, knowing what you were doing today, and I hated like hell coming home to find everything gone. But...well...thanks."

She seemed mesmerized by the pencil she was rolling between her fingers. "I wasn't sure how you'd react."

"You want the honest truth?"

She looked up and met his gaze. "Always."

"I was so mad I wanted to howl. Now, I don't. Janice dropped by."

Surprise showed in Melissa's eyes. "She did?"

"Yeah. She said you told her not to, but she couldn't stay

away. In a weird way, seeing her all broken up about things made it easier for me."

"I'm glad." She looked at him as though checking for fever symptoms. "How do you feel now?"

"Like somebody worked me over with a baseball bat."

She nodded. Not even surprised.

What he had to say next had his stomach on fire. "I also want to apologize for last night." He sighed heavily. "For my…it was nothing to do with you…I felt…" How the hell could he explain what he'd felt when he didn't understand it himself? He wanted Melissa so badly his teeth ached. And he felt guilty. And scared. God, there it was. He was scared. Scared of feeling again, loving again and getting hurt.

"It was too soon," she said to the pencil.

"No. Damn it, Melissa, it's not too soon. It's been three years."

"Chronological time doesn't mean so much. You're not ready."

"Yes, I am." And he knew he was. He was eager, in fact, to take Melissa in his arms and prove to her exactly how ready. He crossed to her in two strides and dropped to his heels in front of her, so he could look up into her down-turned face. He raised just his index finger and traced the shape of her cheekbone.

Her lips opened slightly on an intake of breath, and just like that, lust slammed into him like a speeding locomotive. "Oh, baby, I am ready," he said, pulling her shoulders until, with a startled exclamation, she tumbled into his lap.

She started to gasp his name, but he stopped her mouth with his lips, kissing her for all he was worth. She sat there in his lap, letting him kiss her, but barely responding. Dimly, he realized he'd hurt her last night. Made her feel he didn't really want her. Words wouldn't express what he needed her to know. He took her hand and placed it firmly on the one part of his body that would tell her, in no uncertain terms, exactly how much he wanted her.

He felt the little huffing gasp against his lips when her hand closed over him. Then her arms came round him and she kissed him back. Oh, the sweetness of that trim body alive with passion. Kissing him back, her tongue slipping boldly into his mouth.

His need mounting, he cupped her cheek, let his hand follow the line of her jaw and neck, the way his eyes had followed it earlier, and dipped into the jean shirt she wore to cup her breast.

"Mmm," she sighed as he rubbed and kneaded the firm round globe. Wanting to see what he was touching, wanting to put his mouth there, he slipped his hand back out and started undoing her shirt buttons.

As soon as she realized what he was doing, she pulled away, glancing at the kitchen light overhead. "Not here."

He didn't care. The kitchen floor was fine. The front lawn was fine with him. "Let's go upstairs." He tried to kiss her again, but once more she retreated, and, grasping the kitchen table, pulled herself to standing

She pressed her hands to her cheeks. "No, I can't. What if one of the children needs me?"

"Doesn't your door have a lock?" He gave her back the same line she'd used on him last night.

"No. After Stephen left I took it off. Alice went through a stage where she liked playing with the locks. I didn't want her to get locked in by accident. None of the bathroom doors lock, either. I'm sorry."

Even as frustration raged through his blood, a glimmer

of humor peeped through. "We're as bad as a couple of horny teenagers worrying about their parents coming home. I'd invite you to make out in my car, but I walked."

She made a production of rebuttoning her shirt and patting her hair back into place. "It's probably for the best, anyway." She was doing that nurse voice that ticked him off every time she used it on him.

"I'm telling you, I'm ready. I'm so ready, I'll have to have a cold shower and read all the stock market listings before I can sleep."

"Your body's ready, which, if you don't mind me saying so, isn't a real breakthrough in a man. But, I don't think the rest of you is ready yet." She glanced at him, her blue eyes so clear and yet troubled. "You've been pretty honest with me, and I appreciate it. Seth, you need to know," she dropped her gaze to her hands. He noticed they were clasped tight. "I've never been with anyone but Stephen. I—you're not the only one who's got some demons here." She looked up again and he felt she'd forced herself to meet his gaze. "Let's be careful, okay?"

He was shocked at her admission. Then flattered at the implication. But she was right. He had no business messing with this woman until he knew exactly what he was after.

"Whatever is going on here, I don't think it's casual."

She chuckled softly, the sound surprising him. "No," she said. "Sometimes I wish it were."

"Well—"

She picked up his left hand and tapped the gold wedding ring he still wore. "Good night, Seth."

CHAPTER FOURTEEN

THE MAROON VOLVO pulled into her drive Sunday morning around eleven. She wasn't sure, after last night, whether Seth would come, and if it was only the two of them involved, she doubted he would have made the trip. But he'd promised Matthew they'd practice baseball and for that reason alone she'd pretty much expected him to show.

He looked tired, with tiny crinkle lines fanning from his eyes. She'd expected that, too.

"Hi," she said to the trio coming up her drive.

"Can we do makeovers?" the girls wanted to know.

"Is all your homework done for school tomorrow?"

Twin eye rolls greeted her. "Yes."

Suddenly, she remembered the first day they'd arrived at her house bristling with bad attitude. How had they become so dear to her in such a short time? She smiled at the pair of them. "Okay, then. Makeovers it is."

She gave her attention to their father, but he was having trouble maintaining eye contact with her. She wondered if he'd slept at all in his redecorated room. "Are you okay?"

"Yeah."

Seth had the box of home handyman stuff he'd bought her for her birthday, which he set on the front porch. She was so used to seeing him in business clothes that she took a moment to enjoy the sight of him in jeans and a gray athletic T-shirt with a navy hoodie over top. He wore a ball cap and perched on top of the box of household fix-it stuff were two leather baseball gloves and a grubby looking ball.

Matthew came bounding to the door, his excitement beaming from him. "Hey, buddy," Seth said.

He took in the gloves and ball at a glance. "Where's the bat?"

"We're going to start with throwing and catching. The bat's next time."

"Okay."

"Would you like some coffee?" Melissa asked. The poor man looked as though he could use some.

She wished she hadn't offered when she saw Matthew's face fall. She realized with a pang of sadness how much it meant to him to have an adult male take an interest in him.

Fortunately, Seth saw it, too. Or maybe he didn't want to chat with her over coffee. He said, "Maybe later. You ready Matthew?"

Silly question. He'd been ready when he woke her at seven asking if Seth was here yet. He wore his oldest jeans and a sweatshirt with the name of his school on the front. "I forgot something," he said and pounded back upstairs, emerging in less than a minute with his own ball cap on his head.

"Have fun," she called, as they sauntered down the drive together.

They looked good together, she thought. Almost as though they fit.

"Will you be back for lunch?" she yelled.

"Na-ah. We'll probably grab something out."

"Okay."

Please let it go well, she pleaded silently as she went to gather the three girls.

She let them have free rein with her nail polish drawer, and each of them had a manicure. Alice, who'd never had polish on her tiny nails before, was beside herself with excitement.

"Dad said you and Auntie Janice decorated his room," Laura said while she was having bright red polish painted on her nails.

"That's right," Melissa answered, doing her best to keep the brush strokes straight on the small nail. Laura and Jessie had tiny, delicate hands. She wondered whether they'd inherited those from their mother. "Are you okay with that?"

"I guess."

"Dad said a swear word when he went in there last night. I heard him," Jessie said. "But this morning, when he showed us, he said he likes it."

"Do you like it?" How did they feel about having all of Claire's personal items moved?

"It's okay."

"You know, we saved all of your mother's things. They're stored at your Auntie Janice's house. Any time you want to see them, they're there."

"Okay." Well, Melissa thought, she wasn't sensing hysterics or hostility. She had the impression that the girls had accepted their mother's death. Of course, the loss would always be there and probably would always hurt, but they were healing—a lot more easily than their dad.

After manicures, they moved to lipstick and hair. It was fun taking the time to play with all the girlie stuff. After that, they washed up and ate lunch. "I wonder how the boys are doing," she said.

"Dad loves baseball. He made us go on a team last year, but we hated it so we quit. He made us practice all the time. Matthew's going to be, like, totally bored."

But when the guys rolled in around three, it was clear that Matthew was anything but bored. His eyes were vivid with excitement. "Guess what, Mom," he said, bounding into the kitchen. "I'm a natural. Seth said so."

"That's grea—"

"And we had jumbo hot dogs and I had two refills of Coke and next time Seth says we're going to practice hitting. With the bat. Can we do that tomorrow?"

"I have to work tomorrow. But we'll do it again soon."

"Sweet."

Melissa and the girls were making sugar cookies. The table was littered with scraps of dough and Laura, Jessie and Alice were decorating cookies in weird and wonderful ways she'd never thought of.

"If you wash up, you can help decorate cookies, Matthew," she told him.

"Or you can help me. I'm doing some home handyman chores."

She looked up in surprise. "Today?"

"Sure. Why not?"

"I can help with chores," Matthew said, ultra cool. As though he'd handled power tools every day of his life. She wanted to hug him, but knew enough not to.

Seth fetched the box from the front porch, and soon he and his helper were replacing the hinge on her kitchen cabinet. "You know," she said, "this seems like a very sexist division of labor."

Seth sent her a glance from his tired, blue-gray eyes and halted in the middle of screwing in the new hinge.

"Girls, do you want to help with some handyman stuff or decorate cookies?"

The twins rolled their eyes in identical motions. "Cookies."

"Cookie," Alice parroted.

"Matthew? Do you want to do handyman stuff or decorate cookies?"

"Handyman stuff." There was an unspoken but implied "*like, duh!*"

Seth managed to stow most of his smirk. "If you ask me, some things are hardwired."

"Well, every man should learn how to cook," she stated.

"And every woman should learn some basic home repair and auto maintenance."

She nodded.

"But not today."

Later, when he was upstairs redoing the grout in the kids' bathroom and Matthew was sanding one of the cracks they'd patched, she had a chance to get Seth alone.

She liked the way he looked, leaned over the bathtub, his body stretched out, his arm muscles defined.

"Thank you," she said.

He glanced up at her. "For what?"

"For today. With Matthew."

"Don't thank me. He's a great kid. I had fun."

She perched on the closed lid of the toilet. "How are you? After yesterday."

He turned back to his work. He smelled like healthy working man, a little warm and sweaty. "Okay."

"How did you sleep?"

"Like shit."

What could she say? He kept working. She felt dismissed.

"Well, I'll let you get back to it."

She'd walked all the way out of the bathroom when he stopped her. "Melissa?"

"Yes?"

He held her gaze, looking sad and tired. "I'm working on it."

"Good," she said softly.

"Hey."

She turned again to see him scramble up off the bathtub and wipe his hands on his jeans. He'd apparently been doing that a lot—they were getting pretty disgusting.

"Come back in here a minute."

She did, feeling her stomach flip. Once she was inside, he shut the bathroom door, making the space seem ridiculously small all of a sudden.

He appeared frustrated and confused as he cupped her face in gritty hands. He kissed her as though he couldn't help himself. She responded for the same reason.

"If it was only sex, this would be a lot easier," he said.

"I know."

"I feel something for you. I don't know what it is, but there's too much at risk to do anything stupid." His hands tangled in her hair and he kissed her again, taking his sweet time.

Oh, she thought, maybe it could be just sex. If they were careful, and discreet, why not?

Except that it was already too late. She had no idea what she felt for Seth, but it was more than lust, though that was a huge ingredient in the confusing mix. It was more than friendship, though he was her friend. It couldn't be love. Not yet, so that left her as puzzled and frustrated as the man currently nibbling at her earlobe and running his hands over her body.

HOW MUCH LONGER DID he think he could wait?

That was the question that was taking up a lot of Seth's time recently. Melissa was sweet and sexy. A terrific mother. And she was good for him. The first few days after Melissa and Janice had redone his bedroom were tough. He hadn't been able to sleep.

It was like a miniversion of the way he'd felt after Claire died. But, somehow, he'd come through it. And he was honest enough to admit that he felt as though a heavy burden had been lifted.

He'd pushed the bed back to its accustomed place because he hated the way those almost too-creative women had placed his furniture, but other than that he'd left everything as they'd done it. He was even thinking about painting the walls in his bedroom, something they hadn't had time to do.

Already his clothes were creeping over into Claire's side of the closet, and he had to admit that it was easier to find stuff.

He glanced at his desk clock, grateful it was a squash day and he could exercise away some of his sexual frustration. He grabbed his racquet and bag.

They hadn't had their date, he and Melissa. After all that had happened, he couldn't imagine a dinner somewhere and then dropping her off at her home. They'd gone too far for that.

The question of Melissa bothered him all morning, along with a question Jessie had asked him over breakfast.

The tiny rubber ball bounced and ricocheted around the enclosed squash court like the idea that had taken root in his mind.

He spiked the ball hard, heard the rubber squeak, protesting against the wall and scudding off into that sweet unreachable corner. Ron, his opponent, lunged and grunted as the ball eluded him.

"Good shot, buddy."

He continued punishing the ball, driving relentlessly until both he and Ron were sweat-soaked and gasping.

"Feel better?" Ron asked him after they'd showered and were walking out of the club together.

"You know, I do," he said, limping away to his car.

"Why are you limping?" Melissa asked as he hobbled into her hallway later that afternoon, inhaling the scent of warm spices. "Are you hurt?"

"Nah. I pulled a muscle playing squash."

"A hamstring?" She was all full of concern. "I could rub it for you."

"A groin."

"Oh." Her face bloomed with delicate color, and the uninjured part of his groin perked up at her suggestion. She peered at him, caught the grin he didn't even try to hide and rolled her eyes at him. "Try ice."

He followed her into the kitchen, helped himself to a speckled brown cookie right off the cooling rack and sighed with pleasure as he bit into the crunchy spice cookie. Man, that woman could cook. And always from scratch. He, who'd only recently mastered the secrets of cake from a box, could appreciate the fine art of real baking.

Yep. There were a lot of things he could appreciate about Melissa.

And lots of things he could only appreciate if she were naked. It had been two weeks since the disastrous weekend of her birthday, and he hadn't stopped thinking about her in very non-babysitter terms.

Their little chats when he dropped off and picked up the

girls were charged with unspoken messages, their glances passionate. He must be crazy to try to ignore the obvious.

He wanted that woman in the worst way, and unless he was way more out of touch than he believed, she wanted him, too.

She'd put the kitchen island between them and was trying very hard to appear unflustered by their conversational exchange about his groin.

"Why don't you call the girls?" she asked. "They're downstairs."

"Not yet. I want to talk to you."

Her forehead creased with anxiety. "They're not in trouble at school again, are they?"

"It's not about the girls. It's about us."

"Oh." She scrubbed at cookie pans that already gleamed. How to start? How to get out what he wanted to say? "This arrangement. It's not working. I—"

The pans clattered into the sink, and her head sprang up. "But the girls are happy here. Aren't they?"

"They love you."

Her face lit up then, as pink and iridescent as one of the perfectly tended rose buds in her garden. "I love them, too." Pleasure and relief coursed through her voice. She was so pretty, with her lips parted and eager, that he longed to kiss her.

"You know what Jessie asked me this morning?"

"What?"

"She asked me if I was going to marry you."

The color faded from her cheeks. "Well, kids think everything's easier than it is."

She slammed the shiny cookie pans into the dish drainer, then sprinkled baking soda in the sinks and started scrubbing.

He grabbed her wrist to still the frantic scrubbing. "I've

been thinking about it all day. It makes sense. We're friends, we love each other's kids, they get on great. And there's obviously a powerful physical attraction here. Why don't you? Marry me."

Even as he felt a jolt of shock vibrate through his bones at his own words, she jerked away, leaning against the island and glaring at him.

"That's not funny."

"It's not supposed to be." His lungs felt like collapsed balloons. He'd pulled a Brady Bunch, after trying to avoid even thinking about blending their families, doing everything he could to prevent Melissa and her kids from getting ideas about him. He'd pulled a childhood TV happily-ever-after blended family out of his pocket and handed it to Melissa. And, surprisingly, it didn't seem so terrible now it was out in the open. In fact, them getting married made a lot of sense. Melissa could keep her lifestyle, her kids could stay in the same school. And Laura and Jessie would have Melissa around permanently.

And he'd finally get Melissa in bed.

There were a lot of positives here.

Melissa didn't seem to be seeing it quite his way. In fact, she looked as though somebody had died. "Why are you doing this to me?" she whispered, her eyes overbright.

"It could work, Melissa. You're a terrific person." He scoffed another gingersnap. "You make excellent cookies, and the twins love you."

"What about you, Seth. Do you love me?"

She had him there. He wasn't sure what he felt about Melissa, where lust left off and love began. But she was a woman receiving a marriage proposal, and she deserved certain things. "I think I'm falling in love with you." It caught a little in the back of his throat, like a stray speck of cinnamon, but he got the words out.

For a long moment she stood there staring at him, a slow flush mounting her cheeks.

"No, you're not. You're still in love with Claire. I can't ever compete with that."

CHAPTER FIFTEEN

MELISSA WORKED IN THE garden feverishly, but she couldn't find the peace she sought. All she saw was Seth's stricken face when she'd turned him down.

Married? Was he out of his mind?

Daffodils were starting to bloom. The earth was becoming workable enough to get a head start on the weeding and think about the new growing season.

He'd said he was falling in love with her. Convenient. What if he stopped falling before he got there?

She wasn't any clearer about her feelings than Seth was. There was so much baggage between them they could open a luggage store. Stephen was still missing and presumed to be in the Czech Republic. She and the kids hadn't received so much as a postcard. More than the money, she wanted some kind of closure. And as for Seth, he was trying so hard to make everything right, for the twins, for her and Matthew and Alice.

And yet, there was undeniably something good happening. It hovered in the air like an early hint of spring when they said good morning. It teased them with longing when they said good night and their eyes met over the noisy confusion of the four kids all talking at once in the entrance hall.

Was that something love?

Or was it loneliness? Need? Sexual desire rising up like the new shoots in her garden?

She plopped down in the damp earth, the smell of rich dirt and growing things all around her. Idly, she watched a disturbed worm upend itself and burrow back down.

Her anger had finally dissipated, and she realized his proposal hadn't been the clumsy act of charity she'd first thought. But it wasn't a sincere proposal from the bottom of his heart, either. His eyes had registered shock when he'd spouted out the words. No. He hadn't planned to ask her to marry him. It had come from somewhere deeper inside himself.

Maybe he did love her. She didn't know and neither did Seth. She was no surer of her own feelings. The only thing she knew for certain was that she wouldn't make another mistake.

The trouble was that she definitely had feelings for him. A lot of them purely carnal. The whole sex thing shimmered and teased, promising her a lush paradise in the middle of her desert of a love life. What if it turned out to be a mirage?

If only they loved each other, marriage would be the perfect answer. Still, even if Seth didn't love her, he'd become her closest friend. And she'd hurt him.

She was going to have to apologize.

"IS SOMETHING WRONG with the phone, Mom?" Matthew asked, hunched on the floor sorting his new collection of baseball cards.

"No."

"Then why do you keep picking it up and putting it down?"

A glib answer came to mind, but she suppressed it. "I have to apologize to Seth. I said something that hurt his feelings. But I'm having a hard time working up the nerve."

Her son nodded wisely. "That's like when my teacher made me tell Josh I was sorry for making his lip bleed. He was real mad—I thought he might hit me. But after I said sorry, it was okay. And I felt better."

"You made Josh's lip bleed?" Her voice started to rise.

"Only by accident. Not on purpose."

"Oh, my gosh. I should call his mother. Why didn't you tell me?"

Her son put on an expression she'd seen on Seth's face a hundred times. "It's a guy thing, Mom. Forget it."

Since Seth had taken an interest in Matthew's baseball career, there was a whole new attitude coming from her son. One she didn't always approve of. "And how did this 'guy thing' happen exactly?"

"I was showing Josh how to steal a base by sliding in on your stomach—'cept he hit a rock."

"A rock? Your school field is grass."

"The big kids were using it. So we made our own diamond."

"And the rock?"

"Was third base."

"I see."

"That's why the teacher made me say sorry. Then I didn't feel so bad. You should phone Seth, Mom. You'll feel better."

She hugged him to her. "Sometimes you're grown-up smart." She turned back to the phone and punched in Seth's number, restraining herself from hanging up like a coward. After an eternity of ringing, while she cleared her throat and swallowed about six times, Seth's answering service picked up.

How do you apologize to a machine? she wondered helplessly as the silence stretched. "Seth, it's Melissa," she spat out at last. "I wanted to, um, apologize for earlier. I think I was abrupt. I—you surprised the heck out of me." Another pause. He was probably standing right there, listening to her make a total fool of herself. "Maybe we can talk tomorrow. Maybe you'd like to stay for dinner?"

She pictured him, a dark, angry presence, too mad to pick up the phone. Why wouldn't he at least let her tell him in person how sorry she was? "I'm not sure what we're having. I was thinking maybe pot roast..." Now she was babbling, making things even worse. "With mashed potatoes. Maybe green beans." Another pause. "I'm sorry, Seth. And thank you."

Her hands trembled slightly as she replaced the receiver.

"Well, Mom, do you feel better?" Matthew's imitation-adult voice brought a smile to her lips.

"Yep. I feel better. Thanks for the good advice."

He swelled with pride before her eyes, picking up his cards and putting them away before she got around to reminding him to get ready for bed.

The man who dropped the twins off the next morning was the same man she'd imagined standing by the phone refusing to speak to her the night before. He wouldn't meet her gaze. Spoke curtly and didn't even set foot in her house.

"Did you get my message?" she finally asked him, knowing damn well he had.

"Yes," he said to the door frame.

"Can you come for dinner?"

"I'm not sure. I'll let you know." Then he was gone.

"What's the matter with Daddy?"

"He's mad at me."

"Wow. He never gets that mad at us." Well, that was comforting.

All day she waited for his call.

She received a curt message from him at three o'clock. He'd known darn well she would be picking the kids up from school then and wouldn't be home. Her heart sank. He wouldn't even talk to her. Surprise widened her eyes when she finished listening to the message. She had to rewind and listen to it again, to be sure she'd heard right.

He'd accepted her invitation. And a lovely evening they were going to have with him glowering, refusing even to glance her way. She'd be the one getting gastric trouble next.

Even though she felt gloomy and a little nervous, or maybe because of it, she got Matthew and the twins to help her drag the kitchen table into the dining room and laid the table with linen.

The girls cut daffodils and a few early irises from the garden and made a centerpiece for the table. Matthew sliced the bread, Alice globbed butter on it. And Melissa put her heart and soul into a pot roast and salad that said, "I'm sorry."

He arrived punctually at five-thirty. After dithering all afternoon about what to wear, Melissa opted for something casual. She didn't want him to repeat his ridiculous proposal. She wanted to get back to the warm and promising friendship they'd had.

Now, as she walked to the door, she wished she'd at least put on a skirt. Not that it mattered. He wouldn't be looking at her anyway, she remembered.

She opened the door and was taken by surprise. He was looking straight at her, big and formidable, the light of war in his eyes. He crossed the threshold. "Where are the kids?"

"In the kitchen."

Before she could move, he grabbed her face between his hands and kissed her. Not tenderly at all, like she was used to, but roughly. If frustration had a flavor, she tasted it on his lips and tongue.

The door was still open, for goodness' sake. Anyone could walk by. As Seth showed no signs of letting go of her, she relaxed into his kiss, allowing herself to enjoy the moment and the strange excitement of his anger channeled into passion.

"We can't go on like this," he said, when he finally lifted his head.

Her heart was pounding and she was having trouble drawing breath. To diffuse the potent emotions swirling around them, she tried for a little light humor. "No, we can't." She reached past him and shut the door. "The neighbors will get ideas."

But he refused to be sidetracked. "I can't stop thinking about you."

"Really?" The thought of the CEO of her bank mooning over her was the sweetest balm to her ego.

He cracked a small smile. "Today, in our executive meeting, I called Mitzi Youngall, our marketing director, Melissa. I've known the woman for six years."

"You did? Cool."

"Mitzi didn't think so."

Seth flattering her was infinitely better than Seth mad at her. Maybe they could get their friendship back, after all. "Anything else?" She let her fingers trail through his dark hair, intimately aware of the weight and warmth of his hands resting lightly on her hip bones.

"Well, since you're fishing for compliments, let's see... Oh, yeah... I dreamed about you last night."

"You did?"

"Uh-huh." He whispered the words against her mouth. "It was a very erotic dream."

Her eyes drifted shut and her lips parted as she waited for him to kiss her again, deep and hard. Instead, she felt his lips trail up her cheek to nibble on her ear lobe, then his tongue ran round the circumference of her ear before be whispered, "I have an idea."

She could hardly concentrate on the words for the delicious shivers coursing through her body as his warm breath teased the wet flesh. "What?"

"Let's make my dream a reality."

"But where...I mean—"

"I was an idiot. I tried to rush you. I'm sorry."

"No. I'm sorry. It was lovely of you to propose, and I was rude and ungracious."

"I don't think either of us can think straight until we get some time alone. I've booked us into a resort for next weekend. For a very dirty weekend."

"You have?" Excitement and nerves warred within her. "What about the kids?"

"I've booked a babysitting agency that was recommended by a good friend. They'll send someone over for you to interview. And Janice said she'd check in on the kids."

"Janice? You told Janice?"

"Sure. You know what she said?"

"I can't imagine."

"She said it's about time. She thinks it's a great idea."

"But, but…" She wished he'd get back a few feet so she could think. "I'm not marrying you."

"So you said. Maybe a dirty weekend will change your mind."

"Egotist." She was half-laughing, and totally tempted.

He grinned. "What this relationship needs is some good, healthy sex. No strings attached." He'd come up with the perfect way for them to explore the attraction between them without any obligations. On either side, she realized grimly. It had been a long time since she'd had sex. And much longer since she'd thought of it as "good" or "healthy." If she was a total disappointment, he could walk away.

"What if it…ah…doesn't work out?"

His mouth opened, and she waited for some sassy answer, but instead he said, "Then we'll know. And we can go back to being friends."

Friends. The word had a hollow ring. But then, Seth as a long-term prospect didn't look good, anyway. This could be a big step in the healing process for both of them. It would put another man between her and her bitter memories of Stephen. And it would show Seth that he was ready to start dating again. Swallowing the quiver of nervousness she nodded. "I agree. Provided I approve of the babysitter, you've got yourself a deal. One weekend away. No strings attached."

"I'll be counting the hours till next Friday."

"Come on in the kitchen. The kids will wonder what we're doing out here."

"They're smarter than you think. You already know about Jessie. Matthew asked if I'm your boyfriend."

Her mouth fell open. "Matthew? He talked to you instead of me? What did you say?"

"I said I'm working on it."

"Oh... Was he upset?"

"Seemed happy about it."

"Huh."

They entered the kitchen, Melissa with her cheeks feeling undeniably warm.

"Hi, kids," Seth said. Hugging all three girls who'd come running at once, and making a point of leaning over to Matthew, who stood a pace or two back, to ruffle his hair.

What a nice family they made, Melissa thought as she dished up dinner. Laura proudly carried the salad she'd helped make into the dining room, followed by Jessie with the fruit punch, Matthew with the bread steaming in its basket and Alice, who refused to be left out, wobbling behind, her eyes glued to a tottering jug of salad dressing with fierce concentration.

It wasn't the first dinner they'd eaten together at her place, her family and the O'Reillys. But it was without a doubt one she would always remember.

It was the way Seth looked at her. Every glance held a secret, taunting message. Even though the conversation at the table was general, and mainly child-centered, there was a second conversation going on. It was unspoken. As subtle as the accidental-on-purpose brushing of his fingers against hers when he asked Melissa to pass him the salad. As subtle as an innuendo.

"Delicious," he pronounced, and the way he rolled his tongue over the word had Melissa suspecting he wasn't talking about her food at all. When she peeked up at him, he winked, and she swallowed so hard she choked.

"You okay, Mom?"

"Just choked on a crumb," she gasped, gulping fruit

punch. But an ocean of fruit punch wouldn't be enough to quench the desire the man across from her had kindled.

He didn't try to play footsie with her, or any other obvious action that she could have shut down with a sharp kick. He was so subtle, she wasn't even sure if she was imagining the undercurrent. And yet, when she looked at him, she was convinced he was deliberately teasing her.

Resolutely, she kept her gaze on the children or her plate. That worked for about five minutes until Seth's voice asked her oh so politely if she'd pass the bread.

"Jessie, pass your father the bread. You're closer," she retaliated, and got nothing but a sly grin for her pains. He knew exactly what he was doing to her, and he was enjoying every minute.

Come to think of it, so was she.

She didn't even get a kiss when he left. Not that it would have been appropriate in front of the children, of course. All she got was a slow, teasing, hidden pat on the derriere as he headed out the door. "Thanks for a terrific dinner. We'll have to do it again, when we have more time." *Like an entire weekend,* his eyes telegraphed.

When her children were in bed, she toyed with her garden design for a while, but it was hopeless. She could hardly hold a pencil straight she was so keyed up. She'd agreed to a weekend of sex with a man she'd already decided she wouldn't marry.

A weekend spent with a man not her husband or even officially her boyfriend might not shock many people, but it shocked Melissa. It teased of the forbidden. It was a nice change to think of herself as a woman a man desired enough to spirit away for an entire weekend. It was better than dumped ex-wife, struggling single mom and the other epithets she could come up with.

She abandoned her design work and ran lightly up the stairs to her bedroom. In the back of her closet was a cream and gold box. In it was a nightgown she'd bought a few years ago, shortly after reading an article in a woman's magazine entitled, "How to Rekindle the Fire in Your Marriage," or something along those lines.

She'd discovered that Stephen had been kindling a lot of fires outside his marriage before she ever put the nightgown to the test. It had sat in the back of her closet, all but forgotten—kind of like her sex drive. Quickly, she stripped and slipped the gown over her head. Just the feel of the silk shimmering against her flesh made her feel voluptuous and sexy. It wasn't all that revealing, being ankle length with a silk and lace bodice that hinted at cleavage rather than displayed it.

Feeling younger than she had in years, Melissa padded across the carpet into the bathroom where she could see herself in the full-length mirror, and flipped on the light.

Her first flush of excitement died when she studied her reflection more carefully. It seemed like her nipples had slipped down about half an inch since she'd bought the gown. And that was definitely a hint of tummy bulge glaring at her where the light hit the silk.

With a sinking heart she turned around and craned her head over her shoulder for a back view. To her critical eye it looked as though more than her breasts had sagged.

Maybe she should call the whole thing off.

And then she thought about the way Seth gazed at her, the way he made her feel. Anyway, he couldn't reject her. She'd already rejected him. So she could just relax and have a good time.

Just relax. Have a good time.

Ten days. She had ten days to prepare. How fit, toned and perked could one woman get in ten measly days—without major surgery?

She didn't have a moment to lose.

Delicately replacing the silk nightgown in the rustling tissue, she dug out an old pair of sweatpants and a T-shirt, crept back downstairs and raided the DVD collection. Right at the back was a workout DVD designed by a bouncy starlet. Rarely viewed.

At the end of half an hour she wanted to kill the starlet.

Every muscle in her body trembled, and sweat trickled into her eyes. She tasted carpet fibers from when she'd collapsed, facedown, on her twelfth push-up. Only the vision of Seth seeing her in that gown (cause there was no way in hell he'd ever see her naked) kept her going.

"Five more, four more...feel the burn," that chirpy voice urged her on.

Gasping and exhausted, she rolled off the floor after the longest hour of her life and struggled to the kitchen to drink a gallon or so of water.

Before dragging herself up to bed she made a note on her calendar. Workout Video. On every little square of the nine days leading up to next weekend.

HE COULDN'T STOP thinking about sex. It was kind of embarrassing to be as randy as a teenager at his age. But he no sooner had to glimpse Melissa, think about her, or even dream about her, than he was off in erotic fantasy.

He'd dreamed about her again last night. If his dreams had ratings, he wouldn't be old enough to watch this one. He savored the wispy fragments of the dream as he shaved, wondered if the real Melissa would ever do that with her mouth.

"Daddy, we're out of Dino Puffs." Laura's imperative tones coming from downstairs swept away the last of his dream.

"Eat the Corn Flakes."

"I only like Dino Puffs."

"All right. I'll be down in a minute." He wiped his face, stepped into the bedroom and rooted in his briefcase for his Day-Timer. Carefully wrote "Dino Puffs" on his daily to-do list.

So much for dreams.

Soon to be dreams no more, he reminded himself. He was still amazed Melissa had agreed so easily to spending the weekend with him. Maybe she was feeling as randy as he was. Lust spiked through him at the thought. It was Monday, his Day-Timer reminded him. Monday of the week that would lead to Friday, where he'd penciled D.W. across the calendar square. Like he'd forget. The dirty weekend was his top item of business for the week. He smiled at the mostly empty to-do list. There were plenty of things he planned to do starting Friday—and none of them would show up on any list.

He whistled while he hauled the last loaf of frozen bread out of the freezer and made toast, in such a good mood he pretended he didn't notice that the radio wasn't tuned to his news station but to some teeny bopper hip-hop garbage. He even found himself laughing when the girls jumped up from the table in unison, grabbed air mikes and mouthed along to "Born To Be Bravo," milk mustaches and all.

The radio announcer voiced over the last bars of the song with some smarmy hype, and he stopped listening, scanning the newspaper business section while he chomped his own toast.

A twin shriek had him dropping the paper to watch as the girls fell over each other, lunging for the phone.

"Let me have it."

"Got here first."

"It's speed-dial 2."

"I know….it's ringing!"

"A-a-ah! Let me listen!"

They were both jumping up and down like identical demented pogo sticks.

"What the…"

"SHHH!" the pogo sticks hissed in unison.

"I can't stand it. Do you think we were the sixth caller?"

"I don't know. We're on hold. But we got through."

"I can't stand it. Oh, my—"

He watched the eager flush change to abject disappointment. Laura pulled away and Jessie said, "Okay. Thanks, anyway," into the phone before replacing the receiver.

"We were so-o-o close. Eighth. He said we were eighth."

"What is going—"

"Shh!" Laura said again, and dashed to the radio to turn up the volume.

"Congratulations!" The DJ boomed across his kitchen. "You're the sixth caller."

Some girl, who could have been either of his daughters, screamed, "I can't believe it! You're kidding!"

"No, I'm not," the DJ promised her, and she screamed again.

"You and your three best friends will be going to see the Bravo Boys in concert when the Bravo World tour hits Seattle next month."

"I can't believe we were so close," Jessie wailed.

"And that's not all. Our very special prize package includes a backstage visit with the boys and an autographed CD."

More screaming from the radio. More groaning from the twins. Seth was getting a bad feeling in the pit of his stomach, and his good mood was ebbing. "What was that all about?"

"The Bravo Boys concert. You can win tickets from the radio," Laura informed him.

"I figured that part out. The bit I don't get is what you two would do with tickets." He kept his voice carefully neutral.

A desperately anxious, pleading expression suffused both faces. "Please, Daddy. Please, can we go? If we win the tickets, it won't cost a thing."

"You girls are ten. Do you seriously think I'd let you go to a rock concert at ten years old?"

"But Daddy, it's the Bravo Boys."

"Maybe when they grow up to be the Bravo Men, you'll be old enough to go. Finish your breakfast or we'll be late."

"Janet Suche's mother's letting her go."

Deliberately, he switched the radio back to his news station. Although he could have saved himself the effort. The world could have ended and he wouldn't have heard a thing over the commotion in the kitchen. Cajoling turned to pleading turned to shouting, until he finally snapped, "Not one more word. Go upstairs and brush your teeth."

"I bet Mom would have let us go," Laura sobbed as she stomped out of the kitchen.

CHAPTER SIXTEEN

"JAPONICA, I THINK," Melissa mused aloud, sketching a low bush into her design.

"Apple tree," Alice murmured gravely, a beat behind her mother, her chubby fingers busy with a green crayon, a look of utter absorption on her face.

It had been a hell of a week. The twins were snarly and miserable because they couldn't go and see that ridiculous boy band they were so hot for. Matthew was snarly and miserable because he was missing his weekend baseball clinic with Seth—even though Seth had come home from work early on Wednesday—in the rain—so he and Matthew could fit in their practice.

The weather all week had been as miserable as the kids. Rainy and dreary.

Only Alice remained sunny, but at three she hadn't got the hang of laying on a guilt trip yet. A couple of years and she'd be right up there.

Plus, this landscape design thing was starting to build. She'd been up until midnight almost every night this week working on designs for a second display home by the same company doing another subdivision, and on designs for several of the new homeowners.

All of which was good since it took her mind off the big

weekend. The sun had suddenly arrived, which seemed like a good omen, but now there were only hours to go and she was as nervous as she'd ever been. Ridiculous. Seth was a nice man she'd known for months. It was a weekend away to relax.

She almost laughed aloud. Relax? Oh, yeah. That was going to happen.

Maybe she should call it off. Now. Before anyone got hurt. Or rejected.

Or had to bare their sorry ass in front of a stranger.

She sighed and explained to Alice once again that nice Mrs. Lowenthal, whom the kids had already met and liked, was coming to stay with her. Alice hadn't been too sure about the arrangement until she'd found out that the twins were staying over, too. This made the weekend a major treat for her.

Melissa was all packed, every muscle sore from her week-long fitness marathon. She was shaved, plucked, exfoliated, manicured and pedicured.

Damn it, she was as ready as she'd ever be.

It was normal to be nervous taking on a new lover, she reassured herself. Once she got that first time out of the way, she'd be fine.

Mrs. Lowenthal got there not long after the kids got home from school and they all shared a snack together. Then Seth arrived and gave everybody a hearty hello. He barely looked at Melissa, but when he did she felt breathless. The gleam in his eyes was unmistakably carnal.

No, she thought, *relaxed* would not describe how she felt.

"How come we can't come again?" Matthew asked in his best whiny tone.

"Shut up, dork," Jessie said.

Instead of chastising her, Seth ignored the interruption and spoke to Matthew. "Because it would be boring for you guys. We're looking at gardens to give your mom some ideas for her work." He flicked a glance at his watch. "And we should go now, so we can get some good hours in before dark."

Matthew stared at Seth as though he was completely letting down the guy team. "Gardens? A whole weekend of gardens?"

Mrs. Lowenthal rose with tactful timing. "Have a wonderful time. We're going to be fine. I've got games and books and movies, and the older girls are going to help me take care of the little one, aren't you girls?" They nodded. "And Matthew, as the man of the house, will have a great deal of responsibility."

Matthew still looked belligerent, but she could see his chest swell with the implied compliment. Yes, she thought, Mrs. Lowenthal was going to be fine.

Seth was wearing a fine wool shirt, open at the neck, and jeans she hadn't seen before. She wondered if they were new.

After they'd kissed everybody and got into his car, she said, "I can't believe you lied to those children. Gardens indeed."

He pulled smoothly out of the cul-de-sac and headed for I-5. "I did not lie. I have a surprise for you."

He wouldn't say any more, and she decided to sit back and enjoy the spring sunshine in the Pacific Northwest—and the fact that she had Seth all to herself.

They headed north, and she realized she didn't even know where they were going. Nor did she care. They had plenty to talk about, including the kids and her business ideas. One thing about Seth—he was an excellent sounding board, she'd found. He listened to her, and his advice was always sensible. "You know," she said, turning her head to look at him, "You are my favorite banker."

He lifted her hand from the seat between them and pressed it to his lips. "And you are my favorite client."

"Delinquent payments and all?" She was making her payments now that the grace period was up, and managing to scrape by. But she still had middle-of-the-night terrors when she wondered if she was going to make it.

They left the highway and meandered through farmland. It wasn't until she saw the first sign that she clued in. She laughed. "The Skagit Valley Tulip Festival?"

"Gardens," he said smugly. "I promised you gardens."

Soon they saw them. Fields and fields of tulips. Rainbows of tulips in every color. "Do you know, I've never been here before?" How odd. It wasn't far from home and she, who loved flowers, had never made the trip.

"I'm glad," he said. "I want everything this weekend to be different."

Her stomach lurched. *Everything?*

He followed the signs, parked in a slightly muddy lot and they got out of the car.

Then he reached for her hand and the warmth that both soothed and aroused her was in his gaze. He brushed her lips in a quick kiss and walked her into the rainbow of flowers.

She read all the signs and wandered every path. She couldn't believe the colors. It was almost magical.

He wanted to buy her a bunch of tulips on their way out, and she couldn't decide between the cheerful yellow, soft pink, brilliant purple and creamy white. So he bought her a bunch of each. And then they drove on to a resort she'd seen written up in magazines and had always wanted to visit.

Layton Lodge was on a large, wooded property over-looking the ocean. It offered first-class accommodation, a renowned restaurant, golf, tennis, wilderness hiking trails and a spa.

"Tell me you haven't been here, either," he said, as they drove through the gates and she voiced her excitement.

"No. I never have."

He let out a sigh of relief. She understood how he felt. "You?"

"No." He gripped her hand for a moment, over the colorful riot of tulips. "Fresh start."

Their room was wonderful. Overlooking the ocean, fur-nished with modern luxury in mind. Of course, like most hotel rooms, this one was dominated by the bed. A huge bed. A monstrous bed. The king of king-size beds. As though the room were obsessed with sex.

He tipped the bellboy and, as the door shut behind the pimply young man, silence descended.

She knew he was looking at her but felt too shy to return his gaze. She walked over to her suitcase, sitting so neatly on a built-in rack, and unzipped it. The sound was as loud as a scream in the quite room.

"Would you like a glass of wine?" Seth asked her as she removed her toiletry case and headed for the bathroom. She turned and saw a tray with wine and fruit that seemed to have come with the room. "I made a dinner reservation for eight."

"Yes, please." At least it would give them something to do before dinner.

The bathroom was marble luxury. She put her bag on the counter and filled drinking glasses with water for the tulips.

She fussed around, putting water glasses full of tulips all

over the room. Then, it took all of two minutes to hang her single dress and her robe. She hesitated before deciding to leave her underwear and the silk nightgown where they were.

She rezipped her case and, with nothing left to do, crossed the room to accept the glass of wine Seth had poured. She caught him staring at her and took a big gulp of wine. "Are you as nervous as I am?" she finally asked.

"I don't think so," he said, with a shred of humor.

"I'm a wreck."

"Don't be."

She gazed at him. "It's been so long," she whispered.

"For me, too."

"There's been no one since…?"

A flicker of pain crossed his face. "No."

She reached for his hand, feeling stronger now that she knew he was struggling, too. "We don't have to do this if you don't want to."

He squeezed her fingers. "Funny, I thought that was going to be my line."

Putting her glass down, she reached for him, touching his face. Kissing him, realizing the sex thing was going to be a big issue until they dealt with it. "Maybe we should just go to bed and get it over with."

She felt his hands run up her back, tangle in her hair. He tumbled her to his lap and deepened the kiss. "No," he said, when he finally lifted his head, his eyes dark with passion and his lips wet from her mouth. "I've wanted you from the first day I saw you." He kissed her again. "There will be no 'getting it over with.' I plan to take my time with you."

Tremors of desire ran over her skin at his words. And the passion she'd locked away for so long suddenly burst its bounds. She moaned, deep in her throat, and kissed him back.

"Melissa," he whispered into her hair, his hands unsteady as he reached for her pale blue sweater, pulling it up and over her head with help from her own unsteady hands.

She'd imagined their first time together would be tonight, after dinner, that she'd change in the bathroom and emerge in her full-length nightgown with her hair and teeth brushed. Not that she'd find herself tangled in her sweater and jeans, feverish with need, that she'd be tugging him out of his clothes with abandon, as restlessly and urgently as he was stripping her.

She tasted wine on his tongue and the same need she felt racing through her veins. When she nearly toppled off the chair, she grabbed for the table just in time. He laughed. She'd never heard him sound so carefree. He scooped her up, jeans and all, and carried her to the bed.

He finished undressing her slowly, kissing random parts of her as they emerged. Her shoulder, the slope of her breast, her belly, her hip, her knee. She'd imagined making love with him would be searing and emotional. But it was fun. Maybe there was a strong current of searing emotion underneath what they were doing, but right now she felt like those tulips. Fresh and just coming into bloom.

When they were both naked, he said, "Hang on a second," and walked, unembarrassed and gorgeous, to his case. He returned with a box of condoms. Thank goodness. Her last anxiety fled. She'd bought a few herself, but she was glad he was taking care of it.

As he placed the box on the bedside table she couldn't help teasing him, "The jumbo box?"

He grinned down at her. "I bought two of them."

Then he kissed her slowly, his bare body coming against hers so she felt her entire body taking part in that kiss.

She wrapped herself around him, giving and taking comfort, intimacy and pleasure. Oh, such pleasure. He found her secret places, learned her body as she learned his. When he entered her she had an awful moment when she caught a glimpse of raw pain in his eyes. As though he couldn't bear to let her see his hurt, he closed his eyes and kissed her fiercely.

She had seen, though, and she even understood. He was making love with another woman. He was pushing his wife a little further away. Even as the knowledge of his emotional pain hurt her, she gave him what solace she could. She was here, and warm and alive. After that first bad minute, she felt him come back to her from that dark place where he'd been. And then he made love to her like she'd never been loved before.

Ultimately, they cancelled their dinner reservation and ordered room service, Which they ate in bed.

CHAPTER SEVENTEEN

FOR A BEWILDERED MOMENT, Melissa didn't know where she was. Soft light filtered through strange curtains, displaying unfamiliar furniture and a room that wasn't her own. As she reoriented herself in the hotel room, and consciousness returned fully, so did her memory of last night.

Last night...

A smug little smile pulled at her lips while she thought about last night. She snuggled backward a little closer into the warm weight of Seth sleeping beside her in the bed. She heard a rustling movement and then felt his lips on the nape of her neck in a sleepy caress. "How are you feeling this morning?" he whispered.

"If I were a cat, I'd be purring," she admitted. She turned her head to gaze at Seth, almost unable to believe she could experience so much uncomplicated pleasure in one night. She caught the tail end of a very self-satisfied grin as he tried to swallow it.

"Bet I could make you purr louder," he challenged, trailing a hand to her breast.

"Ow," she said, as she felt his stubbled cheek rub against her tender skin. "You need a shave."

He kissed the place he'd scraped, making her sigh, then he said, "Don't move," and bounded out of bed and headed for the bathroom.

Without knowing she was doing it, she snuggled over onto his side of the bed, where it was still warm from his body and smelled faintly of him. Through the open bathroom door came the sounds of water swishing, then Seth's voice, distorted as though he were talking while shaving. "What do you want to do today?"

She wanted to stay in that bed and make love. She was all keyed up and waiting for him to finish shaving. Had he lost interest so quickly? In a voice that sounded like one of the twins after she'd been told "no" to the Bravo Boys concert for the fiftieth time, she answered, "I don't know."

"I thought maybe we'd drive to La Conner for breakfast. A very late breakfast," he said, striding out of the bathroom and toward the bed with an expression on his face that told her he hadn't lost interest at all.

"Oh, *after*." She flipped up the covers to let him back in the bed. "That would be good."

Then he kissed her and she forgot all about La Conner. All about everything but the sensations bubbling through her body. The soapy clean scent of shaving cream and the taste of toothpaste on his lips. With a sigh of utter pleasure, she closed her eyes and began drifting toward the stars.

Some time later, she awoke for the second time.

"They'll be serving dinner, not breakfast, if we don't get going soon," she mumbled against Seth's ear.

"Room service," he huffed into the pillow.

"Not again," she giggled. "Anyhow, I need a break," she groaned, struggling to a stand. "I've found muscles I didn't know I had."

The bathroom seemed to have moved four miles farther from when Seth had made the trip earlier. She felt his eyes on her naked back and wanted to cover her drooping posterior and bolt. But pride, and something else—a new-found sense of herself—held her to a slower pace. More a speed walk than a fifty-yard dash.

"Did anybody ever tell you you have a great ass?" His voice stopped her at the bathroom doorway.

"Not in about a hundred years."

He chuckled. "Bet they were thinking it. I know I was."

Since she couldn't think of a thing to say, she shut the door. Had nine days of video workouts done that much for her figure? She twisted around to get a better look at her backside in the mirror. It looked about the same as it had a week ago. But if he didn't care, why should she?

She made a face at herself in the mirror. Then did a double take. Was that really her? That woman with the tousled hair, swollen lips and bright, sparkling eyes? That was the face of a woman who'd spent the greatest night of her life making love to a considerate, inventive and hu-morous lover.

She stepped into the shower and let the hot water pummel her naked body. She experienced a new awareness of the way the water felt against her skin, the way the soap slid across the slope of her breasts, the way her flesh glowed pink and healthy as she toweled herself after.

She emerged with the slightest twinge of shyness. It was, after all, full daylight now. No more darkness and closed-eyed caresses. They'd be looking each other in the eye all day. Talking. And all the time, this new sex thing would be between them.

But she hardly had time to be shy. Seth handed her a cup of coffee, kissed her shoulder and took her place in the bathroom. Soon she heard the shower, and took the oppor-tunity to swiftly dress in a pair of khaki pants and a sweater.

The intimacy of dressing in front of him seemed too much like marriage, somehow.

Taking her coffee out to the balcony, she stared out at the view over the golf course to the wilder forested areas. Pretending to be totally absorbed in the lofty soaring of a couple of bald eagles high above the trees, she managed to ignore Seth dressing until the rattling of keys and change told her he was pretty much done.

"Hungry?"

"Starving."

"There used to be a great little seafood restaurant. I wonder if it's still there. Claire and I went once and I had the best crab chowder." He pulled the door open and smiled at her. "Do you need a coat or anything?"

She shook her head and forced herself to smile back. "I've got one in the car." *Claire*. He'd mentioned her name. He was taking her to a restaurant he and his dead wife had been to together.

While they walked through the plush corridor and waited for the elevator, he talked on about La Conner and what she'd see there, but she couldn't take any of it in. He'd mentioned Claire's name. Just like you would an old and dear friend. Not with anger or pain. The memory hadn't spoiled his day at all.

Maybe he'd been telling her the truth. Maybe he had moved on.

"Pretty slow elevator for a brand new hotel," he grumbled. He had his car keys in his right hand. When he extended his left to jab at the elevator call button, she was shocked by what she saw.

"Your ring. Your wedding ring. It's—"

"Gone." He regarded the naked ring finger self-consciously. "I didn't think it would be right to wear it. With you, I mean. I wanted us to have a fresh start."

"Oh, Seth." At that moment, the delinquent elevator chose to arrive, and a noisy family carrying tennis equipment witnessed a teary-eyed Melissa throwing herself into Seth's arms and heard the words she'd once sworn she'd never utter to another man. "I love you."

His sad, sexy eyes glowed. "I love you, too." And then he kissed her.

"Should I hold the elevator?" a teenaged male voice croaked.

"Get over here, Marvin," his mother scolded. And in a marginally quieter tone, "They're making up from a fight. Like your father and I do sometimes."

"Dad never kisses you like that."

I LOVE YOU. Such easy words to say. They might have been oiled, they'd slid so easily out of her lips before she could stop them. She could have kicked herself. Now the casual, weekend was spoiled.

For once in her life she'd thrown caution to the wind and dashed off for a wild weekend—and what happened? She awoke to find herself in love. A scary kind of love that felt as deep as her bone marrow. And as permanent.

As they strolled down the narrow main road, hand in hand, she could picture them five or ten or twenty years from now. Like one of those retirement ads on TV, she imagined her and Seth, gray-haired and lined, in a tasteful, air-brushed way, heading off into their golden years.

She wanted to scream.

This was supposed to be a wild, glorious, sinful, no-holds barred, maybe-I'll-call-you-again-sometime-and-then-again-maybe-I-won't kind of weekend. If she could take back those three little words, she'd grab them and stuff them carefully away. And the most humiliating part was that she'd said them first. Oh, he'd parroted them readily enough. What was the poor guy supposed to do with a doubles tennis team witnessing their little clinch outside the elevator?

"Penny for them," Seth spoke at her side.

"Hmm?"

"That's what my English grandmother used to say. 'A penny for your thoughts.'"

"They're not worth a penny." She sighed. "You know, if your grandmother had put her penny in the stock market when it first opened, it'd be worth millions of dollars today. Millions. I read that in a budgeting book I borrowed from the library." A bitter laugh shook her. "I couldn't afford to buy the book."

He released her hand and his arm came round her shoulders in a squeezing hug. "It hasn't been easy for you and the kids. I know that. But it will all change when we get married."

She nearly stumbled. "I thought we weren't getting married."

He looked at her, puzzled, and she heard her own stupid words echo around them both. "I thought I'd changed your mind."

"I wish I could go back in time and deposit that penny. That would change everything."

"It wouldn't change this," and turning her to him, he kissed her. A real honest-to-goodness, toe-tingling kiss, right in the middle of the busy, tourist-crowded street.

She tried to separate her head from her heart, but the damn thing was banging away inside her rib cage, making her light-headed. How could she possibly think straight? "I mean, there wouldn't be any hidden agendas between us."

"You mean you're marrying me for my money? I should warn you, my grandmother spent that penny." He was teasing, but only half. She saw the serious expression in his eyes. "There's no inherited fortune. I'm in pretty good financial shape—" he made a comical expression "—as you'd expect from your banker. But all I have is what I've saved and invested from my earnings over the years. We'll be comfortable, but not jet-setters."

"I don't care about that. All I want is a good life for my kids. But money always comes between us. What happens if we get married and we fight? Will you think, she only married me to get out of debt?"

"Of course not. That's like you thinking I only married you to make our babysitting arrangement permanent."

"Bingo."

A growl of frustration came from her right. "Sometimes I wish I could meet that ex of yours to pound his head in."

The idea made her so gleeful she knew she should be ashamed of herself. "You do?"

"You picked the wrong guy first time out. It happens. He was a pig. What can I say? Some men are pigs. But not all of us. Don't let him spoil what we have."

"I don't want us to marry out of desperation. Either of us."

"I know desperation. I've been there. I could draw you a road map of the place." His fingers traced up and down her neck under her hair, his eyes gentle and understanding. "I know this scares the hell out of you, but you must know you helped pull me out. I'd been there so long I'd forgotten I could leave."

"Oh, Seth—"

"But, I don't love you because of that…well, maybe I do in part. But only a part. I don't love you because you're great with my girls, but that's part of it, too. I love you because you're a terrific woman. Gorgeous and sexy and brave. I love you because I'm better with you than I can ever be without you."

"I feel that, too. But Seth, I'm scared."

"Trust me. Trust us. We can do this—but not on an empty stomach. Here's the restaurant I was telling you about."

How like a man, she thought to herself with a smile. He could only take so much intimate talk, then he needed a breather. Truth was, she kind of needed one herself. They were starting to unpack their emotional baggage, one bag at a time.

And before she knew it, he'd used his breather to settle them into the restaurant and they were sitting at a table drinking coffee and eating fresh salmon omelets.

And discussing the future. From the way Seth was talking, it seemed they were engaged.

Every time the little quavery voice in her head sounded its fearful alarm, she'd put a determined smile on her face and remind herself of Seth's words. She did trust him. And she did love him.

And of course, he must love her. He'd told her so, hadn't he? Not only with words, but with little thoughtful gestures and the expression in his eyes when he glanced her way. He'd loved her with his body deep into the night. So, she quelled the voice that said it was too soon. He wasn't ready.

Seth was the answer to all her hopes and prayers. She was delighted. Really, she was.

Maybe she was having so much fun being single and

enjoying an attractive man simply for sex that she wasn't quite ready to be a wife again.

"Eat up. You'll need your strength for tonight," he taunted as she pushed the last bit of food around her plate.

She felt absurdly shy at his words and the images they immediately conjured in her mind. She might have blushed, except that the blood all seemed to have rushed to the intimate parts of her body. "Didn't you get your fill last night?"

"Sweetheart, with you I don't think I could ever get my fill. Just to help you get in the mood, I've booked you a full massage and I don't know what else. Some kind of spa package."

"You did? For when?"

"This afternoon. I promised you a decadent weekend, didn't I?"

She gave a soft chuckle. "I'm really starting to like being your weekend mistress."

"Well, it's a short-term assignment."

She blinked.

"Until we get married."

Abandoning the last of her breakfast, she sipped the fresh coffee their waitress had poured. "I don't know. We shouldn't rush into anything. This is a big step for both of us. We're not impulsive people." She glanced up with a wry grin. "Look how long it was before we made love."

He reached for her free hand and ran a thumb over her knuckles. It was his left hand. The mark where his wedding ring had rested for so long was a shade paler. He'd only taken off one woman's ring a day ago. Was he really ready to replace it? "How do you see this playing out, then?"

When she raised her eyebrows, he continued. "Do I kiss

you in front of the kids? Do we have complicated sleep-over arrangements every time we want sex? Are you going to be okay with Matthew and Alice seeing me come out of your bedroom some mornings but not others?"

Slowly, as the impact of his words sank in, she shook her head.

"I know it's a little soon for us. I get that, but I can't see another way for us to be together other than to get married. And I don't think either of us is going to be comfortable carrying on in front of the kids unless we're married."

She did want to marry him, and she knew she'd be good for him. Instead of arguing, as part of her knew she should, she gave in.

"I may become your wife, but promise me you'll always treat me like your mistress when we're alone."

He chuckled, deep and sexy. "I don't have a lot of personal experience with mistresses—"

She cocked a severe eyebrow at him.

"Okay. I don't have any. But I think a man's mistress is supposed to do anything he tells her to—of a sexual nature, I mean."

"Really?" Little shivers of excitement raced up and down her spine. "Like what?"

He gave her a few ideas, and suddenly she couldn't wait to get back to the hotel and follow his instructions explicitly.

CHAPTER EIGHTEEN

HE FELT AS EXCITED AS a kid at Christmas. After escorting Melissa to the door of the day spa—where they seemed to do a lot of very expensive things with mud and seaweed—he'd dashed to his car and headed to a nice little jewelry store he'd noted earlier.

He'd seen the trepidation in Melissa's eyes and knew she was scared silly to get married again. To him, putting a ring on her finger was like getting a signature on a contract.

Marriage was the answer for both of them. Now that he'd made his decision, he wanted to get the thing done. He'd push for an early wedding, too. Once they were hitched, she could get rid of that too-big house of hers and her financial burdens. He had plenty of room.

"May I help you, sir?" asked a buxom, middle-aged woman with twinkly blue eyes behind some heavy-duty glasses.

"Yes, I—" Now that he was here his collar felt too tight. He raised a hand to automatically loosen his tie, only to discover he wasn't wearing a tie. Or collar. How could an open-necked polo shirt be choking him? "I'm—uh—looking for an engagement ring."

The woman slid the glasses off her nose and let them dangle from the silver chain around her neck. Something about the motherly way she regarded him made him breathe a little easier. "I see."

He got the uncomfortable feeling she did see. More than he wanted her to. "And the bride to be? Will she be joining you?" The woman squinted toward the door behind him.

"No. I want to surprise her."

"All right then. Of course, you can return the ring if she wishes a different style, or—"

"She throws it back in my face?"

The woman's laugh was musical and young. He found himself grinning. "I hope it won't come to that. But, yes, we'll take it back for any reason. Now, what did you have in mind?" She led him to a staggering display of glistening, glittering gems. All neatly paired with wedding bands. The imaginary collar tightened another notch. Absently, he rubbed his own ring finger, only recently naked.

Was he ready for this? He remembered picking out Claire's ring. God, he could almost hear her giggle beside him, ghostly and far away. They'd gone together and chosen the set of rings that currently resided in a safety deposit box for when the twins grew up.

After a long silence, the woman said, "This isn't your first marriage, is it?"

He dropped his hands, pondered getting huffy with her, and looked up to see such a warm expression on her face that he felt a momentary urge to bury his head in her ample bosom and tell her all his problems. "No. I'm a widower."

"I'm sorry," she said quietly. "And the lady?"

"Divorced."

"I see." She glanced down to unlock a display case containing rows of black velvet trays, each one loaded with diamond twinsets.

"Whew. I don't know where to start," he said, swallowing against the constriction in his throat.

The woman eyed him with professional interest. "Why don't you tell me a bit about her."

"Well, I love her, of course. That's why we're getting married." He said it in his bottom-line voice. So there'd be no mistaking his sincerity.

Two thin-penciled eyebrows rose. "Naturally. I was thinking more of her interests. That can have a bearing on jewelry. If she's a plumber or competitive swimmer you'd want one kind of setting. If she's a model or stockbroker you'd want quite another."

"Oh, I see. Well, between us we have four active kids. She loves to cook. And she's building a business as a landscape designer."

"She'll be getting her hands dirty, then." The woman's perfectly manicured hands, sporting quite a glitter of their own, fluttered over the trays and, selecting a ring, removed it and placed it on the glass display case.

"No," he said. "Too showy."

"What are her hands like?"

"Huh?"

"Are her fingers short and thick or long and slender?"

"She has beautiful hands." He flashed back to the way they'd looked trailing over his body last night, and almost groaned. "Ah, long and slender for sure."

"Take a look through these and see if anything strikes your fancy. The prices are all marked on the bottom."

He realized all at once that this was a more delicate operation than he'd foreseen. He had no idea what Melissa had worn when she was married the first time. He was determined to get something completely different. He reviewed what little he knew of Mr. Stephen Theisen and immediately figured the guy would buy something huge and flashy, and probably full of flaws. He wouldn't care so long as it was shiny and big.

"I want a perfect diamond," Seth said. "Something elegant but understated."

From the smile the woman beamed his way, he felt like he'd passed some kind of test. She opened a small drawer and pulled out a jeweler's loupe and a square, black velvet tray. She plucked two diamond engagement rings out of the lot then scanned the rest of the offerings and picked a third from another tray.

With only three brightly winking rings in front of him, Seth felt better. She picked the first one up and squinted at it through her scope. "One very slight occlusion," she informed him. "Really, as close to perfect as you can get in this size. It's just under a carat. The setting is very simple, no claws or curlicues to get in the way of gardening or child-rearing."

He knew the moment he saw it that was the one. He pictured the diamond on Melissa's finger, and it felt right. It wasn't a showy ring, but it was both simple and elegant. And, like Melissa, nearly flawless.

He studied the other two because he felt he ought to have a reasonable comparison, but he came back to the first.

"I'll take it," he said.

She polished the ring and placed it neatly in a compact box on a plush bed of black velvet.

"Wish me luck."

"Oh, I do, sir. Both of you. I hope you'll be very happy. We can alter the ring to fit, obviously, so bring her in tomorrow to size the shank properly. And, if she wants to change it…" The woman shrugged, obviously thinking if Melissa wanted a different ring than the one Seth had chosen, she must be insane.

He gave himself a pep talk all the way back to the hotel. Melissa was good for him, good for the girls. He was crazy about her and about Matthew and Alice. He was doing the right thing.

He was.

Back in their room, he realized he couldn't sit still and wait for her, so he tucked the ring into his toiletry case, left her a note and went down to the gym, where a punishing workout helped keep his body, if not his mind, occupied.

After the workout, he sat outside on a bench, feeling the crisp breeze dry his sweat, drinking a bottle of water and staring at the ocean. So long as he stayed here, nothing changed. The minute he walked up to his room, he entered a new phase.

He blew out a breath. That was good, he reminded himself. Good.

He finished the water and knew Melissa would have been back for a while. Feeling every one of his muscles, he rose stiffly and made his way upstairs.

He had his room key, but knowing she was already inside, he knocked.

The second she opened the door, all his apprehension vanished. The woman standing in front of him was stunning. Gorgeous and sexy, and he was crazy about her.

"You look fantastic," he said, "for somebody who spent an afternoon covered in mud and seaweed. How do you feel?"

"Like a new woman. Thank you, Seth," she whispered, her red lips curving deliciously. "I feel…pampered."

"You're beautiful." She was, too. In a simple black dress he'd never seen before that fit in all the right places. Her hair and makeup were different than he was used to, more obvious and very, very sexy.

"What was the best part?"

"Mmm. The massage. Definitely, the massage. Did you find something to do while I was being pummeled and painted?"

"Yep."

"Tennis or golf?"

"I did some shopping, then went for a workout." Now that the time had come, he felt his collar tightening again.

Her professionally made-up eyes widened, then crinkled when she giggled. "Shopping. Right. Every man I know can't wait to go shopping."

"Let me shower and change, and I'll show you."

"All right."

"Can you find something to do for a bit?"

"I'm going to do something I rarely do at home. Absolutely nothing," she said, and sank into the comfy chair in the corner and put her feet on the ottoman.

He'd been torn between presenting the ring in the restaurant, which they'd rebooked for tonight, and doing it privately. But as soon as he was showered and dressed, he knew he had to do it here and now and get the whole thing over with. When he was with her he had no doubts. Why would he? Any man would be lucky to find a woman like Melissa.

He dug the jewelry box out of his toiletry case, opened it and studied the ring for a long moment. He'd never imagined doing this a second time in his life. Closing the lid carefully, he dropped the box into his pocket and emerged into the room to find Melissa exactly as he'd left her, looking perfectly blissful.

Clearing his throat, he felt as foolish as a boy asking out a girl for the first time. He didn't have a clue how to act or what to say.

She glanced at the clock when he walked into the room. "We're a little early for our dinner reservation, but maybe we could take a walk first."

"I want to show you something."

"All right."

"I—uh, bought you a present."

"But Seth, you've already given me so much. This weekend, the spa—I saw the prices in there."

"You've given me much more, Melissa." His collar was so tight it seemed to choke him, making his words come out hoarse. "You gave me hope. And a future." It was now or never. He slipped the jeweler's box from his pocket and held it out. "Please marry me."

For a moment she stared at him. Then slowly she extended those beautiful hands he'd come to love, red-tipped at the ends from a fresh manicure.

They trembled as she took the velvet box. She didn't open it right away. He could have sworn she was praying, or making a wish. Then she lifted the lid.

"O-o-oh, Seth." She stared at the ring, and he knew he'd guessed right. "It's perfect. But…are you sure?"

He took a couple of jerky steps toward her. "Yes. Trust me." And as he slipped the ring onto her shaking finger, her tears spilled over.

"I'm going to ruin this very expensive professional makeup application," she cried, sniffing and brushing the tears away with her hands.

"If we don't get out of this room, I'm going to ruin it even more." He kissed her lips swiftly. "Come on. Let's get a bottle of champagne and the best dinner in the house."

She admired her ring in the light, and he told her how good it looked on her finger. Which it did. She could be a hand model.

They made their way to the restaurant, which was decorated in cedar and glass, with huge windows overlooking the restless ocean.

When they were seated at a quiet window table for two, he ordered champagne and waited until it was bubbling in two glasses to toast her. "To us," he said simply.

She sipped, watching him over her glass.

"You haven't answered my question, you know."

Her eyes dropped to the ring sparkling on her finger.

"Will you?" he asked softly.

"Are you sure this is what you want? Really sure?"

He stifled every qualm. "Absolutely."

"And you're positively sure you love me? I won't ever marry another man who doesn't."

It must be love, this feeling he had for her. This combination of raging sexual desire, gratitude for all she was doing for him and the girls, and this indefinable sense of need. "I love you, Melissa."

She took a deep breath and closed her eyes for a moment. When she opened them they were bright with excitement and a tinge of fear. "Yes. I'll marry you. And I promise to love you forever."

Forever.

Till death do us part.

The unaccustomed twinkle on her left hand snagged his attention and offered him a safe way to back off from the intensity of this conversation. "We can exchange the ring if you want to pick out something else."

She beamed at him, totally eclipsing the diamond's sparkle. "This is exactly what I would have picked myself. Well, I would have chosen a smaller diamond. Are you sure we can afford this?"

He lifted her hand and kissed it. "I hope I have absolutely nothing in common with your ex. One thing we sure as hell don't have in common is financial recklessness."

"You have better taste in jewelry, too. I should have realized he was all wrong for me when he gave me the ring. It was so—obvious. Like him, showy on the outside, not worth much when you got deep." She sighed. "I didn't get nearly as much as I'd hoped when I sold it."

He'd guessed right. Oh, he had the unlamented Stephen's measure.

"Well, one problem we are never going to have is exspouses interfering with our marriage or causing trouble with the kids."

A tiny frown marred her smooth forehead. "I hope not." He didn't know whether she was referring to Stephen or Claire. He didn't press for details.

"Another good thing is how nicely we mesh. My daughters will have the mother they need, Matthew will have somebody around the house who likes guy stuff, and you won't have to worry about money the way you have been."

"Hey, don't knock my hard times. I've learned a lot about making do with less. It's got to be such a habit, I kind of like the challenge and I'm proud of my new frugal skills. This dress, for instance, that you admired earlier?" She smiled mischievously. "Four bucks at the thrift store."

He threw back his head and laughed. He had to. There she sat, the most elegant and beautiful woman in the room, looking easily like a million bucks. In a thrift store dress.

"It's not funny. I figured out the difference between buying this dress and a brand-new one, and decided investing in my children's college education would be a better use of my money."

"Sweetheart, you were meant to be a banker's wife."

"I've learned a lot in the past couple of years. I'm through pretending to be something I'm not."

While she ate her fresh halibut surrounded by crisp vegetables and he plowed into his rack of lamb done with an amazing sauce made from local berries, they talked, for once not about their kids, but about themselves.

"Will you still keep looking after other kids?" he asked her.

Obviously, she hadn't thought very far into the future— well, they'd only been engaged for an hour. She put her head to one side and regarded him. "I think I'll have to for a while. I made a commitment to the kids and their parents. I can't close up shop too soon. I can wind the child care up by the end of the school year. I think that's fair."

"More than fair," he agreed, wondering how he was going to like having a day care in the house he called home.

"What about your landscape design business?"

Those gorgeous, lake-blue eyes that had been regarding him widened and he saw a flash of panic. "I love what I do. I'm not giving that up."

"No. Of course not. I don't want you to. I was thinking that if you want to start expanding, adding some of those other services, well, you'd be in a better position to do it. That's all."

Her expression showed her relief. "Oh. For a second

there I thought you were going to tell me you wanted a stay-at-home wife."

"Melissa, I want you to be happy. And whatever makes you happy is fine by me."

She leaned closer. "I think I just fell a little deeper in love with you."

He snorted. "I haven't started getting on your nerves yet. It'll happen."

"I know. I'm kind of looking forward to it. There's so much intimacy in somebody's annoying little habits." She laughed softly. "Stephen used to do this thing—" Then she clapped her newly ringed hand over her mouth. "Oh, God. I'm sorry. What a tactless thing to say."

He finished chewing and swallowed. "Not really. He was part of your life for a long time. What did he do? I'll make a note never to make the same mistake."

She leaned forward and spoke softly. "He threw his dirty clothes at the laundry hamper. About sixty percent of the time they went in. The rest of the time they'd be draped over the edge, or socks would lay where they landed around that hamper. I'd end up picking up the stuff. It drove me nuts."

"I don't do that."

She grinned at him. "Good. What about Claire?"

Suddenly, this conversation wasn't such a great idea anymore, but he was the one who'd wanted her to go on when she'd tried to stop it, he reminded himself. What could he do but share something about Claire the way she'd so easily done about her ex?

"She, uh—" What? He tried to think of Claire as the woman he'd married, the woman he'd lived with day in and out for nine years. The woman she'd been before she got sick.

And there it was. A memory as clear as the food in front of them. He sipped wine and then said, "She wasn't the neatest person in the world. And she liked to sew."

Suddenly, he was grinning at the memory of her surrounded by scraps of fabric. Orange and black as she worked feverishly at two identical pumpkin costumes for Halloween. "She made great stuff for the kids. Costumes and clothes. She was really careful about pins and needles and things because of the girls. But she wasn't too neat about anything else. There would be slivers of fabric and pieces of thread everywhere. For weeks after. And that sewing machine would sit in the middle of the dining table until we had somebody coming for dinner or I couldn't stand it anymore and put it away."

Melissa touched his hand, jarring him back to the present. "I'm so glad you told me that. I was getting scared that she was perfect."

He shook his head. "No. She wasn't perfect. But she was a good woman. The best."

"And you'll always love her."

"Yes, but that doesn't mean—"

"I know. I know. I don't want to take that away from you. Not ever. What we have is our own."

The moment was so intense he felt that he needed to escape from all that emotion for a bit. "Anyhow, what I was saying earlier is that if you want to branch out and expand your business, I'm behind you all the way."

"Thank you for believing in me. But, no. I'm not ready yet, and when I am, I think I'll go to the bank and get a loan. This is something I need to do myself."

"Good for you. Dessert?"

She shook her head. "Uh-uh. I'm stuffed."

"Coffee?"

"I couldn't."

"Sex?"

She giggled. "Oh, yeah."

CHAPTER NINETEEN

MELISSA OPENED HER EYES, conscious of a feeling of well-being. Today, she knew exactly where she was. Already the warmth of Seth's naked body wrapped around hers was familiar.

With a pang of regret, she decided they'd have to wait until they were married to spend any more nights together. Today was the last day they could simply devote to each other for a while.

Married. A wedding. In her mind she'd skipped over that part and simply pictured her life going on pretty much as always, only without the money worries, and with Seth in her bed every night when she went to sleep. And every morning when she woke up. She sighed. She'd have to get that lock on the bedroom door fixed. And turn the guest room into a bedroom for the twins. She'd get them to help her decorate. That would be fun.

"Penny for them," Seth mumbled in her ear, his voice sleep-groggy.

"I was wondering how quickly we could get married."

"I thought you liked being a mistress." He nibbled her ear lobe. "You're certainly good at it."

He traced a finger lazily round one nipple and her body started turning to liquid, just like that. She felt him hardening behind her and wiggled her hips against him. "I do like it, but I won't get any more practice until we're married."

The nibble turned into a bite that made her cry out and the hand on her breast went rigid. "What?" he demanded in a tone so peevish she smiled into the pillow.

Shifting so she could see his outraged face, she said, "How do you suggest we conduct an affair with four kids?"

"We're engaged. I—but—they'll know we're getting married."

"I can't do it, Seth."

He flopped onto his back with a grunt, crossed his arms under his head and stared moodily at the ceiling. "Tell you what," he said at last. "I'll meet you at city hall tomorrow at lunch. No, wait a second, I've got a meeting at one. Tuesday, then. We'll get married Tuesday."

"What about the kids?"

"They'll be at school."

"No. I mean, they'll want to be there. I want them there."

"Well. We could go after school, get married, and take them out for pizza afterward."

She chuckled helplessly. "That is, without a doubt, the most pathetic idea I've ever heard."

"Who cares about the marriage part? I want to get to the wedding night."

"I care. The kids'll care. This is forever, Seth. I want it to feel like forever."

He groaned again, sending her a pleading look. "This isn't working up to one of those magazine-type weddings with three hundred guests, is it?"

"Oh. No. I had that kind of wedding once. I don't want

it again." She hesitated a moment. "What kind of wedding did you have? The first time?"

"Same. Crowds of relatives I didn't know from Adam. Speeches. Bridesmaids. God knows, I love you, Melissa, but I'm begging you. Don't put me through that again."

She laughed.

"There were plastic bells on every table. Swear to God. Plastic bells."

"Paper roses. My mother sat at home night after night and made one hundred and seventy-five paper roses." She sighed. "No. I don't want to go through that again, either. But I wouldn't want to hurt people's feelings. Janice would want to come. So would my neighbor, Pam." Her heart sank. "And my Dad."

"My parents will fly in from Florida."

"It's already getting complicated."

"I've got a great idea. Let's take the kids away some-where—Hawaii maybe—and get married. They can be part of it, and we don't have to invite anybody else to the wedding. Then, when we get back, sometime we'll have a party to celebrate."

"Can we really go to Hawaii? I've always wanted to."

"Nothing easier. I'll call my travel agent tomorrow. Let's say, two weeks from now?"

This was feeling so much like a fairy tale it was scary. But it was good scary. She could picture them, the six of them, posed against a tropical sunset like a postcard.

"I love this idea. We'd be legally married, so that would take care of the sleeping arrangements, and then we could have a garden party to celebrate when we got home. It's perfect, don't you think? Gardens are my thing." She glanced at him from under her lashes. "I might even get some business out of it from all your stuffy friends."

"How do you know my friends are stuffy? You've never met any of them."

"That's right. I haven't." They'd probably all known Claire, though. They'd compare her, of course, to her predecessor. How would she stack up?

"You'll meet them soon enough."

"What have you told people about me?" she asked, feeling deliciously girlish.

"I haven't told them anything."

"Oh." It was crazy to feel disappointed. She hadn't told anyone about Seth, either. Well, apart from Pam. And she and Pam had discussed it endlessly. Sure, she had her business and kids and the usual things, but falling in love with a new man was the most significant and exciting part of her life at the moment. He was definitely top of mind.

Oh, well, she reminded herself. Men are different. They don't love to communicate the way women do.

"Two weeks to wait," he complained. Before she knew what was happening, he'd flipped her on her back and rolled his full length on top of her, a very wicked expression in his eyes. "Better get our fill in now."

Then he kissed her, and she thought what a long time fourteen days was. And then she couldn't think at all.

"HAWAII!" the three older kids all screamed at once. Little Alice's voice echoed right behind them, "Hawaii!" Then she whispered to Jessie, "What's Hawaii?"

The kids had seemed pretty enthusiastic that their parents were getting married. But their reaction to the trip to Hawaii almost had the San Andreas fault quivering in response.

"Shh." He glanced out the living room window. "You'll have the neighbors calling 9-1-1."

"Dad, can we get bikinis? Ple-ea-ease?"

"B-bikinis?" He glanced to Melissa for inspiration. "Aren't you a little young?"

"Everybody wears them, Dad." And then, obviously following the line of his own gaze, his oldest turned to Melissa. "Right, Melissa?"

She shot him a questioning glance, but he shrugged. Bikinis. What did he know? He knew one thing, it was going to be a hell of a lot better having Melissa around to help with the girls.

She answered their question with a question of her own. "You girls know about sunscreen?"

An eager "Uh-huh" duet was the reply.

"If you promise to wear sunscreen every second we're in Hawaii, I'll talk to your father about the bathing suits."

They'd obviously already figured him for a total pushover. He could tell the way they were hugging Melissa and thanking her, then trying to decide whether they should buy the bathing suits before they went or get them in Hawaii. Damn it. He was their father. He felt a need to assert himself. "Not those things with shoe laces down the backside," he commanded.

"Wha-at?"

"Do you mean thongs?" Melissa asked, a dimple teasing her cheek.

Four identical eyes rolled heavenward. "Oh, Dad."

Matthew, who'd been practicing surfing on the couch cushions, crouched and leaped into the air, riding an imaginary wave. It dumped him soundly on the ground, where he rolled and bounced up again. "When do we go?"

"In two weeks."

"Woo-hoo. Wait'll I tell Ryan Doran. He thinks he's so cool cause he went to Disneyland for Christmas. I'm going to Hawaii, *and* getting a new dad."

Something funny squeezed in Seth's chest. It was pretty obvious he placed a distant second to two weeks in Hawaii, but Matthew seemed totally willing to accept him as a surrogate father. He and Melissa hadn't got as far as figuring what the kids would think about them becoming a blended family. He'd mentally budgeted a few thousand for counseling fees, and here everybody seemed delighted.

Everybody, that is, except Laura, who'd suddenly gone pale.

"Two weeks?" she asked in a hollow voice. "Will we be in Hawaii on the nineteenth?"

"The nineteenth?" He glanced at Melissa but she looked as puzzled as he felt. "No. We leave on the twenty-first. Why?"

"The Bravo Boys," Jessie said. "Their concert is on the nineteenth."

He felt his jaw clench. "And on the nineteenth you'll be sitting here at home. Because there's no way on earth I would let you two go to a rock concert."

Jessie opened her mouth and Seth gritted his teeth even harder, but he was saved by Laura, who took one look at his face and dragged her sister out of the room. He heard them whispering and muttering all the way up the stairs.

"What?" He challenged Melissa, who was grinning helplessly.

"I was wondering if we could postpone the wedding a little. Say, until they've finished being teenagers."

"At least with two of them, and two of us, the odds are

a little more favorable." He flopped down on his favorite chair, and wondered fleetingly whether Melissa would make him move it when she brought her own stuff over. He had to admit that what she hadn't sold was in a lot better shape than his own stuff.

He surveyed the living room, noting the dingy, finger-marked paint and how shabby the furniture was. Mostly because he let the kids pretty much have free run of the house when they were home. He couldn't ask Melissa to move in with the place looking like this. They could have a decorator come in and put a new touch on the place. She'd like that.

He watched her bend over and replace the couch cushions Matthew had upended before roaring off some-where with Alice in tow. He opened his mouth to tell her not to bother, then closed it again and decided to enjoy the view. If it weren't for four very good reasons all over his house, he'd be sneaking up behind his new fiancée right now and messing up those sofa cushions again.

"I want you," he said low in his throat.

Her hands, busy smoothing the cushions into precise geo-metrical lines, stilled. He saw the diamond wink on her finger, heard her sharp intake of breath. Then she turned to face him, and he knew without words that she wanted him, too.

He stood and in two strides had her in his arms.

"We can't," she murmured into his ear.

"Lunch tomorrow. Can you get a babysitter for Alice?"

She sent him a teasing smile. "You have a meeting tomorrow, remember?"

Puzzlement turned to self-conscious laughter as he recalled his crazy idea to get married on their lunch hour. "Right. I remember."

"But Alice and her little friend have play school on Tuesday, if you could take an early lunch."

"I'm hungry now. Okay. Tuesday, then. I'll run home for a nooner."

She chuckled, a deep sexy sound that made him kiss the side of her neck and try to get a hand up her shirt.

A slap took care of the hand. "Are you going to make a habit of nooners when we're married?"

"Damn right. Morning, noon and night. You and I have a lot of celibate years to make up for."

"Mmm." She didn't seem to dislike the idea, so he tried sneaking his hand back up her shirt and got another whack for his trouble.

Regretfully, he gave up and pulled away. "Tuesday."

She smiled, her face slightly flushed. "Tuesday."

"Oh, well. If we can't have sex, let's eat. I'll order some pizzas for dinner and we can celebrate with the kids."

"Well, all right. But we'll have to leave early. I want to bathe Matthew and Alice tonight."

"You're such a good mother."

She pinkened with pleasure at the compliment. "I'll try to be a good mother to Jessie and Laura, as well."

"Don't worry. We're going to make this thing work."

He couldn't help wondering who he was reassuring.

CHAPTER TWENTY

A *NOONER*? Sex in broad daylight? Melissa felt both excited and foolish. She wasn't even sure if he'd been serious when he'd suggested it. And really, she shouldn't waste her time when she had the house to herself. She should be catching up on work.

But then, she reminded herself piously, even she was entitled to a lunch break.

Should she make him lunch? The etiquette of a nooner completely baffled her.

Not to mention the correct apparel. Should she wear a negligee and stand at the bottom of the stairs holding a martini, a trail of rose petals leading to her bedroom? Or wear jeans and a T-shirt and give him a chicken sandwich, and let events proceed as they would?

She sighed, following the paring knife, which went round and round the apple, spiraling like her thoughts. The telephone interrupted her reverie.

"Hello?"

The voice on the other end of the phone made her gasp and spoil the unbroken circle of peel. "Seth. I was thinking about you."

"Me, too. What are you doing?"

"Making apple sauce cake. I'm peeling the apples."

"Peeling the apples." He sounded like he was laughing at her. "Haven't you ever heard of canned apple sauce?"

She shook her head, even though she knew he couldn't see her. It was a good thing she was marrying him. He needed her. "It's not the same." Suddenly inspired, she continued with forced casualness. "Maybe I'll let you try a piece tomorrow…." She let her voice drift at the end, sort of like a half question. Hopefully his response would let her know if it was a negligee or jeans date.

"Sweetheart, I can't make it tomorrow. I'm sorry."

"Why not?" It suddenly didn't matter what she was supposed to wear. She really wanted a nooner. Disappointment seeped over her.

He sighed deeply on the other end of the phone. "Our bank financed a combination residential and commercial development in California that's got a bad feel to it. I'm going to fly down and check it out, meet with the developers before we advance any more funds. I leave tomorrow, and I'm swamped getting things cleaned up before I go."

"How long will you be gone?"

"I don't know. A few days."

The apple was wobbling in her fingers, and she realized her hands were shaking. It bumped into the sink and she put the paring knife down with a snap. *He's not like Stephen. He's not.* But the term *business trip* to her was synonymous with extramarital affair. And they weren't even married yet.

"Are you okay?"

"Yes. I'm fine. Just, ah, disappointed." *I trust him. I trust him.*

"Me, too."

"Can you come for dinner tonight?"

"No. I'm scrambling here to get everything ready."

"Oh."

"I have to ask you a favor."

She picked up the paring knife and started idly pressing it into the peeled apple in the sink. "What is it?"

"Can I leave the girls with you until I get back?"

"Oh. Sure, of course."

"You've still got a key to my house?"

"Yes." He'd given it to her a couple of months ago when one of the twins had forgotten her homework. He'd told her to keep it.

"Sweetheart, I don't even have time to pack the girls some clothes. Do you think you can manage?"

"Sure."

"You sound funny. You're not mad about tomorrow?" He lowered his voice and she imagined him sitting at his desk, with that awful Stella trying to listen from her desk outside. "If there was any way I could see you, you know I would."

"Yeah." The pressure in her chest was increasing. She needed to be honest with him. "I have some trust issues around business trips. It's not your fault."

"Oh, Melissa, I'm sorry. You know I'd never do anything to hurt you. You can trust me."

There was a pause. "I know," she finally whispered.

"Look, I'll—" She heard an urgent voice in the background.

"I'll be right there," he snapped. She heard the sigh of frustration. "I have to go." He lowered his voice and murmured, "I love you."

"I love you, too," she said, but he'd already gone.

"DO YOU THINK Anne's going to marry Gilbert?" Jessie wanted to know.

"Blech." Matthew made gagging sounds and accompanying retching gestures.

"You are such a child," Laura said. It wasn't clear if she was referring to Matthew or her sister, younger by a couple of minutes. "Of course she's going to marry Gilbert. He's her soul mate."

Melissa smiled. "I'm not going to tell. I've already read all the *Anne of Green Gables* books." She wasn't sure how the routine had started, but since the first fateful day she'd tried to interest the twins in something other than the Bravo Boys and handed Laura *Anne of Green Gables,* the series of books about the turn-of-the-century orphan girl from Prince Edward Island had become part of their lives.

At first, Laura had asked so many questions and read so many passages aloud that Jessie had wanted to read the book, too. Melissa ended up reading the book aloud, chapter by chapter, on afternoons when the kids were all together. She wasn't sure that Alice understood a lot of what was read, but she curled up in her mother's lap and copied the intent listening pose of Laura.

Matthew pretended utter disgust, but even he'd laughed aloud when Anne, horrified by her red hair, had tried to dye it and it had turned green.

"What did she use again to get it green?" he'd asked with interest.

"Don't even think about it," Melissa had warned.

"But all the teenagers do it."

"You can't have a ring in your eyebrow, either."

"Aw, Mom."

He'd given up trying to get green hair, but he'd started paying attention to the chapters anyway. Now, with Seth away and the girls staying over, they'd taken to reading at night before bed. After they were done the Anne books, they'd decided they were going to reread the Harry Potter series. After Seth's harried phone call earlier in the day, Melissa thought gloomily that they might get the whole series finished before he got back.

She stilled the flutter of panic that occurred every time she thought of him so far away. He wasn't anything like Stephen. He wasn't off having an affair. She knew that. She trusted him completely, but she'd sure be glad when he got home and she could stop reminding herself a hundred times a day about how much she trusted him.

"Gilbert loves Anne," Laura continued. "Like my dad loves you, right Melissa?" It was amazingly warming that even his ten-year-old daughter could tell he was in love with her. Of course he wasn't off on a spree.

"Right." She smiled.

"When's he coming home, anyway?"

"He's hoping to be home by the weekend. His meetings are taking longer than he thought. But think what a surprise he'll get when he sees we've got your room all ready." With the girls' help, she'd removed the wallpaper in the guest bedroom. They'd chosen a bright apple-green color for the walls, and, unable to talk them out of their choice, Melissa had managed to convince them that it would look nice striped. And it did. A little bright, but nice. She'd painted white and green stripes on the walls, helped the girls brighten up an old wooden dresser by gluing on pictures out of magazines. She'd imagined something tasteful, like the Victorian decoupage she'd shown the girls from one of her decorating books. Instead, they'd covered every square inch of the dresser in little Bravo Boys.

They'd learn a good lesson about the fickleness of

fashion trends when they had to scrape off their decoration a couple of years from now. In the meantime, they were happy, and Melissa felt it was important to make them feel at home in their new room.

She'd rummaged through the remnant pile at the local fabric store and raided her own stash of "someday" sewing projects for enough scraps to make each of the girls a new quilt for their beds. It was her idea of a house-warming for them.

It was comforting to know that Seth would be leaving the painful memories in his house behind when they became a family. She wondered if they should redecorate her bedroom as a kind of symbolic gesture. She'd have to ask him when he got back.

Once she had all four kids asleep, Melissa donned her pajamas and crawled into her own bed with the notes from her interview with one of the homeowners in the new subdivision.

The homes there were gorgeous and, unlike a lot of new subdivisions, the developers hadn't gone in and leveled every tree; they were working in as eco-friendly a way as possible. Her designs were a whole lot more inter-esting because she had some natural features to work with. This yard had some huge boulders in the backyard with a couple of big cedars brooding over top. She imagined a pond with a small fountain to keep the water moving. A stone bench, and a lot of shade-loving plants. Ferns, hostas. Some rhododendrons over here. She started scribbling, then stopped. Sure, the rhodos would love the shady garden, but weren't they a little obvious? Who was going to pay for a design you could get from your local garden store clerk?

With a sigh, she settled back among the pillows and let the unease she felt rise up and make its point.

Seth had delayed his trip home by a couple of days. Big deal. He'd told her to trust him and she did. He'd told her he loved her and she believed him.

And maybe if she kept reminding herself how much she believed him, one day she actually would.

Knowing that rest wasn't going to happen anytime soon, she got out of bed and wandered the house. After checking that everybody was asleep and tucked in, she padded to the computer in Stephen's old home office. She'd found some excellent resources for plants and design ideas on the Web.

Having asked Google for help, she visited a lot of garden sites, bookmarked a few, made some notes.

Then she sat back, brooding. Maybe it was being here in Stephen's old office, but she couldn't stop thinking about him tonight. Comparing him and Seth wasn't fair. And perhaps she wasn't comparing them. Maybe—in the same way Seth had needed to accept his wife's death before he could move on—she needed to accept that Stephen had really gone, too. And yet he wasn't dead—or was he? The idea sent a strange shiver down her spine. It was late at night and she was getting maudlin. Of course he wasn't dead. She'd have heard something. Wouldn't she?

Her fingers started typing. Good old Google. She entered his name, certain it couldn't be this easy to track down the man who'd yanked up the roots she'd so carefully planted and disappeared.

It took her less than an hour to find him. His arrogance was astounding. He had a blog all about himself and his new business, exporting antiques and artwork from the

Czech Republic. With his Czech partner, Vladka. The blog led to a Web site for their export business.

She waited for her blood to boil, but strangely it didn't. The feeling was more like a simmer.

Naturally, a person wouldn't have a Web site and a blog promoting their business without advertising an e-mail address. She wrote to him.

Melissa sent an e-mail to her AWOL husband and imagined it traveling from Lakeview, Washington, to Somewhere Unspecified in the Czech Republic. What would he think when he read it? Would he reply?

"DAFFODILS ARE THE HAPPIEST flowers, aren't they?" Melissa said to Alice.

Alice regarded the bright blooms in the vase thoughtfully. "They're yellow."

"Yes, they are. I think yellow is a happy color." Or maybe it was her mood that made everything seem bright. Seth was coming home tonight. And Stephen had replied to her e-mail as she'd somehow known he would. Oh, he was full of apology that he hadn't been in touch, work had been busy, he was having a bit of a cash crunch, but of course he'd be sending her money soon, he sent his love to the kids, blah, blah, blah. Melissa had phoned around. She'd put her problem out there in the network of women, and she'd been referred to a lawyer who specialized in family law. A woman.

For some reason, she felt, even if she never got another penny out of her ex, that a burden had been lifted off her shoulders.

Maybe it was the smarmy, lying e-mail that had made her see so clearly the difference between him and Seth.

Maybe she was simply over him. But that morning she'd gone and bought herself a wedding dress.

"Why? Why is yellow a happy color?" Alice wanted to know.

"Well, it's the color of sunshine, and butter, and what else?"

"Bananas?"

"Good one. What else?"

"Your hair?"

She chuckled, tweaking a lock of Alice's bright hair. "And yours."

While they played an impromptu color game, she sliced the shortbread squares that the kids all loved. Dinner was in the oven. They hadn't discussed it in the rushed phone call, but she assumed Seth would stay for dinner when he came home tonight.

In a little more than a week's time, they'd be married and then he'd be coming home for dinner every night. Excitement and a little skitter of nerves filled her at the thought. Please let this work out.

They had tickets booked, a hotel on the beach, and now she had found a dress. A simple, long, sleeveless dress in primrose. Such a happy color.

She was pulled out of her reverie by the doorbell.

She wiped her hands and walked down the hall and opened the front door. There was a woman on her doorstep and a boat-sized silver Cadillac in her driveway. The woman had on absurdly high heels. For some reason, that was the first thing that Melissa noticed. She wore a stylish, pale gray suit, bleached blond hair in a back combed, upswept style and jewelry glinting off her hands and wrists as she beamed a toothy smile at Melissa and handed her a business card.

"Mrs. Theisen? I hope I'm not too early. I'm Cindi Thornton." The woman had a southern accent with a touch of eastern European.

Melissa stared at her blankly.

"The Realtor? Seth set up the appointment. I don't see his car so I guess I am early." The woman extended a thin hand with cinnamon-colored nails, and Melissa was so stunned she took it. She felt like she was going to have her home sold out from under her by Zsa Zsa Gabor.

"Seth made an appointment with a Realtor? Seth O'Reilly?"

"Sure he did. Did he forget to tell you about it? Honestly. Men." She smiled, displaying big preternaturally white teeth. The woman could be a walking ad for Crest White Strips. "Congratulations, by the way. I can tell you that there will be a lot of very disappointed women when they find out he's getting married."

"Thank you. But why are you here?" A headache was starting behind her eyes.

"To put your house on the market, honey. Seth says it's in excellent shape. In this area and this market?" She flapped one hand back and forth like a middle-aged blond rapper. "It'll sell in no time."

"I think there's been a mistake, Ms. Thornton," she said as firmly as she could.

"Why, that's just plain Cindi. Cindi with an *I*. I like to say that's 'cause I have an 'eye' for real estate." She tittered as though she'd just thought such a lame one up. "And you have a real nice home here."

"Thank you. I plan to keep it. I mean, we plan to keep it. It's Seth's home that will be going on the market."

A sigh, so sincere sounding it could have been genuine,

wafted from between thin, cinnamon-colored lips that matched the nails. "I'm getting the feeling you two never discussed this."

"Well, of course we—" She stopped in midsentence, then slowly shook her head. "I assumed—"

"I'm guessing he did the same thing."

A curtain fluttered in the Carmody home across the street.

"Would you like to come in?" She couldn't stand there explaining this hideous mix-up in front of every nosy neighbor on the block.

"I'd love to. I've always wanted to see inside this house. Real estate's not only my job. It's my addiction."

She stepped into the hall and Melissa shut the door behind her. "Oh," she said, putting a hand to her heart. "You baked. You do that every time we have a prospective buyer and the house will sell like that." She snapped her fingers.

"Make yourself comfortable in the living room. If you'll excuse me, I'm going to call Seth."

"Sure, honey. Don't worry about me. I'll just poke around."

That's what Melissa was afraid of. She bolted into the kitchen, took Alice to the den and flipped on the TV, then grabbed her phone. She called Seth's cell but it was turned off. Called his private line at the bank and got his recording. However, she could press 1 to speak to his assistant, so she did.

"Stella Hornby, how may I help you?"

"Oh, hi, Stella, this is Melissa Theisen. I'm trying to reach Seth."

"Mr. O'Reilly is out of the office. May I take a message?" the frigid voice asked her.

"I know he's out of the office. His cell phone's turned off. I'm trying to—"

"If you'd like to book an appointment, he has space Thursday."

"An appointment, but—no, let me speak to—" Who? Who did Seth talk about at work? Who might actually treat his fiancée like a human being? "Mitzi Youngall. Is she in?"

"I'll transfer you," the arctic voice said.

"If it's not too much trouble," Melissa said sweetly, but her sarcasm was lost since she'd already been transferred. Fortunately, Mitzi answered her phone.

"Hello. I'm sorry to bother you, but this is Melissa Theisen. I'm trying to reach Seth."

"I'm sorry, Ms. Theisen, Seth's not in the office until tomorrow."

Her eyebrows drew together. "I know he's not. I'm trying to reach him on a personal matter."

"Personal?" Curiosity zapped like an electric current across the line.

"Yes. I'm his…girlfriend." Stupid term at thirty-five. Why hadn't she said fiancée? What was the matter with everybody today? What was the matter with her?

Mitzi squealed. "What? Seth has a girlfriend?" Then she gasped. "Oh, I'm so sorry. That was tactless. I'm…ah, kind of surprised that's all."

"I—uh, I didn't realize no one knew."

"Yeah. Um. Did you try his cell?"

"Yes. It's off."

"He checked in earlier, right before he got on the plane. He should be back sometime this afternoon."

"Okay. If you hear from him, can you tell him I'm looking for him?"

"Sure will. It was nice talking to you. I hope I get to meet you soon."

"Yes. So do I." When she hung up, she stared sightlessly out of the kitchen window. No one knew about her. No one. It wasn't only his friends, but the people he worked with every single day. He hadn't mentioned her or their upcoming wedding to anyone at all. Except the Realtor. What did that say about her importance in his life? Maybe if she weren't already so wretchedly insecure she could tell herself he was only keeping his private affairs to himself, but after being dumped by one husband, she really didn't want to be hidden away like a guilty secret by a second.

She walked slowly back toward the living room and found the Realtor in the dining room along the way. "Lovely wainscoting," she said, then looked at Melissa and her smile dimmed. Concern took its place. "Please don't look so worried. This will all work out. Misunderstandings happen all the time between couples. You know, communication is the toughest skill to master in a marriage."

"Yes. I know." And right now the communication she was receiving from Seth was unnerving her.

"We'll sort this thing— Ah, looks like we can sort it out now," Cindi said, and going to the front door, flung it open.

Sure enough, a maroon Volvo had pulled up and a very tired Seth emerged.

He took a step, paused, squinted at the Realtor and then at Melissa. He shook Cindi-with-an-I's hand, gave Melissa a peck on the cheek and said, "I think I forgot to tell you about Cindi coming."

"That's not the only thing you forgot to tell me," she said as pleasantly as she could, considering she wanted to smack him.

CHAPTER TWENTY-ONE

THE CRESCENT WAS EXPERIENCING its after-school rush hour. Kids shuffled, skateboarded and cycled past on their way home. Moms and nannies walked to the school to pick up younger children. With horror, Melissa noticed that Cindi used her boat-sized Cadillac as a rolling billboard for her services. Any minute now, she'd be hailed by some nosy parent or neighbor. She gestured into the house, "Why don't we talk about this—"

"Dadd-ee!" came a twin chorus and there were the girls, with Matthew hot on their heels, sprinting toward Seth.

She steeled herself for the inevitable inquisition about the realty sign on the Cadillac, but they were too wrapped up in greeting their father, in the twins' case, and his hero, in Matthew's.

"Guess what? We're putting on a play at school and I'm going to try out," Laura panted.

"I'm going on the track team," Matthew reported.

"Did you see our new room?" Jessie piped up. "Me and Laura and Melissa decorated it ourselves."

He'd been grinning and hugging the jumping, wriggling bodies, until Jessie spoke. Then he glanced up with mixed horror and embarrassment.

"Come and see." The girls each took one of his hands

and dragged him toward the open door where Alice stood, a big smile on her face and her arms upstretched.

She thought he paused, as though no longer sure of his place, then dragged Alice up high the way she liked. She squealed her approval.

That left Melissa and the Realtor staring at each other. "Why don't I let you two talk about things? You can give me a call when you're ready. I do have the nicest family that would love to locate into this area."

"We'll call you," Melissa said firmly. Then felt like a bitch. The woman was only trying to do her job, and she'd been pretty decent under the circumstances. "Thank you for understanding."

"Honey, I've been married for twenty-eight years." She paused, her car keys glittering in her hand. "Do you want some advice?"

No. But she nodded to be polite.

"Go in and let him have it. Have that fight I can see you working up to."

"Don't worry, I intend to."

"But don't let your pride and your hurt blind you to a good thing."

"I won't. Thanks."

She followed the gang up the stairs to the room she and the twins had been working on every night he'd been away. She could hear their excitement from here.

"Isn't it great, Dad?"

"Do you like the color?"

"Melissa let us put the Bravo Boys on our dresser. She said we could bring our clothes over, too. After we come home from Hawaii, this'll be our new room."

"I...uh..." His hand crept to his belly and he rubbed it

absently. She could see he was in pain. Well, so was she. "I need to talk to Melissa for a while."

"About Hawaii?"

"In private. Laura, Jessie, take the other kids down and put on a DVD or something."

"Melissa always makes us do our homework first."

With a distracted air, he waved them away, and Melissa thought she'd never seen him treat them so dismissively before.

The twins gaped.

She finally found her voice. Or maybe it was somebody else's. It sure didn't sound like hers, with that flat, hopeless tone. "Go watch a movie. It's okay."

"Cool." They thundered down the stairs whispering and giggling. Melissa was pretty sure she heard the dreaded initials *MTV,* but today the Bravo Boys seemed like saints compared to the man she was suddenly alone with in the bright apple-green-and-white striped room.

He walked to the doorway, listened for a moment and then shut the door, closing them in together in the ridiculously girlish room.

"I don't know what to say. I assumed you and Matthew and Alice would move in with me. I've got plenty of room."

"But I'm closer to the school. Everyone's used to being here." And she didn't even mention that the state of her house and garden were a lot more desirable than his.

It turned out she didn't need to. "I know my place needs some updating. I thought we'd get a decorator in."

"But that's always going to be Claire's house." She thought about the way he'd first taken her to the guest room. "I'd feel like an intruder."

His face darkened. "How do you think this place would feel to me?"

"I never thought about it."

"Yeah. It was another one of those conversations we should have had. Forget it." He flicked a glance at the bright walls. "Your place is fine."

But the vise around her heart didn't ease. "How come when I phoned the bank no one knew who I was?"

"What?" His surprise seemed genuine.

"Your secretary offered me an appointment for next week when I introduced myself, and then I got transferred to Mitzi Youngall. You talk about her a lot, so I figured she'd know who I was. She pretty much fell off her chair when I identified myself as your girlfriend."

His eyelids jerked as though she'd come at him with a pitchfork. "I don't talk about my private affairs at work."

"You were planning to get married in a week, and you didn't bother to tell your co-workers? Must have forgotten to pencil it into your Day-Timer." As she finished speaking she noticed she'd spoken of their marriage in the past tense. Her hands felt cold. She glanced down and noticed they were clenched into fists.

"Of course I was going to tell them. I've been busy."

She was working up to mad now. Maybe if she hadn't been married to Stephen Theisen she wouldn't be so angry about her fiancé making sure not to mention her to the people in his life. But she had been married to Stephen, and no one was ever going to treat her so lightly again. "In all the time you spend with these people, you never found a minute to say, 'by the way, I'm getting married in two weeks?'"

He shifted, looking uncomfortable and sad and confused. "I don't want to make a big deal out of it. Frankly, I want to get the whole thing over with."

The silence was so heavy she found it hard to breathe. "Getting married *is* a big deal. It's a big deal to me."

"I didn't mean that the way it came out. Damn it, Melissa. You know I didn't."

"I know only one thing. I'll never, ever marry a man who doesn't love me. *Me!* Not the babysitter or the corporate wife or the cook and cleaner. Me, Melissa. For who I am." Her throat was aching and her nose tickled, but she was determined not to cry. Not today.

"Don't dramatize a misunderstanding. You know I love you."

"Would you want to marry me if you didn't need a mother for your daughters?"

His lips clamped together in his anger-darkened face. She could almost hear him mentally counting before he answered. "We wouldn't have got to know each other if it weren't for the girls."

"No. It was the twins who brought us together, wasn't it?"

"So what? Was I supposed to fall in love with you just because you were beautiful and gazed at me with big helpless eyes? I'm trying to do what's best here for everyone."

"What's convenient you mean. I won't be anyone's convenience. Never, ever again. I can make it without your help, thank you very much."

"And what about the kids? Are you going to deny them a family because you don't feel special?" He sneered the last word. She knew he was hurting, but right now she needed reassurance big-time. Sure, he was scared, too. But she'd been planning a wedding, telling anyone she felt like telling that she was getting married again. The only person Seth seemed to have told was the Realtor.

She sank to the single bed that awaited its green quilt. She felt so cold, she wished the quilt were there so she could wrap herself in its cheerful warmth. "I know this is hard for you. I do understand." She shook her head, cursing herself for a fool. "I even knew you weren't ready. Not for marriage." She swallowed. "It's too soon."

He sat down on the opposite bed. Finally, they were talking about the real issue. She knew the trouble between them wasn't about which house they were going to live in.

"I put Claire's pictures away. All but one. I have moved on."

She smiled a little. She managed that. "I know you have. You've come a long way. But we rushed into marriage so we could sleep together without embarrassing our kids. That's not a good enough reason."

"It's not true, either. We love each other."

She met his eyes. "Do we?"

He shifted, and dropped his gaze.

"I found Stephen."

Seth stood with a jerk, turned away and strode to the window. Stood, looking out. "Where is he?" His voice sounded like it came from a long way away.

"He's in the Czech Republic."

"You were right, then."

"Yes. I found him on the Internet. Can you believe the arrogance of the guy? He didn't even change his name. He's got a new business, a new life." She hesitated. "A new woman. I e-mailed him."

"Did he reply?"

"Yes."

Seth still wouldn't turn around. "Is he coming home?"

She stared at the line of his spine, so straight, painfully straight. "Could you possibly believe that I would want that man back?"

"Melissa, I can't figure out what you want."

"I guess maybe I want closure. I want him to…" She petered out. The truth was she wasn't entirely certain what she wanted from Stephen. Or what was best for the kids. "I want him to take his responsibilities seriously. To pay what he owes us and…" And what?

"What did his e-mail say?" Seth turned back to look at her, at least, but he still had that remote expression on his face. She knew him well enough to understand he'd locked his feelings away behind that facade.

"He said he was sorry, that he'd been meaning to get in touch and threw in a bunch of excuses. He's going to figure something out, he says. He promised he'd take care of us."

For a second she glimpsed the swirl of anger and pain in Seth's eyes and then he clamped his emotions down once more. "And that's what you want?"

"Damn it, I want him to do what's right."

"What's right is for us to get married and make a family. Put aside our own problems and give those kids stability."

She gazed at him, wishing this could be easier. She wanted them to be happy so badly, she was almost tempted to take second best. But something stopped her. Maybe it was selfish to marry for love rather than convenience. If so, she was selfish. "I can't, Seth."

In the silence of the room, she could make out the noise of the television. Oh, God. How were they going to tell the kids?

"I—" She glanced up and the words died in her throat

when she saw his face, so pale and grim she wanted to reach out and make everything all better. Even though his hands were jammed in the pockets of his slacks, she could see they were fisted. He stared out the window, but it was pretty obvious he wasn't admiring the landscape. The younger Melissa, the naive one, would have gone to him. But not this Melissa. Not the woman who had finally learned her own worth.

She shut her mouth and silence ruled again.

Finally he jerked round to face her. "Just don't say anything for a few days. Will you do that?"

"But what's—"

"Please. All I ask is a few days."

He appeared so desperately in earnest that she agreed. It wouldn't change anything, but maybe the time would give her a chance to find a way out of this mess. Get things straightened out with Stephen so she could finally have the closure she needed. Yeah, and maybe Seth would throw a meet-Melissa cocktail party for his friends and co-workers.

Seth left soon after with his girls, and Melissa operated on autopilot, helping Matthew with his homework, getting dinner on the table, dishes done and the kids to bed. She felt shell-shocked. As though some horrible explosion had robbed her of her normal senses. But beneath the numbness, she was fully aware of the pain.

If she'd had any doubt before, she knew now, beyond the shadow of a doubt, that she loved Seth.

There was something else she'd learned in the last few months, as well, and that was that she would survive. All by herself, with no support from anyone. She could give her kids a home and she could make a life for herself.

Her little garden business was growing like chickweed.

She probably had enough work for at least the next year. And by then, Alice would be in kindergarten. With luck and hard work, she could make a go of it on her own.

Losing the love she thought she'd had was cruel. But, if it was only one-sided, it was doomed anyway.

MELISSA STOOD OUTSIDE THE storefront realty office and took a deep breath. Pam's pep talk was fresh in her mind. She could do this. She had nothing to lose.

The planter pots outside probably spilled over with geraniums and blue lobelia in the summer, but right now contained only a couple of dry-looking weeds and a few cigarette butts. They should be full of spring bulbs, she thought, her mind flashing painfully back to the tulip festival such a short time ago, when she'd so foolishly given her heart away. Even in winter, she could keep those pots looking inviting.

Somehow, those empty planters filled her with confidence and she put the same firm smile on her face that the Realtor had greeted her with when they'd first met.

"Hello," she said to the young woman at the reception counter. "I'm here to see Cindi. I have an appointment. I'm Melissa Theisen."

"Okay, I'll check—"

"Melissa. Great to see you," Cindi said, emerging from an office with her teeth gleaming and her hand extended. She glanced behind Melissa. "No Seth today?"

"No," Melissa said, keeping her smile intact and her voice steady. So she'd come under slightly false pretenses. She'd wanted to make sure of an early appointment.

"Well, come on in." If the woman noticed that Melissa carted a portfolio case with her, she gave no sign of it.

Cindi had a desk and computer in one corner of her office, but she motioned Melissa to a round table and padded chairs, then sat opposite. "Can I get you some coffee or tea or anything?"

"No. Thank you."

"Seth called me. He said you two had decided to slow things down a little. I'm sorry. I shouldn't have—"

"It wasn't your fault," Melissa interrupted. "We went into the whole thing too fast. I think we need to make absolutely sure we're doing the right thing before we go any further."

Cindi gazed at her for a moment, then said, "I sold Seth his current house, you know. When he and Claire were expecting the twins."

A shudder tickled her skin. Her mother used to say, "Somebody walked across your grave" when she shivered, but in this case, it was Claire's grave they were disturbing.

She glanced at Cindi, knowing the question was in her eyes but not wanting to ask it. "She was nothing like you. She was one of those bubbly people who talk a mile a minute. You could tell they were happy by the way they looked at each other. I remember thinking, this is one house I'm never going to have to put on the market because of a divorce."

"You were right." She smiled sadly.

Cindi sipped from a coffee mug, then grimaced. Melissa guessed the coffee was cold and she'd forgotten.

"Well, I'm sure you didn't come here to talk about that."

Melissa managed a chuckle. "No. I didn't come here to buy or sell a house, either."

"Too bad. That family I had in mind can't find anything they like. I drove them by your place and they loved it." She let a moment pass before suggesting, "With a little work, they could even make Seth's house work for them."

"I honestly don't know what's going to happen. We're both taking a breather right now and trying to figure things out."

"Well, keep me posted."

"I will, thanks." She took a breath and said, "I'm here on different business."

"A-ha."

With a flash of entrepreneurial zest, Melissa saw her opportunity to sell herself, and before she could talk herself out of it, said, "In fact, *you* could use *my* services."

The professional smile froze. "Really."

"Landscape design. That's what I do. You said yourself, it's easier to sell a house that looks good. I could shape up gardens on properties you're trying to sell."

"Did you do your own garden?" She had the woman's attention, now. And that patronizing *I don't think so* expression had been wiped off her face.

"Sure did. Front and back. I also did several other gardens in the neighborhood that you could look at. And they're finishing the planting this week on the display home near me." She placed her portfolio on the table. "Would you like to take a look at what I can do?"

Cindi pored over the portfolio. She nodded a couple of times. Murmured "Nice" when she got to the display home's garden.

Cinnamon nails drummed the tabletop. A businesswoman's excitement glowed on the Realtor's face. "Smart girl. I own the realty company, you know. Sometimes we mow lawns. I've been known to trim shrubbery myself to make a property more visible. Some people just have no idea how to make their homes look good." She was talking to herself now, Melissa could tell. "I could offer the service and tell clients I'll add the cost to my commission. Then they aren't out of pocket up front. And if the house doesn't sell, it's me who takes the loss. Not the homeowner."

"That's right. I could do a consultation, draw up a plan and let them do the work themselves—that would be the cheapest. Or, I could do it all for them."

"Do you have brochures?"

She shook her head. "I've got business cards. That's all. I've been working strictly on referrals and word of mouth, but I need to expand my business, especially if—" Especially if she was going to be on her own, but she didn't finish the sentence.

She didn't have to. Cindi knew. "I can't make any promises, you understand. I'd have to think about it and talk to some people. But I think you're on to something. Promise me you won't go to any other agents until I get back to you?"

Melissa opened her mouth to agree, then remembered she had a landscape design company to build. "I can wait until next week."

The hard mouth softened in a grin. "You'll do fine in business. I'll introduce you myself to the local business-women's network. I know a great company, two local gals, that do the most darling brochures. They do all my stuff."

Businesswomen's network. It had a nice ring to it. "Thanks, Cindi. If I ever do sell…"

And in that moment, it hit her. In her own way, she was hanging on to the ghosts of her past as badly as Seth was. Did she really want to start a new life with Seth or anyone in the house where so many memories of Stephen remained?

But that was the house where Matthew and Alice had lived their whole lives. What about those memories? And the love and time she'd put into her garden and the house?

And yet, she'd asked Seth to do exactly that. And his memories were a lot more poignant. Maybe she had to stop feeling threatened by the woman who'd loved Seth first and who'd brought the twins into the world. They weren't rivals. They ought to be a team.

She packed up her portfolio, then said fast, before she could change her mind, "I'm making no promises, but if your family would like to come through the house, I might consider an offer."

Cindi's eyes lit up. "Can I bring them by tomorrow?" At Melissa's nod, she hauled a cell phone out of her purse and in minutes a house tour was arranged for ten the next morning.

SETH PICKED THE GIRLS UP that afternoon, as he did every day after he was done work, and he and Melissa chatted briefly about the children's days. They tried to sound normal in front of the kids, but it wasn't easy. When she looked into his eyes, she saw the same confusion and hurt she imagined he was seeing in her own.

She didn't know how long she could keep doing this, seeing him every day when it hurt so much.

Alice decided to have a full-blown temper tantrum that night, and Matthew was stuck on the nine-times table and Melissa—who'd never been strong at math—was having to stop and think as she tried to test him. Some role model she was.

"Nine times nine," she yelled over Alice's howls of outrage. It was time for bed and she'd decided she wasn't going until Matthew went. Melissa knew her little girl was overtired, but it didn't make it any easier to listen to her scream.

"You keep asking me that one. Eighty-one," Matthew yelled back, a lot less bothered by the noise than his mother.

"That's because I'm sure of the answer. Look, keep memorizing the sheet and I'll test you after Alice is asleep." Which better be soon. She was worn out. Exhausted. She wanted that trip to Hawaii so badly she could taste the salt-tinged air and feel the warm breeze on her skin. And right now, she wanted to go alone.

She'd barely got the kids asleep and was sitting in the kitchen thinking she might never get up, when the phone rang.

"Hello?"

"Hi. It's me."

"Seth." Her insides went liquid with wanting—and sadness that it was all such a mess because they were both so scared.

There was a tiny silence rife with all the things they couldn't or wouldn't or didn't know how to say. Finally he said, "I miss you."

"Me, too."

"You sound tired," he said.

Oh, if she'd ever needed a shoulder to lean on, it was tonight.

"I had a rotten evening. Alice threw a temper tantrum and Matthew had trouble with his math."

"He should have called me. I'm a whiz at math. It's my thing."

She traced a pattern on the tabletop with her fingertip. "I don't think it's fair to Matthew to let him start relying on you. If…"

"I don't want to keep doing this. It's crazy. We can't go back to the way things were before, when we were practically strangers. I stand there in the doorway dropping off and collecting the girls and all I want to do is hold you. I can't pretend nothing happened with us."

"No. I can't either. It's too hard."

"Look. I've been thinking. It's a house. Who cares? I can't believe we're putting our future in jeopardy over a house."

She found she was clutching at the phone with both hands, hanging on for dear life. "It's not the house. Is it?"

A heavy sigh. "No."

"I think we rushed into things. We need some time to cool down and think it all through."

"I've had lots of time to think. We've known each other for months. We had a great time on our weekend. Our kids even like each other. How can we let this go?"

She sucked in a breath. "I've got a family coming tomorrow who might be interested in buying my house."

"You have?" He sounded shocked. "I thought we decided your place made more sense."

"I haven't even decided if I'm going to sell it yet. But I'm exploring the possibility of maybe being open to the idea," she said, trying for a light tone.

"It's tougher than you think to let go of the memories, isn't it?" he said after another silence.

"Yes."

"So, what are we going to do about Hawaii? The kids are already dragging out their summer clothes and arguing about what to pack."

She closed her eyes. "Why don't you take the girls and have a holiday?"

"Because I want us all to go. We could all have a holiday and put the wedding on hold."

"That doesn't make any sense. If we're not going to make it as a couple—"

"Don't you give up on us," he practically yelled. "I'm sorry I screwed up with the Realtor. I'm sorry about a lot of things. But don't give up. Not yet."

"I don't want to give up." She loved him so much it hurt, but she wasn't sure enough that he loved her. She had a feeling he wasn't sure, either.

"You won't come to Hawaii?"

"No. But you should—"

"If you're not going, none of us are going."

"I'm sorry." She looked around her quiet kitchen, at the cabinet door he'd fixed and the tile he'd replaced. Already he was part of her life and her home. How could she bear to lose him? "I think I'd better go. I've got some work to finish up."

"One last thing."

"What?"

"Are you still wearing your engagement ring?"

She glanced at the diamond winking from her left hand. "Yes."

"Good."

CHAPTER TWENTY-TWO

THE DOORBELL RANG AT precisely ten o'clock the next morning. The family that stood on her doorstep, along with Cindi, were perfect, Melissa had to admit, as she shook hands with the mother and father and children. After greeting the Realtor and her clients, she pretended she and Alice had to go out, unable to watch strangers going through her house, wondering if it would suit them.

After driving around the block, she snuck up to her neighbor Pam's, and while the kids played, the moms had coffee in the living room where they could watch what was going on at Melissa's house.

Pam wept a little. "It won't be the same without you."

Glumly, Melissa nodded. "I haven't decided anything yet."

Pam brightened at that.

"And the family seems really nice."

While they talked school, kids and gardening, they both kept an eye on the late-model SUV in Melissa's drive. "I don't care if they are nice people. Don't they know how much pollution those SUVs create? It's not like they have to cross a desert to get to the school or downtown Seattle from here." She clucked disapprovingly. "I could never be friends with anyone who drives one of those monsters."

"They've been in there a long time. They must be interested."

"Who wouldn't be?" her loyal friend said. "Your house is gorgeous. And the way you keep it." Pam waved a hand around her own cluttered living room, which Melissa had to coax herself not to dust every time she entered. "Your garden, too. Which reminds, me, Sheila Westover—do you know her? She's got two boys at the school."

"Is she the one who's always organizing those political fund-raising dinners?"

"Used to. Now she's a Buddhist."

Melissa almost spewed coffee all over the carpet. "A Buddhist?"

"She found a truer path to enlightenment, I guess. Anyway, she wants to turn her garden into a meditation center. I gave her your phone number."

"Gee, thanks."

"Hey, it's work. Anyway, she's probably kept a lot of her old contacts. You never know."

But Melissa had stopped listening. "Look, there they go."

Pam craned her neck to get a better view of her potential new neighbors. "That boy looks the same age as Josh and Matthew," she said, gleefully. "Maybe they'll be friends." Presumably, she was rethinking her position on SUV owners.

Cindi waved as the family drove off, then returned to the house. "I think she's waiting for me. What if they want to make an offer? I feel sick."

"You don't have to do anything you don't want to."

Melissa felt foolish. "Yeah. I know. For some reason, it's just so hard to say goodbye to that part of my life."

Her friend's eyes flooded in ready sympathy.

"Anyhow, even if I don't sell my house, I might get some

work from the real estate agent. I think I have more entrepreneurial spirit than I ever knew." Briefly, she relayed yesterday's conversation with Cindi.

"All right!"

"I'd better go. She's obviously waiting."

"Leave Alice. I'll watch her."

"I can't let you keep babysitting for me."

"Hah. I'm holding her hostage. That way you'll have to come and tell me what happened."

As she walked the short distance home, Melissa felt the colony of butterflies in her stomach morph into elephants.

"I've got good news," Cindi sang from Melissa's front door, waving a clump of papers in her thin hand.

The elephants started to stampede.

"They want to offer. I told them you're reluctant to sell so they've given me the top price they can afford." The woman practically crowed like a rooster as she named a dollar figure that made Melissa's eyes bug out. She knew prices had risen in her neighborhood, but not that high. She could put some of the money into her business.

"When? When would they want it?"

"They want to be all moved in before school starts in September. Lots of time."

"Can I have a few days to think about it?"

"Obviously, they're anxious to get things settled. They have to go back to California and sell their house. He's been transferred up here."

"I understand. Give me two days?"

"Sure. Now. About that other matter. I talked with some of my agents and everybody likes the idea of being able to offer your services to our clients. Exclusively, you understand."

Melissa's head was whirling. The woman in front of her was a deal-making machine. From one project to the next with lightning speed. She realized she'd better learn the technique if she was going to make a success of her own business. She managed a noncommittal "Uh-huh," and tried to shift her thoughts from the fear of finding herself imminently homeless, to business wheeling and dealing.

"I'll put up the money to get a brochure done that will describe your services and include our logo and a short blurb. I want to get right on this. Also—"

"I'll want creative control of the brochure," Melissa interrupted.

A beat went by. "Naturally."

All right. Score one for me, she thought gleefully. By the time they'd hammered out a plan, Melissa was feeling euphoric about her new-found skills. And there was a lightness in her chest, like a weight had been lifted.

It wasn't till later, when Cindi had left and she wandered the quiet house once more, that she realized it was the weight of the house itself that had been lifted. The worry, and hopeless aim to keep a house she couldn't afford and that didn't fit her anymore, was over. In that moment she realized she'd made up her mind. She was moving on.

That night, she was the one who called Seth.

"Hey," she said. "How's it going?"

"All right. You?"

She took a deep breath. "We need to tell the kids that we're not going to Hawaii."

"I have a better idea. We go. We get married. We can make this work."

"I can't marry you if I don't believe you love me," she

said, feeling a pain in her chest, as though her heart was literally breaking.

"I do love you. What the hell am I supposed to do to prove it?"

"I don't know," she whispered.

There was another of those awful pauses that punctuated their conversations ever since the day Cindi had first shown up in her driveway. Finally, he said in a low, expressionless tone, "All right."

"MELISSA, YOU HAVE TO marry Dad. We have to go to Hawaii."

Her heart went out to the little girl scowling at her. Laura's eyes were puffy and dark-circled. Too much crying and not enough sleep, Melissa diagnosed the problem without a second's hesitation, knowing she suffered the same ailment. "I'm sorry, honey." She held out her arms, but the older twin took a step backward and scowled even more fiercely.

"You promised! You said we'd be a family. We painted our room."

"It hurts me, too." And it had hurt to see Seth's face this morning when he'd dropped the girls off. Where the twins' stormy expressions gave away all their feelings, his face gave nothing away. He'd locked up all his emotions.

If she'd expected that he might try to win her back at seven forty-five in the morning, in her driveway, she was wrong.

He was in the car, backing down the drive, the kids all in the house when she ran to the car and motioned for him to roll down the window.

"Did you tell them Hawaii's off?"

He nodded. For a second, the blank expression cracked, and she had a glimpse of a man in pain. Then the mask was intact again.

There was half an hour before she had to walk the kids to school. It was going to be a very long thirty minutes.

Maybe another cup of coffee would help.

"You're a bum-head and I don't want you for my sister anyway," Matthew shouted. So much for that peaceful cup of coffee. She ran into the hallway and saw him halfway up the stairs, his face beet-red and his arms waving wildly.

Alice was crying noisily. Jessie sat slumped and quiet on the hall stairs. And Laura, equally red in the face, was about to answer Matthew in kind.

"Stop," Melissa commanded. Her own heartbreak had to be put on hold for now, while she dealt with the very real pain in the young faces all around her.

She picked up Alice and crooned softly.

"But she called me—" Matthew blustered.

"He said—" Laura shouted.

"Stop," she ordered again, in the voice that brooked no arguments. When she was certain the imminent battle was defused, she shepherded all four into the kitchen.

The three older ones sat stiffly on chairs around the table, while Alice clung to Melissa's leg in a way she hadn't for a long time. It took some soothing words that almost choked in her throat, a few animal crackers and some juice before Alice would sit at the table, sniffing quietly.

Melissa prepared three cups of hot chocolate and then poured herself that much-needed cup of coffee. Then she broke one of her rules and put a plate of chocolate chip cookies in the middle of the table. So they ate cookies at eight o'clock in the morning for once. What the hell.

Although she felt a ripple of surprise flow round the table, it was a measure of their distress that not one of the kids reached for a cookie. Glancing at each face in turn, she read shock, anger, fear, disbelief…and from Laura, glaring back at her, blame. Keeping her gaze on the elder twin she said simply, "I'm so sorry about Hawaii. I know how much everyone was looking forward to going." Her voice wavered piteously, and she swallowed hard.

For an instant she glimpsed the naked hurt in the child's eyes, then it was gone. "That's crap."

"Laura."

"My dad still wants to marry you. He said so, and *he* never lies. It's you. You don't want us."

"I do. I do want you. This has nothing to do with you and Jessie. But sometimes adults make mistakes." She stopped to regain control of her voice. "Your dad and I…" What? What could she tell them? She was terrified she couldn't compare to their dead mother? Horribly afraid he was marrying her for convenience? "We need to take more time. It's too soon."

"You pretended you loved him."

"I do love him."

Laura still glared, Jessie had yet to say a word, and Matthew hadn't lost the belligerent, perplexed expression he'd worn ever since she'd explained to him that they weren't going to Hawaii after all.

"If you love him, why don't you get married?" Laura challenged.

"It's not that easy."

"I'm never getting married. It sucks." Laura stared into her hot chocolate. "No Hawaii, no Bravo Boys concert. The whole thing sucks."

Ignoring Laura, Matthew glowered at his mother, his color blazing once again. "We have to go to Hawaii. The kids at school'll call me a liar."

"We'll go."

"When?"

She sniffed miserably. "I don't know, honey. Maybe next year?"

"Next year?" He stormed to his feet, a study in impotent fury. "You're all a bunch of boogers." Then he stomped out of the kitchen.

"I wanna go Hawaii," Alice wailed, snuggling deeper.

"Well, that went well. Call us next time you want another one of these little talks." And with a jerk of her chin, Laura left the table, followed meekly by the still-silent Jessie.

With a sigh, Melissa reached for a chocolate chip cookie.

"I DON'T BELIEVE IT," Pam said in a voice of amazement.

"Don't believe what?"

"You have a butter mold. And it's used—I think."

Melissa pulled a foil sack of coffee beans from the freezer. "Of course it's used. It makes a really elegant star-shaped butter pat. I've also got a fleur-de-lis mold somewhere in that drawer. I don't entertain anymore. Why don't you take them?"

"No. Really. A tub of margarine in the middle of the table is as elegant as I get." She replaced the butter mold and got the coffee spoons out of the drawer. Then she reached for the mugs. They'd done this so often, they had an unspoken ritual.

"I don't know what I'd do without you, Pam."

"Are things any better with the kids?"

Melissa made a face. "Armed neutrality. The twins barely speak to me, Matthew's rude and uncooperative, and Alice pretty much whines every second she's not sleeping."

"It'd be nice to ship them off to camp."

"Huh. Camp David maybe. Someplace where we could figure out how to declare a truce. Maybe I'm not going to be their stepmother, but I love those girls."

She poured the beans into the grinder. After the machine had finished roaring, she measured the freshly ground coffee into the coffeemaker and added cold water.

"And the bodacious banker?"

"He barely glances at me when he brings the girls and picks them up. He treats me like some evil home wrecker."

"Are you?"

"What?" Melissa slopped the milk she was pouring into a jug on the counter.

"I wonder if maybe you panicked. That's all."

The milk puddle blurred before her eyes. "Maybe. It's like we're locked into this pattern and neither of us knows how to get to the next stage, you know?"

"Yeah. I appreciate your scruples, but I'm not sure it would have ruined those kids forever if you'd gone ahead to Hawaii and tried a family vacation. Maybe you'd find out he really does love you."

"I don't know. I already lost one husband to another woman. I'm not going to marry a man who's in love with a ghost." She poured two aromatic cups of coffee, passed one and then drank from her own.

"He offered to move in here," her neighbor reminded her.

"And then I could feel guilty forever more for taking them away from all their good memories. I'm not that awful a person. I'm not."

"Life." Pam shook her head.

She stared out at the rain drizzling down the kitchen window pane. "We would have been on our way to Hawaii in a few days. With the family."

"I can understand you throwing over a handsome, successful man, but giving up two weeks in Hawaii?" Pam shook her head in mock despair.

Melissa gave the requisite chuckle. "Think of the money I saved on sunscreen."

BEFORE THE KIDS WERE expected home, Melissa brushed her hair and freshened her makeup. It was silly, but her mother had always done it and somehow she'd fallen into the habit, too.

In the mirror's reflection, she noticed how tired her face appeared. A couple of lines she'd never noticed before had taken up permanent residence between her eyebrows. She was exhausted. Not only was she trying to police a war zone, she was the proud owner of her own business. Complete with business cards, brochures and letterhead from the ultra-efficient Cindi. If she hadn't begged for mercy, she'd also be the proud owner of a Web site.

And when she had little time for business, the calls had started to increase. Financially, she needed the work and somewhere deep down in her entrepreneurial soul, she was thrilled by each call. But the toll of trudging out to job sites, dredging up enthusiasm and enough creativity to wow clients and design fabulous gardens was leaving her seriously depleted.

The irony was that her favorite current project had turned out to be the meditation garden. The part of her that craved quiet and peace and contemplative solitude yearned for such a place to escape to. And so it was easy to imagine the little trickling fountain, exactly there. The small stone bench here, under the shade of this maple. The lavender there, where its scent would soothe the soul.

And, in between work, she pretended she didn't notice Laura's sarcasm, Jessie's pained silence, Matthew's boisterous rudeness or Alice's whining. The children were working out their feelings. She tried to respect that.

And Seth's brooding anger. Which she knew was directed at himself as much as her.

As for her own feelings, she'd tried to push them into a mental cupboard until she had time for them. Mostly, she was so busy they stayed locked up. But every once in a while, like now, she'd feel the overwhelming sadness.

She picked up Alice from play school and drove home in a daze. What had she done? Was she really considering selling her home? She walked in and prepared lunch and then the girls went downstairs to the playroom.

She was tidying the hall closet when the phone rang. Maybe it was Cindi canceling. But no, the woman's voice said, "Is this Melissa Theisen?"

"Yes."

"This is Janice, Seth's sister."

"Janice. How are you?"

"I'm fine. Listen, I get off early today. I'd love to buy you a coffee somewhere and, um, talk."

Seth's sister wanted to talk to her? "Can I ask what it's about?"

A low laugh came through the phone. "It's about my lunkhead of a brother."

"I can't leave the house. My daughter's napping. Would you like to come here for coffee?"

"Sure. That would be fine." She took the address and told Melissa she'd be there in fifteen minutes.

Melissa ran into the kitchen and put coffee on. There were muffins left from breakfast, so she threw a few in a basket and got out napkins and cups. She felt like she'd had a lot of emotional conversations lately over coffee. Now she was entertaining Seth's sister? What if the woman was coming to yell at her?

Well, she thought, she might just yell back.

But when Janice arrived ten minutes later, she didn't look as though she was going to yell. She was dressed in black wool trousers and a blue blazer and she held a box of chocolates in her hand, which she pushed toward Melissa with a wry grimace. "I had no idea what to bring you, but chocolate always seems appropriate."

Melissa laughed, sensing that a chocolate offering meant she wasn't going to be yelled at. "Thanks, come on in."

"I hope you don't mind me calling. Seth would kill me if he knew I was interfering." The flicker of hope that Seth had sent his sister to mediate on his behalf died.

"I've got coffee on in the kitchen."

"Wonderful. Wow, your house is beautiful."

"Thanks."

Melissa fussed around with coffee and muffins and Janice waited until she was sitting. Then she said, "I know this is pushy of me, and you can throw me out any time, but I wanted to beg you to give my brother another chance."

A feeling like an electric shock zapped through her. "He told you what happened?"

Janice leaned forward looking anxious. "Please don't think he was being disloyal. The thing is, we've always been close and I could see he was upset, so he told me you guys were having trouble."

"Trouble? Janice, I can't believe he told you about us. Frankly, you're the only person he has told. I feel like some dirty secret in his life." She blew out a breath.

"You've known him a lot longer, but I was there when we cleaned out Claire's room. I knew then. I should have known. He was still in denial about her death."

Janice squeezed her hands together. They were plump and freckled, the kind of hands that could soothe a crying child or write for hours on a chalkboard. A teacher's hands. "He's come a long way since he met you."

"I can never be Claire," she cried. "I'm jealous of a dead woman."

The other woman reached forward suddenly and touched her hand. "No. You're nothing like her." She studied Melissa. "You're obviously a more reserved person. Maybe a little more serious. And you're right. He loved Claire with all his heart." She swallowed and her voice grew hoarse. "We all loved Claire. She was like the sister I never had. And when they looked at each other you felt their love. But you know what's funny? When you and Seth look at each other, I get the same feeling from you two. I thought to myself, after I met you, I can't believe he got that lucky twice. And when we worked together that day cleaning out her room, I thought, maybe I'm going to get another sister." She sniffed and Melissa passed her a box of tissues, then pulled out one for herself.

"I never had a sister, either."

"I know he's hopeless, but please don't give up on him yet. He loves you."

"He didn't tell anybody he works with. None of his friends. He didn't tell anybody about me. How can he love me and hide me away like that?"

"He's never been a man to wear his heart on his sleeve. He's more like you, reserved." Janice plucked another tissue out of the box. "When Claire was dying, those terrible last months, he still went to the office every day. He did his job and I doubt any of the customers even noticed anything was wrong. That's the kind of man he is. It doesn't mean he doesn't have deep feelings just because he doesn't show them."

"I don't know, Janice. I'm so terrified of making another mistake."

"I think that's what's really bothering you. More than the house or Seth not telling people. You're scared."

Melissa blinked at her.

"Hey, I'm not criticizing. I'd be scared, too. It's not easy trusting someone to love you forever. But what if it's possible?"

"What if?"

"By the way, our parents are dying to meet you. They wanted to book Hawaii, as well, to be there for the wedding."

She felt her eyes widen. "They did?"

"Sure. Seth told them it's immediate family only. But they can come to the garden party to celebrate your marriage."

"He actually phoned his parents and told them about me? You're not telling me that to make me feel better, are you?"

Janice pulled out a cell phone and even as Melissa waved her hands and protested, she hit a button and the next thing Melissa knew, Seth's sister was saying, "Hi, Mom, it's Janice. I'm here with Melissa Theisen. Of course she wants to talk to you." And she passed over the phone.

"Ah, hello," she said.

"Hello, Melissa. I'm so happy to make your acquaintance. I've written you a letter to let you know how pleased we are that you'll be joining the family. But a phone call is much better."

She sounded a lot like Janice, so Melissa imagined Janice, only older. "It's nice to talk to you."

"I'll get my husband on the extension." Then she yelled, "Van? Van! It's Melissa on the phone. Seth's fiancée."

Within five minutes, Melissa knew that Janice took after her mother and Seth was more like his dad. One was all chatter and plans, the other quiet but sensible. They'd heard so much about her, they said. They couldn't wait to meet her.

They didn't care when the garden party was, they were coming up soon after the Hawaii trip for a visit.

"I'll look forward to it," said Melissa, realizing that Seth had told them the wedding was on but not that it had been postponed. Melissa hadn't mentioned the delay, either.

When she disconnected, she glanced at Janice. "I think I need one of those chocolates."

AFTER JANICE LEFT, MELISSA picked up the phone to call Seth. But she put it down again. She needed some time to think about this. Maybe she'd suggest they set a wedding date for six months away. Give them both time to get used to the idea.

She cleaned up the coffee things and set out cookies, juice and fruit for the kids' snack.

Maybe this can still work, she thought as she heard the front door slam. The kids were late but she wasn't going to start an argument. "Hi," she called out.

"Hi, Mom."

There was a rule that the older kids all had to walk home together. Puzzled, she moved toward the front door where Matthew was kicking his shoes off into the hall closet. He knew she hated him to do that. "Where are the girls?"

"I dunno. They never showed."

She counted to ten. "You know I don't like you walking home alone. You should have waited for them. Maybe they were kept in after school."

"Nope. I went to their class and checked. They left before me."

Unease fluttered in her belly. "If they left before you, why aren't they here yet?"

"I don't know. Those girls in their class are all nuts. All of them were yapping on about the big concert tonight."

Her legs suddenly felt boneless. She slumped to a sitting position on the stairs. "Oh, no. Not the Bravo Boys."

"Oh, yes. The Bra-avo Boys," he mimicked the white-clad crooners. Any other time Melissa would have laughed at the impression. But not today.

A surge of panic wiped her mind blank. What to do? Where to begin? Then reason reasserted itself. There was no cause to believe the girls had gone to the concert. Where would they have got the tickets? How were they planning to get to downtown Seattle and the Key Arena? How would they have pulled something like this off without raising her suspicions?

Then she remembered the hostility. They'd been simmering ever since they found out the wedding was off. And she hadn't exactly been her usual perceptive self, either. She wouldn't have registered strange behavior as anything more than the anger she knew they felt.

"Matthew, did the twins say anything to you?"

"'Bout what?"

"About coming home late today? Or…uh…anything?"

"No. But they gave me a note. At lunchtime."

"Well, why didn't you—" She took a breath. Shouting at Matthew wouldn't help. "Can I see it?"

He dug through his backpack and hauled out a crumpled piece of foolscap with a smear of jam at the top. It was addressed to Melissa.

Hey, Melissa.
   Don't worry. Me and Jessie are going to the Bravo Boys concert tonight. We know how to get there and everything. Tell Dad we will get home late. We are writing this note so you won't worry or get too mad at us.
Yours truly,
Jessie and Laura O'Reilly

"Oh, my God," she said, leaping off the steps and running to the phone.

CHAPTER TWENTY-THREE

"SETH!"

"Hmm?" The way Mitzi's voice had sharpened, he had a feeling it wasn't the first time she'd called his name.

"I've got the layouts for the new brochure. Do you have a minute?"

"Sure. In fact, you're exactly the person I wanted to see."

"That's unusual," she muttered, placing the mock-up on his desk.

He glanced at the thing. "That looks great, Mitzi."

"Are you feeling all right? You always hate everything I do."

"No, I don't. We have differing opinions from time to time. You do a fine job." He smiled warmly. He'd been smiling warmly at everyone today. And the reactions had shocked him. From puzzled looks to nervous grins to Mitzi here, with her mouth hanging open. It gave him the uncomfortable feeling that he might have been less than pleasant the last few days.

"You go out a lot. What's the most romantic restaurant you know?"

"La Pergole." A dimple appeared. "So that's why you've been so weird lately."

"Sorry about that."

"You had a fight and you want to make up?"

"Yeah."

"That's so romantic. No wonder you've been such a grouch." Her face brightened in a playful grin. "As soon as you initial your approval on this brochure you like so much, I'll give you directions. It was written up in 'Best Places to Kiss in the Pacific Northwest.'"

He ignored the blackmail and signed. "Best Places to Kiss"…that sounded good. "How's the food?" Like he cared.

"Mouth watering. You'll kiss and make up before dessert. At least I hope so, for all our sakes."

"I'm sorry I've been kind of…uh…grumpy. It's been a tough couple of—"

The phone shrilled insistently on his desk. He frowned. Stella always held his calls when there was someone with him. Unless it was important. "Excuse me," he muttered to Mitzi. "Seth O'Reilly here."

"Seth. It's Melissa."

Pleasure coursed through him at the sound of her voice. "Melissa, I was just thinking about you."

"I'm so sorry, Seth." She sounded near tears. He made bye-bye motions to Mitzi, who was eagerly listening in.

"I'm sorry, too, honey." Mitzi gave him a thumbs-up and waltzed out with her signed layout.

"Did they leave you a note?"

"Who? What note?" He reached for the extra strength antacid pills his doctor had recently prescribed.

"Oh, God, Seth. It's the girls. They've gone to the Bravo Boys Concert."

"They what?" he shouted, jerking to his feet.

"I—they sent home a note with Matthew. I'm going to drive down to the stadium and try to find them." She had that super-calm voice he remembered from the first day he'd met her when the twins had been so sick. But now that he knew her better, he heard a quaver underneath the calm.

"Don't move. I'll be there in ten minutes."

He sprinted out of his office. "Stella, if the twins call, find out where they are, tell them to stay put, and call me immediately on my cell."

"Trouble?" the startled woman asked.

But he was already through the stairwell door and he didn't pause. Oh, yeah, there was trouble.

When he pulled up at Melissa's house, Matthew and Alice were waiting outside with their coats on. "He's here, Mom," the boy shouted through the open door.

Seconds later, Melissa appeared with her coat and purse, and locked the door behind her. He couldn't believe it. She wasn't planning on bringing a couple of little kids on a manhunt, was she?

Her eyes were wide and anxious as she opened the rear door of the Volvo.

"Wait. Melissa, they'll slow us down." He motioned to Alice, already half in the backseat.

Her tragic eyes widened. "I don't—I'll take my car. We'll meet you there."

But he couldn't do it. He'd only be worried about her and her kids as well as his own two. "No. Get in."

She hesitated.

"Please." He got out and opened the other rear door for Matthew.

She nodded briefly and within a minute they were on their way. "I called the school, but no one there knew anything, except they were at school all day, so they don't have too much of a head start." She was calm.

Businesslike. Whatever fear she was feeling, she had it under control. "I also called the bus line while I was waiting for you. I have the probable route they took. If we can overtake the bus, that's our best chance."

She didn't explain, and she didn't have to. If that concert wasn't sold out, it was damned close. Tens of thousands of concert goers would be milling around. He pictured drinking, drugs, even a riot. Anything could happen. If they could nab the girls before they got off the bus... He pressed down on the accelerator.

He could practically hear Melissa's teeth grinding in the seat next to him. Momentarily, he'd forgotten Alice and Matthew in the backseat. Ashamed of taking foolish risks with those he loved, he slowed the car.

She gave him directions to help him track the bus route, and he followed them.

"I think that's it." Melissa said beside him.

And sure enough, ahead of them was a bus. He pulled in behind and followed it. The tension in the car was palpable as they followed the lumbering vehicle. Several blocks went by before the bus signaled.

"It's stopping," Melissa said.

He nodded. "If there's a place to park—"

Already she was grasping the handle. "Pull in behind. I'll go."

So he did. And she did. After several tense minutes of waiting she returned. Alone. Her head shake was pretty unnecessary under the circumstances.

He watched the bus pull away as she slipped back into the seat beside him. "Given the timing, the driver thinks they've probably already reached Seattle Center. He's going to try to get hold of the other drivers and if anyone remembers the girls, they'll call your cell."

He nodded. Grim. Knowing she was as worried as he was. And that he could trust her completely. She couldn't love them more if she were their biological mother. The thought didn't even surprise him, the way it would have a few months ago. He pulled away from the curb. "Should we call the police?"

"Won't there be police outside the concert? For crowd control?" There was an awkward pause before she resumed, with false brightness. "Not that they'll be hard to spot. Redheaded twins."

"Are Laura and Jessie getting arrested?" Matthew asked hopefully from the back.

"I'm thinking about it."

"Cool. Maybe they'll be on 'America's Most Wanted.'"

He shot a glance at Melissa and they exchanged a look—the kind of look that parents everywhere swap when a kid says something outrageous. There was a world of unspoken communication in that glance. Understanding and the kind of intimacy shared by parents who work long and hard raising children together. He pulled his gaze back to the road, but not before he'd seen her small, reassuring smile. "It'll be okay," that smile said. He had to believe it.

Apart from Alice getting all excited every time they passed a bus—she'd picked up that this was somehow a very special event—the rest of the drive passed in virtual silence. As they drew closer to the stadium, the traffic got heavier, the sidewalks and crosswalks were thronged with people, scruffy-looking deadbeats most of them, as far as Seth was concerned. And bus after bus came from all directions. "What the hell were they thinking?" he finally roared in mingled frustration and terror.

She didn't murmur any safe platitudes, merely reached over to squeeze his hand in sympathy and support. He felt the trembling in her palm and knew she was as anxious as he was.

The traffic was hardly crawling, and somewhere out there with all the riffraff, druggies, drunks and perverts were his precious daughters. He couldn't sit there. "Take the wheel Melissa. I'm going to flag down a cop and get some help."

"Yes. All right."

"Everybody got their doors locked back there?" He craned his neck around and checked to be certain.

"I hate to leave you like this," he said to the outwardly calm woman at his side.

"No. You're right. We can search different areas. Let's make a time and place to meet."

"No. Honey, take the kids home. I'll call you."

"We're not leaving, Seth."

"But—" His cell phone rang. With a quick glance at Melissa he answered, "Seth O'Reilly."

"Daddy," a small scared voice said, bringing an immediate lump to his throat.

"Red. You okay?"

"Yes. We're so sorry, Dad. We didn't—"

"It's okay, baby. Where are you?"

"At McDonald's," she sniffled.

He glanced up, and hallelujah, there it was a few blocks ahead. He'd never been so glad to see those golden arches in his life. "Is it the one near the stadium?"

"Uh-huh."

"Is Jessie with you?"

"Yeah."

"We're on our way. Stay put."

Through the aggressive use of his horn and by shouting the word *emergency* out the window until he was hoarse, he managed to cut his way through the jammed cars. Of course, the restaurant parking lot was full when he finally got there.

"Go on in. I'll park. We'll join you in a few minutes," Melissa said.

"I can see them in the window," Matthew piped up. "Look." And there they were. Two identical curly red heads, in identical dejected poses slumped at a table near the window.

All the relief he felt was mirrored in Melissa's eyes. He didn't have time to say everything he wanted. He leaned over and kissed her lips swiftly. "See you inside."

She was flustered and blushing. He grinned as she pulled away. Then stowed the grin as he marched toward the restaurant.

"Hey, Red," he said softly as he approached.

The twin heads flew up and both girls threw themselves at him. "We're sorry, Dad."

"Please don't be mad."

He hugged them both tightly, not sure which of the three of them was trembling hardest. "I'm glad you're safe. We've been worried sick."

"We?" Laura searched behind him.

"Melissa and the kids are with me. She's parking the car. We started tracking you the minute she got your note."

"I'm sure glad we left that note," Jessie said.

"We weren't going to," Laura admitted.

"Let's all sit down again and you can tell me about it." He sat on the hard plastic chair and listened.

The confession was halting at first. They'd won four tickets from the radio contest. "We wanted to surprise you and Melissa and take you to the concert," Laura said. He'd told them to their faces about fifty times that they were too young for a rock concert, but he refrained from reminding them of that now.

"Then, when we were going to Hawaii we figured we wouldn't be able to go. I mean, I guess you guys getting married and us going to Hawaii is more important than one Bravo Boys concert." He had to hide a smile—she sounded pretty unsure of the equality of the trade-off.

Laura seemed to have stalled, so Jessie took up the tale. "Then you weren't getting married anymore, and it was so awful. Everybody was mad at everybody and we figured you'd say no if we asked again." She shrugged, guilt written all over her face. "So we didn't ask."

"What made you change your mind about going through with it?"

They both blushed. Laura finally spoke. "On the bus it was fun, but when we got here it was awfully crowded. There were lots of kids, but they all had grown-ups with them." She looked at her sister, as if wondering how to proceed.

"Then this guy came up to us," Jessie continued. "He was weird. And he smelled—you know how Uncle Fred used to smell before he started going to AA?"

The familiar burning started deep in his gut. He nodded, dreading what might be coming.

"He hung around and kept trying to talk to us. He said stuff about 'little twinnies' and how he likes redheads cause they're so hot. We were totally grossed out. Then Laura yelled, 'Hi Dad.' I was scared because I knew you'd be mad at us, but she grabbed my hand and started running. It wasn't you. It was somebody else's dad, but we tagged along behind them and pretended we were with them. They came in here, then we hid in the bathroom. We didn't come out for a long time, but the weirdo wasn't here."

"But we were too scared to go back on the street. So we called you."

There was a pause, while he searched for the right words to say. "You were wrong, girls. You know that, don't you?"

Mute nods.

"You've learned firsthand why Melissa and I refused to let you come."

"But lots of families are together. It would have been okay if you guys had come with us."

"But not alone," he reminded her sternly. "I guess you've learned your lesson, though. It wasn't very pleasant what happened tonight, was it?"

Mute head shakes this time.

"I'm also proud of you." The heads jerked up, identical questioning looks on their faces. "You handled a difficult situation very well. That was smart of you, Laura, to attach yourself to a family. And even smarter to call me and stay here until I arrived."

"I love you, Daddy."

"Me, too."

A great wave of tenderness engulfed him. "Me, too," he replied a little huskily.

CHAPTER TWENTY-FOUR

"HOLD MY HAND TIGHTLY, Matthew. We don't want to lose you, too." Melissa let the crowd sweep them along. She had Alice in one arm and Matthew hanging on to the other hand. The golden arches were like a mirage shimmering in the distance. She'd finally found a parking lot that wasn't full, but between the crowds headed for Seattle Center, the one-way streets that she could never keep straight, and her general level of stress, she doubted she'd found the closest spot.

She consoled herself, and her aching shoulders, with the thought that Seth would have more time alone with his daughters before she and her kids intruded. After all, it wasn't like she was anything more in their lives than the temporary babysitter now.

Except for that odd kiss, a little voice reminded her.

That was relief, she explained it away.

And he called you honey, the voice continued.

It was a moment of stress, she countered.

But she couldn't explain away the fact that she and Seth had acted like an experienced mom-and-dad team all through the crisis. And it was a good team, too.

"Can we go to McDonald's house?" Alice chirped when she saw the familiar yellow *M.*

"Can I have a Big Mac?" Matthew added.

She couldn't remember the last time they'd eaten at a place like this. "We'll see," she said. A lot depended on how Seth and the girls were doing.

When they finally reached the door, it opened magically, and there was Seth, precious and familiar, standing there with an expression on his face that made her heart do a funny kind of lurch. He eased Alice out of her arms.

"I asked for a Big Mac, but Mom said 'we'll see,'" Matthew informed him. He caught sight of the girls. "Hey, did you guys get arrested?" he yelled across the crowded restaurant.

Seth laughed, looking years younger than he had an hour earlier and way too sexy for her peace of mind. "Do you mind if we eat here?"

"No. The kids'll love it."

"I had somewhere more intimate in mind for tonight, but…" He shrugged.

More intimate? Who with? The way he was gazing at her, her first guess had to be it was her he'd hoped to spend an intimate evening with. But then, why had he given her no indication that morning when he'd barely looked her way as he'd dropped off the children?

It was a puzzle. As was his good mood after the atrocious stunt the twins had pulled. "Where are you parked?"

"Somewhere in Canada, I think."

He laughed again, shepherding her to where his daughters had Matthew enthralled with their tale of adventure. Alice insisted on sitting with the other kids and, since the table seated only four, Melissa and Seth sat at the next table, munching burgers and fries and Cokes while Seth filled her in.

"I was so scared in the car when I saw all the drug pushers and derelicts heading this way."

"The band's not exactly Megadeth, Seth. I saw lots of families and young children on our way here."

He licked a dab of ketchup from the corner of his mouth, looking thoughtful. "The girls have four tickets, already. I wonder, now that we're here..."

She nodded. "I think they were punished enough just experiencing such a fright. They'd be so thrilled to see the concert."

"And you?" He grinned.

"I wish I'd brought my earplugs."

"Will Alice be all right?"

"She had a long nap this afternoon. And she knows those Bravo Boy songs by heart."

"Right. Don't say anything yet. I'll run across and see if I can get two extra tickets."

"You know you'll be paying scalper prices?"

"Don't remind me."

She watched him stride out, tall and confident, and a pang of sadness pierced her. He was exactly the man she would choose, if only she could be certain he was free to be hers.

With a hopeless sigh, she drank the last of her cola and cleaned away the remains of their meals. After that, she insisted all the kids take a bathroom break and wash up. By the time they'd finished doing that, Seth had returned and given her a thumbs-up.

He didn't say anything, merely held the two tickets out in his hand and waited. Laura clued in first and gave a shriek that stilled conversation in the restaurant. "You mean we can go?"

"Melissa and I decided you've learned your lesson. And,

since we're all here now, anyway…" The girls, then Matthew threw themselves at Seth. Alice, who hated to be left out, followed suit. He swung her up in his arms and the six of them headed out.

"We won't be able to sit together," Melissa warned Seth in an undervoice. "We should decide now who—"

He stopped her with a kiss. "Have faith."

She hadn't been big on that lately. Maybe she'd give faith a try.

And sure enough, when they got to the crowded arena and found their way to the four seats the twins had won, Seth went ahead and she saw him chatting to a couple of teenagers who obviously had the adjoining seats. By the time Melissa and the kids reached him, he had six seats together.

"How on earth did you get those kids to change seats with you?"

"I told them we need to be together because we're a family," he said, looking at her in a way that made her heart flip. "And then I gave them a hundred bucks."

Melissa hadn't been to a concert in years, and, in spite of herself, got caught up in the enthusiasm. To her mind, the Bravo Boys in concert were as nauseating as they appeared on TV, only bigger. And louder. A lot louder.

But the kids' enthusiasm was infectious, and when "Born To Be Bravo" finally came on, they all joined in. Seth caught her eye and mimicked the movements of the lead singer, making her stop singing as a giggle choked her.

He grinned, and behind the backs of their own singing and dancing quartet, pulled her close. Surprise widened her eyes. "Thanks for being a good sport," he said, and kissed her.

Her heart started banging in time to the band's frantic

percussion, and the kiss—which had started out friendly—deepened suddenly. They were grasping each other, gripping and hugging wordlessly while the music blared around them. The cacophony created a sort of intimacy, since it was impossible to be heard. "I missed you," he yelled into her ear.

"Me, too," she shouted back.

They left when Alice began to droop. The concert wasn't over, and yet there wasn't a peep of protest from the three older kids. They really had learned a lesson tonight.

The walk back to the car didn't seem so long with Seth carrying the sleepy Alice, and soon they were all buckled in and driving home. For the first little while it was almost as noisy inside the car as it had been at the concert.

"That fireworks thing was so cool."

"He saw me, I know he did—I did that Bra-avo arm thing, and Benny did it right back at me."

"I bet they got paid a million bucks. At least."

"Who cares, Matthew. You are so lame."

"Not as lame as gushing over some guy with dyed hair and earrings," her stung son retorted.

And so it went on as they drove through Seattle and headed for Lakeview. Slowly, the energy level depleted, and long before they reached home, the back of the car was silent but for the snuffling sounds of children sleeping.

She and Seth didn't talk much. She felt jumpy and uncertain, scared to break the mood and yet determined not to fall back into the bad old patterns. She was a strong woman, she'd discovered that. She loved Seth. She doubted she'd ever love another man as deeply, but if his heart wasn't hers, then she couldn't continue. It was as simple, and as painful, as that.

But it had been nice tonight. She laid her head back and stared out the window as the streets grew more familiar. It had stopped raining hours ago, but the heavy sky threatened more drizzle.

"You took a wrong turn, Seth. You must be getting sleepy, too."

"Can I take you on a little detour? There's something I want to show you." She noted the intense tone under the casual words as she automatically agreed.

She was almost certain they were headed for his house. What was he planning to show her? She kept quiet and waited, her tension mounting as they neared his house. When they turned into his crescent, she looked sharply at him, but he refused to return the glance.

He didn't drive into his driveway but angled the car and left the engine running.

"What are you—"

She gasped as she saw, illuminated in his headlights, a familiar real estate sign. Cindi's, the same one that was featured on her brochure. A red Sold sticker was slapped across the front.

"I love you, Melissa. I couldn't think of a better way to show you."

"But where—"

"I accepted an offer this morning. I didn't want to tell you about it until the house was sold. It's as close as I can come to proving what I feel." He took her hand and his eyes shone in the dim light of the car. "Please marry me."

"And if I don't?"

He flicked the lights off. Darkness filled the car. "Then the girls and I will find a place on our own. You told me to move on. You were right. It was time. With you or without you, I'm moving on, physically and emotionally." She heard the catch in his voice, and knew how tough it was for him to talk about this. "I loved Claire. I'd have stayed with her forever if she hadn't died. But she did. It wasn't until you cleared out her stuff that I realized I hadn't let her go." He stopped and she felt a lump form in her throat. "Now, I have."

"But it was her home. Your memories are there."

"I'll always have my memories. They move with me. Claire will always be a part of me and of the girls, but you showed me that I can respect her memory and still live a good life." He touched her face. "Acceptance. I finally got there."

"I hope you'll share those memories with me. I owe her so much. I wish I could have known her."

She felt him nod. Then, after a moment of silence, he said, "Oh, one other thing."

"What?"

"I'm taking you for lunch one day soon and giving you a tour of my office. You can meet everyone."

"Really?"

"Mitzi's going to kill me if she doesn't get to meet you soon. She's the one who recommended the restaurant I was planning to take you to tonight."

"And on the way we'd drive by your sold house?"

"I'm such a man of mystery." He paused, then said, "God, I love you."

He really did love her! But there was one thing she had to set him straight on. "We haven't talked a lot, lately. I think you should know that I'm taking on a lot of work with my garden design business." She tried to keep the pride out of her voice as she said those last four words, but it was tough. "I won't be there every day when the kids come home from school. Sometimes there will be a sitter."

The lights flashed on again and he turned to face her, an amazed grin on his face. "Do you by any chance think I want to marry you to save myself your day-care fees? Because let me tell you, that was highway robbery."

"It was not. Where else would they get such nutritious food, a trained medical—" He shut her up by the simple method of kissing her senseless. And she was kissing him back.

Her hand was around his neck, the lights were out again, and they were going at it like lovers who'd been apart too long. "I'm going to have to write these down," he mused when they stopped for breath.

"Pardon?"

"I'm writing my own chapter on 'Best Places to Kiss in the Pacific Northwest.' So far tonight, I've got the McDonald's parking lot, the stadium during a rock concert and the car out front of my house. What do you think?" he asked, pulling her close once more.

"I think you'd better rebook those tickets for Hawaii right now."

"I never cancelled them," he said with smug satisfaction. "And while we're gone, the movers can take our stuff over to your place."

She rested her head on his shoulder. Heard a tiny snore from the direction of the backseat and smiled. "That was a broken home."

"Hey, I did a lot of work patching up that place."

"I know. Matthew said it wasn't our home that was broken, it was our family."

"I'm a handyman, remember?"

"The thing is that Cindi's got this nice family wanting to buy my house. Maybe it's time for all of us to move on and find our own home. For a fresh start."

"Do you have any idea how tough it is to find a home in this neighborhood?"

"Follow my directions," she said, excitement filling her as she realized she had the perfect solution.

"I'VE ALREADY DONE THE GARDEN," she said, as they drew up in front of the display home for the new subdivision. "All the lots are sold now, so they'll be selling the display home." She turned in her seat. "I've been inside and it's gorgeous. Four bedrooms and a den that could be a fifth bedroom if the twins ever want their own rooms. The main floor has a big kitchen and family room, and downstairs there's room for a playroom, even a home theater if we want one."

"A fresh start, for all of us."

"What do you think?"

"Cindi's going to get three commissions, is what I think."

She laughed and leaned over to give him a quick kiss. "Let's wake the kids and tell them they've got only two days."

"Two days?"

She smiled. "To pack. There's a wedding in Hawaii to get to."

* * * * *

Experience entertaining women's fiction
for every woman who has wondered
"what's next?" in their lives.
Turn the page for a sneak preview of a new book
from Harlequin NEXT,
WHY IS MURDER ON THE MENU, ANYWAY?
by Stevi Mittman

On sale December 26, wherever books are sold.

Design Tip of the Day

Ambience is everything. Imagine eating a foie gras at a luncheonette counter, or a side of cole slaw at Le Cirque. It's not a matter of food but one of atmosphere. Remember that when planning your dining room design.

—Tips from *Teddi.com*

"Now that's the kind of man you should be looking for," my mother, the self-appointed keeper of my shelf-life stamp, says. She points with her fork at a man in the corner of the Steak-Out Restaurant, a dive I've just been hired to redecorate. Making this restaurant look four-star will be hard, but not half as hard as getting through lunch without strangling the woman across the table from me. "*He* would make a good husband."

"Oh, you can tell that from across the room?" I ask, wondering how it is she can forget that when we had trouble getting rid of my last husband, she shot him. "Besides being ten minutes away from death if he actually eats all that steak, he's twenty years too old for me and— shallow woman that I am—twenty pounds too heavy.

Besides, I am *so* not looking for another husband here. I'm looking to design a new image for this place, looking for some sense of ambience, some feeling, something I can build a proposal on for them."

My mother studies the man in the corner, tilting her head, the better to gauge his age, I suppose. I think she's grimacing, but with all the Botox and Restylane injected into that face, it's hard to tell. She takes another bite of her steak salad, chews slowly so that I don't miss the fact that the steak is a poor cut and tougher than it should be. "You're concentrating on the wrong kind of proposal," she says finally. "Just look at this place, Teddi. It's a dive. There are hardly any other diners. What does *that* tell you about the food?"

"That they cater to a dinner crowd and it's lunchtime," I tell her.

I don't know what I was thinking bringing her here with me. I suppose I thought it would be better than eating alone. There really are days when my common sense goes on vacation. Clearly, this is one of them. I mean, really, did I not resolve less than three weeks ago that I would not let my mother get to me anymore?

What good are New Year's resolutions, anyway?

Mario approaches the man's table and my mother studies him while they converse. Eventually Mario leaves the table with a huff, after which the diner glances up and meets my mother's gaze. I think she's smiling at him. That or she's got indigestion. They size each other up.

I concentrate on making sketches in my notebook and try to ignore the fact that my mother is flirting. At nearly seventy, she's developed an unhealthy interest in members of the opposite sex to whom she isn't married.

According to my father, who has broken the TMI rule

and given me Too Much Information, she has no interest in sex with him. Better, I suppose, to be clued in on what they aren't doing in the bedroom than have to hear what they might be doing.

"He's not so old," my mother says, noticing that I have barely touched the Chinese chicken salad she warned me not to get. "He's got about as many years on you as you have on your little cop friend."

She does this to make me crazy. I know it, but it works all the same. "Drew Scoones is not my little 'friend.' He's a detective with whom I—"

"Screwed around," my mother says. I must look shocked, because my mother laughs at me and asks if I think she doesn't know the "lingo."

What I thought she didn't know was that Drew and I actually tangled in the sheets. And, since it's possible she's just fishing, I sidestep the issue and tell her that Drew is just a couple of years younger than me and that I don't need reminding. I dig into my salad with renewed vigor, determined to show my mother that Chinese chicken salad in a steak place was not the stupid choice it's proving to be.

After a few more minutes of my picking at the wilted leaves on my plate, the man my mother has me nearly engaged to pays his bill and heads past us toward the back of the restaurant. I watch my mother take in his shoes, his suit and the diamond pinkie ring that seems to be cutting off the circulation in his little finger.

"Such nice hands," she says after the man is out of sight. "Manicured." She and I both stare at my hands. I have two popped acrylics that are being held on at weird angles by bandages. My cuticles are ragged and there's marker decorating my right hand from measuring carelessly when I did a drawing for a customer.

Twenty minutes later she's disappointed that he managed to leave the restaurant without our noticing. He will join the list of the ones I let get away. I will hear about him twenty years from now when—according to my mother—my children will be grown and I will still be single, living pathetically alone with several dogs and cats.

After my ex, that sounds good to me.

The waitress tells us that our meal has been taken care of by the management and, after thanking Mario, the owner, complimenting him on the wonderful meal and assuring him that once I have redecorated his place people will be flocking here in droves (I actually use those words and ignore my mother when she rolls her eyes), my mother and I head for the restroom.

My father—unfortunately not with us today—has the patience of a saint. He got it over the years of living with my mother. She, perhaps as a result, figures he has the patience for both of them, and feels justified having none. For her, no rules apply, and a little thing like a picture of a man on the door to a public restroom is certainly no barrier to using the john. In all fairness, it does seem silly to stand and wait for the ladies' room if no one is using the men's room.

Still, it's the idea that rules don't apply to her, signs don't apply to her, conventions don't apply to her. She knocks on the door to the men's room. When no one answers she gestures to me to go in ahead. I tell her that I can certainly wait for the ladies' room to be free and she shrugs and goes in herself.

Not a minute later there is a bloodcurdling scream from behind the men's room door.

"Mom!" I yell. "Are you all right?"

Mario comes running over, the waitress on his heels. Two customers head our way while my mother continues to scream.

I try the door, but it is locked. I yell for her to open it and she fumbles with the knob. When she finally manages to unlock and open it, she is white behind her two streaks of blush, but she is on her feet and appears shaken but not stirred.

"What happened?" I ask her. So do Mario and the waitress and the few customers who have migrated to the back of the place.

She points toward the bathroom and I go in, thinking it serves her right for using the men's room. But I see nothing amiss.

She gestures toward the stall, and, like any self-respecting and suspicious woman, I poke the door open with one finger, expecting the worst.

What I find is worse than the worst.

The husband my mother picked out for me is sitting on the toilet. His pants are puddled around his ankles, his hands are hanging at his sides. Pinned to his chest is some sort of Health Department certificate.

Oh, and there is a large, round, bloodless bullet hole between his eyes.

Four Nassau County police officers are securing the area, waiting for the detectives and crime scene personnel to show up. They are trying, though not very hard, to comfort my mother, who in another era would be considered to be suffering from the vapors. Less tactful in the twenty-first century, I'd say she was losing it. That is, if I didn't know her better, know she was milking it for everything it was worth.

My mother loves attention. As it begins to flag, she swoons and claims to feel faint. Despite four No Smoking signs, my mother insists it's all right for her to light up because, after all, she's in shock. Not to mention that signs, as we know, don't apply to her.

When asked not to smoke, she collapses mournfully in a chair and lets her head loll to the side, all without mussing her hair.

Eventually, the detectives show up to find the four patrolmen all circled around her, debating whether to administer CPR, smelling salts or simply call the paramedics. I, however, know just what will snap her to attention.

"Detective Scoones," I say loudly. My mother parts the sea of cops.

"We have to stop meeting like this," he says lightly to me, but I can feel him checking me over with his eyes, making sure I'm all right while pretending not to care.

"What have you got in those pants?" my mother asks him, coming to her feet and staring at his crotch accusingly. "*Baydar?* Everywhere we Bayers are, you turn up. You don't expect me to buy that this is a coincidence, I hope."

Drew tells my mother that it's nice to see her, too, and asks if it's his fault that her daughter seems to attract disasters.

Charming to be made to feel like the bearer of a plague. He asks how I am.

"Just peachy," I tell him. "I seem to be making a habit of finding dead bodies, my mother is driving me crazy and the catering hall I booked two freakin' years ago for Dana's bat mitzvah has just been shut down by the Board of Health!"

"Glad to see your luck's finally changing," he says, giving me a quick squeeze around the shoulders before turning his attention to the patrolmen, asking what they've got, whether they've taken any statements, moved anything, all the sort of stuff you see on TV, without any of the drama. That is, if you don't count my mother's threats to faint every few minutes when she senses no one's paying attention to her.

Mario tells his waitstaff to bring everyone espresso, which I decline because I'm wired enough. Drew pulls him aside and a minute later I'm handed a cup of coffee that smells divinely of Kahlúa.

The man knows me well. Too well.

His partner, whom I've met once or twice, says he'll interview the kitchen staff. Drew asks Mario if he minds if he takes statements from the patrons first and gets to him and the waitstaff afterward.

"No, no," Mario tells him. "Do the patrons first." Drew raises his eyebrow at me like he wants to know if I get the double entendre. I try to look bored.

"What is it with you and murder victims?" he asks me when we sit down at a table in the corner.

I search them out so that I can see you again, I almost say, but I'm afraid it will sound desperate instead of sarcastic.

My mother, lighting up and daring him with a look to tell her not to, reminds him that *she* was the one to find the body.

Drew asks what happened *this time*. My mother tells him how the man in the john was "taken" with me, couldn't take his eyes off me and blatantly flirted with both of us. To his credit, Drew doesn't laugh, but his smirk is undeniable to the trained eye. And I've had my eye trained on him for nearly a year now.

"While he was noticing you," he asks me, "did *you* notice anything about him? Was he waiting for anyone? Watching for anything?"

I tell him that he didn't appear to be waiting or watching. That he made no phone calls, was fairly intent on eating and did, indeed, flirt with my mother. This last bit Drew takes with a grain of salt, which was the way it was intended.

"And he had a short conversation with Mario," I tell him. "I think he might have been unhappy with the food, though he didn't send it back."

Drew asks what makes me think he was dissatisfied, and I tell him that the discussion seemed acrimonious and that Mario looked distressed when he left the table. Drew makes a note and says he'll look into it and asks about anyone else in the restaurant. Did I see anyone who didn't seem to belong, anyone who was watching the victim, anyone looking suspicious?

"Besides my mother?" I ask him, and Mom huffs and blows her cigarette smoke in my direction.

I tell him that there were several deliveries, the kitchen staff going in and out the back door to grab a smoke. He stops me and asks what I was doing checking out the back door of the restaurant.

Proudly—because, while he was off forgetting me, dropping by only once in a while to say hi to Jesse, my son, or drop something by for one of my daughters that he thought they might like, I was getting on with my life—I tell him that I'm decorating the place.

He looks genuinely impressed. "Commercial customers? That's great," he says. Okay, that's what he *ought* to say. What he actually says is "Whatever pays the bills."

"Howard Rosen, the famous restaurant critic, got her the job," my mother says. "You met him—the good-looking, distinguished gentleman with the *real* job, something to be proud of. I guess you've never read his reviews in *Newsday*."

Drew, without missing a beat, tells her that Howard's reviews are on the top of his list, as soon as he learns how to read.

"I only meant—" my mother starts, but both of us assure her that we know just what she meant.

"So," Drew says. "Deliveries?"

I tell him that Mario would know better than I, but that I saw vegetables come in, maybe fish and linens.

"This is the second restaurant job Howard's got her," my mother tells Drew.

"At least she's getting *something* out of the relationship," he says.

"If he were here," my mother says, ignoring the insinuation, "he'd be comforting her instead of interrogating her. He'd be making sure we're both all right after such an ordeal."

"I'm sure he would," Drew agrees, then looks me in the eyes as if he's measuring my tolerance for shock. Quietly he adds, "But then maybe he doesn't know just what strong stuff your daughter's made of."

It's the closest thing to a tender moment I can expect from Drew Scoones. My mother breaks the spell. "She gets that from me," she says.

Both Drew and I take a minute, probably to pray that's all I inherited from her.

"I'm just trying to save you some time and effort," my mother tells him. "My money's on Howard."

Drew withers her with a look and mutters something that sounds suspiciously like "fool's gold." Then he excuses himself to go back to work.

I catch his sleeve and ask if it's all right for us to leave. He says sure, he knows where we live. I say goodbye to Mario. I assure him that I will have some sketches for him in a few days, all the while hoping that this murder doesn't cancel his redecorating plans. I need the money desperately, the alternative being borrowing from my parents and being strangled by the strings.

My mother is strangely quiet all the way to her house. She doesn't tell me what a loser Drew Scoones is—despite his good looks—and how I was obviously drooling over him. She doesn't ask me where Howard is taking me tonight or warn me not to tell my father about what happened because he will worry about us both and no doubt insist we see our respective psychiatrists.

She fidgets nervously, opening and closing her purse over and over again.

"You okay?" I ask her. After all, she's just found a dead man on the toilet and tough as she is that's got to be upsetting.

When she doesn't answer me I pull over to the side of the road.

"Mom?" She refuses to meet my eyes. "You want me to take you to see Dr. Cohen?"

She looks out the window as if she's just realized we're on Broadway in Woodmere. "Aren't we near Marvin's Jewelers?" she asks, pulling something out of her purse.

"What have you got, Mother?" I ask, prying open her fingers to find the murdered man's ring.

"It was on the sink," she says in answer to my dropped jaw. "I was going to get his name and address and have you return it to him so that he could ask you out. I thought it was a sign that the two of you were meant to be together."

"He's dead, Mom. You understand that, right?" I ask. You never can tell when my mother is fine and when she's in la-la land.

"Well, I didn't know that," she shouts at me. "Not at the time."

I ask why she didn't give it to Drew, realize that she wouldn't give Drew the time in a clock shop and add, "...or one of the other policemen?"

"For heaven's sake," she tells me. "The man is dead, Teddi, and I took his ring. How would that look?"

Before I can tell her it looks just the way it is, she pulls out a cigarette and threatens to light it.

"I mean, really," she says, shaking her head like it's my brains that are loose. "What does he need with it now?"

Silhouette®

nocturne™

**WAS HE HER SAVIOR
OR HER NIGHTMARE?**

HAUNTED
LISA CHILDS

Years ago, Ariel and her sisters were separated for
their own protection. Now the man who vowed
revenge on her family has resumed the hunt, and
Ariel must warn her sisters before it's too late.
The closer she comes to finding them, the more
secretive her fiancé becomes. Can she trust the man
she plans to spend eternity with? Or has he been
waiting for the perfect moment to destroy her?

On sale December 2006.

SNHDEC

In February, expect MORE
from

HARLEQUIN® *Romance*®

as it increases to six titles per month.

What's to come...

Rancher and Protector

Part of the
Western Weddings
miniseries

BY JUDY CHRISTENBERRY

The Boss's
Pregnancy Proposal

BY RAYE MORGAN

Don't miss February's
incredible line up of authors!

www.eHarlequin.com   HRINCREASE

Don't miss
DAKOTA FORTUNES,
a six-book continuing series following the Fortune family of South Dakota—oil is in their blood and privilege is their birthright.

This series kicks off with
USA TODAY bestselling author
PEGGY MORELAND'S
Merger of Fortunes
(SD #1771)
this January.

Other books in the series:

BACK IN FORTUNE'S BED by Bronwyn James (Feb)
FORTUNE'S VENGEFUL GROOM by Charlene Sands (March)
MISTRESS OF FORTUNE by Kathie DeNosky (April)
EXPECTING A FORTUNE by Jan Colley (May)
FORTUNE'S FORBIDDEN WOMAN by Heidi Betts (June)

Visit Silhouette Books at www.eHarlequin.com   SDPMMOF

REQUEST YOUR FREE BOOKS!

2 FREE NOVELS PLUS 2 FREE GIFTS!

HARLEQUIN®

Super Romance®

Exciting, emotional, unexpected!

YES! Please send me 2 FREE Harlequin Superromance® novels and my 2 FREE gifts. After receiving them, if I don't wish to receive any more books, I can return the shipping statement marked "cancel." If I don't cancel, I will receive 6 brand-new novels every month and be billed just $4.69 per book in the U.S., or $5.24 per book in Canada, plus 25¢ shipping and handling per book and applicable taxes, if any*. That's a savings of close to 15% off the cover price! I understand that accepting the 2 free books and gifts places me under no obligation to buy anything. I can always return a shipment and cancel at any time. Even if I never buy another book from Harlequin, the two free books and gifts are mine to keep forever.

135 HDN EEX7   336 HDN EEYK

Name	(PLEASE PRINT)	
Address		Apt.
City	State/Prov.	Zip/Postal Code

Signature (if under 18, a parent or guardian must sign)

Mail to Harlequin Reader Service®:

IN U.S.A.
P.O. Box 1867
Buffalo, NY
14240-1867

IN CANADA
P.O. Box 609
Fort Erie, Ontario
L2A 5X3

Not valid to current Harlequin Superromance subscribers.

Want to try two free books from another line?
Call 1-800-873-8635 or visit www.morefreebooks.com.

* Terms and prices subject to change without notice. NY residents add applicable sales tax. Canadian residents will be charged applicable provincial taxes and GST. This offer is limited to one order per household. All orders subject to approval. Credit or debit balances in a customer's account(s) may be offset by any other outstanding balance owed by or to the customer. Please allow 4 to 6 weeks for delivery.

HSR06

Two classic romances from
New York Times bestselling author

DEBBIE MACOMBER

Damian Dryden. *Ready for romance?* At the age of fourteen,
Jessica was wildly infatuated with Evan Dryden. But that was
just a teenage crush and now, almost ten years later, she's in
love—truly in love—with his older brother, Damian.
But everyone, including Damian, believes she's still
carrying a torch for Evan.

Evan Dryden. *Ready for marriage?* Mary Jo is the woman
in love with Evan. But her background's blue collar, while
Evan's is blue blood. So three years ago, she got out of his
life—and broke his heart. Now she needs his help.
More than that, she wants his love.

The Dryden brothers—bachelors no longer. Not if these
women have anything to say about it!

Ready for Love

Debbie Macomber "has a gift for evoking the
emotions that are at the heart of the
[romance] genre's popularity."
—*Publishers Weekly*

*Available the first week of December 2006,
wherever paperbacks are sold!*

MIRA®

Silhouette®

SPECIAL EDITION™

Logan's Legacy Revisited

THE LOGAN FAMILY IS BACK
WITH SIX NEW STORIES.

Beginning in January 2007 with

THE COUPLE
MOST LIKELY TO

by

LILIAN DARCY

Tragedy drove them apart. Reunited eighteen
years later, their attraction was once again
undeniable. But had time away changed
Jake Logan enough to let him face his fears
and commit to the woman he once loved?

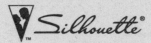

Romantic
SUSPENSE

INTIMATE MOMENTS™

Excitement, danger and passion guaranteed

In February 2007
Silhouette Intimate Moments®
will become
Silhouette® Romantic Suspense.

Look for it wherever you buy books!

Visit Silhouette Books at www.eHarlequin.com   SIMRS1206